Where Dragonflies Dream

Moira Yeldon

A catalogue record for this book is available from the National Library of Australia

Linellen Press
265 Boomerang Road
Oldbury, Western Australia
www.linellenpress.com.au

Acknowledgements

A big thank you to the Book Editors Group at The Society of Women Writers of WA for assessing my manuscript. Thanks to fellow writers and members of the Romance Writers of Australia and South Fremantle Writers' Centre who have read and shared snippets of this book.

Thanks to the many friends and family who supported me on my writing journey and allowed me space to complete the task. I couldn't survive without their ongoing belief in my writing and the many supportive beta readers who gave up their time to spend on my manuscript. Pauline, Debra, Christine, Anne, Natalie, and Kaye, I am forever indebted.

Special thanks to the editors who helped to make my work shine, Catherine Hungerford, Shelley London, Gail Harper, Mairead Hackett and Carmen Thornton.

Thanks to the friends who have allowed me to borrow tiny pieces of their lives and enhanced the compelling content of my fiction.

Thank you, Helen Iles of Linellen Press, for editing and publishing my work.

Other Books by Moira Yeldon

Chasing Marigolds
Where Sunbeams Fall

For Dan

Contents

The Butterfly

Grasping a small handful of dirt, Debra allowed the grains to trickle through her fingers before releasing them into the dark void. She found it hard to comprehend the coffin contained her lifeless husband who was once larger than life, bursting with endless energy. Even now she half expected to hear Alex's gruff voice rising from the freshly dug red soil grave: 'Why don't you just get on with your life? It's not as if I didn't warn you.'

Ambitious and competitive by nature, at fifty-two, Alex had given up on everything and left her, seeking peace in another realm, a place where he could be free of pain and never-ending dialysis. His trauma started in Brunei when he'd been mugged and left to die in a ditch, but it ended in Perth when he could no longer cope with living.

As her own life force energy drained away, her shoulders sagged from the weight she'd been carrying these last few years. Readjusting her feet on the loose soil, she shook the dirt from her peep-toe shoes, feeling lost in the borrowed black skirt with the flimsy fabric that billowed around her legs. Her mind felt just as fragile.

She listened to the mournful caw of a black crow and wished she, too, could fly away to a place and a time before the pressure of Alex's illness had weighed her down.

A large orange butterfly hovered in front of her face, and she recalled another funeral, one with many butterflies yet a much smaller coffin. As she remembered Mala, her lip trembled. It had been years ago, yet she could still see her tiny baby as if it was yesterday.

Beside her, Sam stood firm, a larger handful of dirt in his tightly clenched fist. Not wanting to stare at the deep hole that had swallowed his father, he looked away; his aim skewed. Some of the dirt landed on the priest's pristine white robe; he quickly bent to brush it off. Debra put her arm around Sam's stooped shoulders, finger smoothed his wrinkled shirt and twisted collar. The young man, also feeling the stress of his father's illness while fighting his own demons, pushed her away and staggered back to the relative safety of the group. Unprepared for his reaction, she teetered, and her shoe heel caught in the hem of her long skirt. She stumbled and looked up to see the priest's shocked expression. But he quickly averted his eyes as she gazed at her wraparound skirt sliding down her hips, revealing long bare legs and a flash of lacy underwear. Snatching at the flyaway fabric, Debra re-tied the straps around her waist as Simon stepped in to steady her with his large solid frame. He linked his arm in hers. 'Hang in there, sis,' he said.

Liz moved in too, taking her sister's other arm. 'It's okay. We've got you, Deb.' She'd insisted on lending Debra the skirt. 'You'll never want to wear it again so no point buying something new,' she said.

Liz helped to refasten the skirt and the priest looked relieved. But it was ill-fitting, like most things in Debra's life right now, and she struggled to feel at ease.

Around the graveside, they huddled together, family and friends, a silent throng as they waited for words that would bring meaning to this inexplicable event.

'I can't imagine what she's going through,' Liz whispered to Simon under her large black hat. She was barely in touch with her own emotions, and she'd had a week to witness the raw grief, to share her sister's anguish. But, like Debra, she was left with unanswered questions. What was Alex thinking? Did he consider Debra and Sam at all? How would they manage without him?

A few people stood in the shade of the large gum tree, while others moved in closer to hear the priest's comforting words. At last, his monotone faded away and there was nothing more left to say. Dirt trickled out of Debra's strappy shoes as she tried to escape the sweaty, suffocating crowd before Liz ushered her towards the car.

When they arrived home, they were met by the familiar hedge, stray tendrils of scented jasmine trying to ensnare them as they passed. But as they opened the front door, there was no Alex waiting to greet them.

A crowd tried to fill the void with their overwhelming presence, noisy chatter, and endless food offers. From the kitchen, the smell of hot party pies and quiches wafted into the living room, joining the table covered with platters of fruit, curried egg sandwiches, cakes, and savouries, enough to feed twice the number of people present. Through a blur of faces, she noticed a few of Alex's work colleagues and some of his older friends, most of whom had been absent in recent years. She heard the murmur of platitudes as people whispered to her son, 'Sam, you're the man of the house now.'

What on earth makes them think Sam could take care of a household when he's shunned the responsibility of being an adult in recent years? He's barely able to get out of bed; wanders only as far as the bathroom. At twenty-three, the last thing he wants is to worry about others when he can't take care of himself.

'Here, you need something to eat, love. Keep up your strength.' An elderly neighbour thrust another plate of sandwiches in front of Debra's face, hovered with her pitying expression. More well-wishers smothered her with their good intentions. 'Are you okay?' they asked.

Of course, I'm not okay. Just leave me alone, she wanted to scream.

Her sister Liz, sensing she was about to snap, gently directed her towards a quieter corner of the garden. They sat on a wooden seat beside the sun-bleached Italian fountain, where water trickled from the mouth of a smiling cherub. On any other day, this peaceful setting would have soothed her, but today all she felt was the loss of her husband and the disappointment of broken promises. Despite the endless coins she'd once tossed into the Trevi fountain, there were no guarantees when it came to happiness or marriage.

'I know you're angry, but they're trying to help, Deb. We worry about you. First Mala, now Alex. You don't deserve this.'

While it had been more than twenty years since Mala died, Debra still remembered the shock of losing her baby. Sudden, with no previous warning, she recalled the constant ache in her chest, the primal cry that escaped her throat. Unprepared for the grief, she'd struggled with the pressures of daily life and a toddler who still needed her care.

'At least with Alex, you had years to prepare for his inevitable decline … even though it was sooner than we expected.' They all remembered when Alex was mugged and drugged overseas and his subsequent kidney failure.

'And yet when it came, it was so final. Not a shock but a realisation of something I'd dreaded.' At that, the well burst, and there was no stopping the emotions that poured out.

Sometimes, her tears were a mere trickle, other times a gushing waterfall, which surprised her when she was least expecting it.

'Emotions can be overwhelming, Deb, but I think what you're feeling is normal.'

'I worry about what I'm not supposed to be feeling. The relief that it's over. Also, the guilt. Is that normal?'

'All emotions are important if they help you get through this. But it's not your fault. Don't beat yourself up.'

'I know people mean well but I'm so tired. I haven't slept soundly in years, not since Alex first became ill.' She slid along the wooden seat, leaned down and rested her head on the armrest. At the sight of a large woman panting under the weight of a casserole dish she was carrying, she cringed. She'd run out of patience and fridge space. The last thing she wanted was another casserole – they reminded her of happy family gatherings, especially at this time so close to Christmas. Now there were only the two of them, and neither of them wanted to eat. How would they cope with Christmas?

When she asked Simon the same question as she walked into the house, he'd placed his arm around her shoulders.

'Everyone is leaving, Deb. It's time to say goodbye. When they've gone, you'll get quiet time to grieve. At least you can catch up on some sleep. There's no need to worry about Christmas yet.'

But she already knew she'd be focused on who was missing this year rather than who was sitting around the table with them for Christmas lunch.

'I feel as if I've been grieving for years, in anticipation of being alone. I've been worrying about how I'll pay the bills. How will I take care of this big place on my own?'

'You know Liz and I are here for you. Will you be all right?'

'I don't get much choice, do I? But I worry about Sam. He's already been through so much. I don't know how he'll cope with this.'

'Just take it one day at a time.' He slowly ushered her towards the front door where guests were huddled, waiting for her to bid them goodbye. 'Sam may well surprise you. It might be what he needs to turn his life around.'

She waved goodbye to the last of the guests who hugged her so tightly she could barely breathe. After they released her, she searched for Liz and Simon. They looked at her without asking the same question they knew she didn't want to hear.

I know they care, but right now, I need time to make sense of his death and my life.

All the fears she'd anticipated had materialised and they were worse than she'd ever imagined. It was like she was on a roller coaster, hurtling through sadness one minute, anger the next and, of course, the constant guilt, as if her past actions had caught up with her and this was to be her punishment. As they waited for the transplant that never came, the one small miracle, the belief that he might improve, the glass full of wishes had shattered and the genie had disappeared.

Debra searched for Sam, who suddenly appeared from the garden where he'd been slinking amongst the bushes. With Alex gone, there was only Sam. Perhaps there would be more time to build a meaningful relationship together now. From here on, there would only be the two of them with many bridges to mend.

***

Sam had been silently observing the day's events from a distance as he tried to make sense of his father's death. He'd chewed back most of his fingernails while discreetly keeping an eye on his mother. He'd seen her sitting by the fountain, slouched on the garden bench; at the graveside, he saw her reaction to the butterfly. She'd told him many times about the butterflies at Mala's funeral, but as he'd been barely two when his baby sister had died, he'd only had his mother's memories to rely on. Not only did they release a box of butterflies, but his parents also had a butterfly motif engraved on her headstone. That was not long before they'd packed up their life in Australia and gone to live in Brunei.

While he may not have fully understood the complexities of death back then, he sensed the grief surrounding him at the time. He sensed it sometimes when his mother was talking about the past. Her blank face fixed like a screen saver, would suddenly time out as if her thoughts were elsewhere. As he grew older, he caught her gazing at photos of Mala, and knew he would never be enough no matter how hard he tried. He had survived, but Mala hadn't. After experiencing this recent family death, he wondered if he would feel the same rejection this time. Would he be able to fill the void his dad had left in their lives?

As his father's quality of life had deteriorated, the chances of getting his own life back on track had eroded with each passing month. Aware of his own decline, it was as if his dad wanted to live vicariously through Sam's success.

'Ever thought of playing golf, Sam? You might enjoy it. How about you give surfing a try.' Alex's face brightened at the prospect of each new venture, but Sam's remained deadpan.

Yeah, right! Dad may have loved participating in these activities but not me. Confined to dialysis regimes, his father no longer had the energy or inclination for these sports. While Sam knew how hard that must have been, it wasn't his responsibility. He had enough crap in his own life without taking on his father's problems.

'You can make a lot of money from sport, Sam.'

Alex Grainger would have pursued this opportunity if he could. Sam, on the other hand, viewed himself as a plodder. He lacked the innate competitive streak his dad assumed he should have. A nature lover like his mother, he preferred sitting quietly, observing all around him.

He looked down at his father's shoes – which he hadn't managed to fill despite his thick woollen socks. His mother had polished them that morning, insisting they would look better than his rubber thongs.

'A lot of people will be there. Friends of your dad. You should make an effort, Sam.'

After the funeral, when everyone had left the house, he'd escaped to the nearby riverbank, sat on a grassy mound as an ungainly pelican glided gracefully in to land on the water's edge. From the largest to the smallest, he noticed the dragonfly's scurrying flight across the water. As Sam delved into deeper realms, he always questioned and saw beyond what lay on the surface, the tiny creatures, like dragonflies, were always worth a second glance.

Yes, I saw the butterfly today at the funeral. If I'd been busy striving the way Dad wanted me to, I would have missed it. I would have been moving way too fast, not caring, not seeing, not taking the time to observe this gentle gift of nature.

As Sam had sat at the water's edge, he'd reflected on his life so far. He hadn't always been focused on nature or living things. There was a time in his teens when he'd questioned whether life was worth living at all. He'd certainly thought about the alternatives and there were a few options he almost tried. When he saw his mum crying at the funeral, it reminded him of those earlier times. It was because of her he'd changed his mind. She used to stare at him, plead with him to change. Clenching her fists, she'd screech like a bush stone-curlew, and ask him the same questions over and over.

'What are you doing with your life, Sam? Where've you been, Sam? I'm really worried about you. Why can't you get yourself some decent friends?'

If he slipped out somewhere she'd wait for him to come home and ask the same annoying questions. He rarely took the time to answer. There seemed no point. But he pitied her all the same. Since his dad died, he'd had nightmares and a whole load of old crap had resurfaced.

Last night he remembered a time when he was seventeen and was pushing his skateboard around the neighbourhood. Shaggy, who chased him all the way, started to tire. He knelt and patted his dog, fingered the matted black and white fur behind the Collie's ears, scratching her favourite places. She'd been with him since a puppy, and she too knew his sensitivities. She understood when he was angry and kept her distance. She sensed when he was upset and nudged in closer, licking his hands.

'Here, Shaggy. Lie down.'

He'd balanced his skateboard on the kerb and perched himself next to it. Across the road at number 37, Mrs Wilson turned on house lights as she prepared the family dinner. His mum was probably doing the same at number 42. His stomach churned with dread at the thought of his mum cooking him special meals he rarely felt like eating.

At that stage in his life, he didn't feel much at all. No longer afraid of the dark, he ignored the cold biting into his thin pants and shirt. Unlike his mum, he thought, *I'm tough. I'm immune. Nothing can hurt me.* Shaggy nuzzled into his side, sniffed at his pockets.

'Go away,' he yelled and shoved her. 'I've got nothing for you.'

When he was seventeen, he rarely slept. Instead, he enjoyed roaming with other members of the pack under a full moon.

'Stick with us, bro. We own this neighbourhood,' they'd said. With their matted hair and unwashed clothes, they appeared tougher than they were, but marking out their territory was as close as they came to their wolfish kin. For the first time he had a sense of belonging and no longer needed to sit alone at school with other kids staring at him.

The silvery blackness of nightfall provided a certain security for him that the stark light of day could not guarantee. Daylight hours were often filled with endless questions he couldn't handle from parents and teachers. It was always the same old crap.

'What are your plans for the future, Sam?'

How would he even know that when he didn't know his immediate plans? He had no idea what the next day or week would bring. A chill wind ruffled the long hair on the back of his neck, and his nostrils stung as he deeply inhaled on his reefer. He turned his gaze skywards and pulled the black hoodie over his head.

The first time he'd snuck out at night he'd been scared shitless. He was much younger then. When he tried to climb out his bedroom window, the flyscreen fell to the ground with a loud thud. *Well, that's sure to wake the old girl. But nothing will wake the old man.* His dad was drugged most of the time. Sedatives, he said. *Yeah Der! What right did he have to lecture me about drugs? At least he won't notice if I chop a bit more off his garden hose.* With a Swiss army knife, he'd sliced off another short piece of hose, ramming it into a hole he'd cut on the side of a plastic Coca-Cola bottle. Behind a large lantana bush, he'd half-filled the plastic bottle from a bucket of water. He would need it later that night when he got back. Right now, he wanted to catch up with the gang.

'We don't want you in our group,' the cool kids at school had told him. He didn't talk the right language, his face didn't fit, he was no good at sports, and he struggled with schoolwork. There was a time when a few of the "four-eyes" let him hang out with them. They sometimes let him copy their math homework, but nowadays, he was rarely in class.

Well, fuck 'em all, he'd thought. *I now have a group who doesn't judge me. They might be dropouts but at least they accept me as I am.* He no longer wandered alone but was part of the pack. While the animal inside him was restless, the fluffy one beside him sniffed around his pockets.

'Stop it, Shaggy. You're pissing me off.' He'd pushed the dog away and she yelped.

As he snuck around the lantana bushes at the back of the house, he could see his mum through the kitchen window. He could hear her talking on the phone and seized this opportunity to creep in quietly.

'I worry about him … He's so furtive … always ducking around corners. No, I never know where he is.' Her voice cracked, and she paused to catch her breath.

He'd hurried to grab everything he needed. Mum wouldn't be on the phone for long if Shaggy had her way. She would nuzzle into Mum wanting to be fed. But Mum seemed in no hurry to hang up and was now sobbing loudly into the phone. Shaggy stood whimpering at Mum's feet, licking her legs, before barking loudly to get her attention. As Sam hovered between the kitchen and the back door, his mum looked up from the telephone.

'I have to go.' She slammed down the phone.

As Sam tried to sidestep her, she placed herself between him and the back door.

'Sam, we need to talk.' She wiped her face with her apron.

'I'm going out,' he mumbled into his shirt collar.

'But where, Sam? Where?' She scanned every part of his body as if checking to see if he was still her kid. Then a more desperate tone tempted him with food. 'I've made your favourite lasagna, Sam. It'll be ready in five minutes.'

There was something about the way she slumped against the bench. He hated to see her like this, but he had to get away.

'Give me a fuckin' break. I'm not hungry. I'll eat when I get home.' He pushed her out of the way and ducked around the table.

He hated it when his mum made him feel guilty. Even the late-night antics in the park weren't as much fun. He also hated school.

'Are we keeping you awake, Sam? Are we disturbing you?' the teacher smirked, and the other kids joined in the laughter.

He'd been hearing voices in class, whispers behind his back, kids laughing at him amongst themselves. Everyone seemed to be talking about him these days and he couldn't shut out the noises in his head.

There were times when he crept into the kitchen for snacks in the middle of the night, and found his mother standing there in the darkened room.

What the fuck was she doing there? Waiting for him? It didn't make sense. It was as if she could read his mind. She was always there, waiting, watching, talking about him to her friends.

And then she was at the kitchen door. *No easy way out, nowhere to run.* A strangled sobbing struggled to escape her throat. It was replaced with the scary bird cry that grew louder and louder.

'Eeeghhh.'

He thrust his fingers in his ears and ran out the door to join the pack. Thank Christ his friends were normal.

Since his dad's funeral, he could still remember the scary screeching sounds his mum used to make. His stomach tightened as he remembered the noise. At least she wasn't making those sounds now.

What right did Dad have to end his life anyway, when I've tried so hard to deal with mine? And what about Mum? Will this be enough to send her off the deep end?

The Only Truth is Music

'We're going to call the new band 'Loose Enders',' Mike Jasper announced determinedly to his wife.

She laughed. 'It sounds like a sexual dysfunction! 'Lost Chords' might be more appropriate.'

For some time, they'd been trying to think of a name more in line with their current demographic and identity – a group of middle-aged men living in Sussex with leisure time to spare.

'What a load of bollocks, Jacquie,' Mike huffed in defence. 'This is a new beginning for us. It'll be like old times living in Brunei when we played to an adoring expat crowd.' But it got him thinking, and his lips pursed at her comment. If she'd said it reminded her of sexual inactivity, he could understand it, but sexual dysfunction was way off the mark. He wanted to remind her how long it had been since she gave him an opportunity to prove her wrong. But he swallowed his hurt to concentrate instead on their latest windfall.

The newly reformed band members had just been asked to do a gig for a sixtieth birthday party, and the host had requested sixties-style music. It was their first paid gig in a while, and it was a great opportunity to play some of their favourite songs.

'This guy is a bit of a tosser,' said his muso mate Bob before he hung up the phone. 'He probably won't know sixties from seventies music.'

Mike thought they might even sneak in a few hits from the eighties without too much complaint. As a drummer, Bob was intuitive at picking up the tempo; he knew how to follow the rhythm. He also had good instincts when it came to knowing what people wanted, and he was used to keeping people happy. Fortunately, Mike had his income from teaching to rely on as the music scene had offered only slim pickings in recent years. This sixtieth gig was well worth celebrating. After ending his phone conversation with Bob, he was keen to pass on the good news to Jacquie.

He whistled as he climbed the stairs of their Worthing home, and his long, lanky legs skipped every second step. He rushed into the bedroom and called out to her but was answered by the sound of water splashing from the shower. Jacquie's small case was sprawled open on the bed and several paper gift bags lay beside it. Opening the smallest bag, Mike peeped at a perfume bottle, still in its black cardboard box. The exclusive branding was not familiar to him, but he noted the elaborate wrapping tied with gold ribbon.

He pulled out a pile of delicate lingerie from the second bag, nestled among tissue paper. He let each flimsy item slip through his fingers, and gazed at a silky black G-string, sheer white bikini briefs trimmed with ribbon and lace. Two bras fell out of the bag, one black, one white. He grimaced as he read the price tags still attached. *Holy shit! How could such a small item warrant such a high price?* He quickly stashed them in the bag, then strode into the bathroom.

Through the steamy fog of the shower screen, he glimpsed and heard Jacquie as she belted out tuneless lyrics to Britney Spears' *Hit me baby one more time*. He grimaced at her discordant tone but shrugged. She was oblivious to him and the outside world.

'Hi, Hon. I'm home,' he yelled and moved closer to the shower screen.

She spun around, acknowledging him with a small wave, but continued to lather shampoo into her hair and massage her scalp. He left her in a fog of herbal essence and walked out into the study. Spread out along one shelf, well-worn music sheets took pride of place while plastic folders were strewn across a chair. As he searched through some of the old song sheets, he recognised songs they'd performed years ago, remembered various gigs and functions they played at and the accolades they'd received. There was also a night when they were booed off the stage as their drunken drummer stuffed up big time, but that was in the early days before they were known as 'The Banned'.

Now this one is from the seventies, he mused, and lifted a Dire Straits album, *Sultans of Swing*. 'Steve will love this as he can blend in his own sax rendition.' He scanned the lyrics, hummed the tune. *It's uncanny*, he thought, *how music can bring you back to the places you were when you last heard the song*. His fingers tingled at the thought as he strummed the strings in his mind. He recalled when he played in The Banned with his old mates in Brunei, remembered the fun times they'd shared as they enjoyed their idyllic expat lifestyle in an exotic, tax-free haven. As he taught in schools that closed at midday, his afternoons were free to pursue his number one love – music. His band chose to play their own version of Dire Straits and adopted *Sultans of Swing* as their theme song.

They chose it as a satirical salute to the Sultan of Brunei who, like them, was still young, about to take a second wife, and introduce her to his world of unlimited wealth and power. For the guys in the band, it was enough for them to be young and carefree, their world full of swing. What they had was a world of opportunity free of mortgages and school fees. He and Jacquie were not yet preoccupied with rising food and petrol prices, a need for two jobs, two cars and a larger house to suit two growing daughters. They'd accepted the lifestyle without question. They didn't need to know how long it would last.

But there was no way to stop the invasion of middle age. Even the Sultan of Brunei was not immune from aging. Like him, he was probably now past his prime. No doubt he, too, asked the same question: Where had those carefree days gone? Time marched on regardless, to a tempo and rhythm none of them would have expected.

Recently, Jacquie showed him a newsletter from someone who was organising a reunion for expats who lived in Brunei during the seventies.

'Beth Worthington!' exclaimed Jacquie as she tossed back her fringe. 'I can't believe she's still living with her husband. They must have been in Southeast Asia at least twenty years now. She detested her husband then. How has she survived living with him all this time?'

'Well, we're still together,' he'd sniggered. 'Perhaps we should go to the reunion. We could find out what became of all those people you detested.'

Jacquie stared at him with arched brows. 'You won't get me going back there. But I guess you're keen to meet up with some of your female colleagues, like Debra and your sailing buddy. What was her name, Jo? I prefer holidays where I can choose my own destinations.'

He'd not thought of either of these women in recent times but was more concerned about Jacquie's need to choose her own holidays. It was always her choice of friends, her private hobbies. It was now obvious he was living as a privileged guest in Jacquie's exclusive world.

He grabbed his guitar, tuned it, picked out a few notes, a familiar chord here and there. As he strummed the Dm chord, a wistful sound radiated from his fingers to his ears and into his chest. Why was it those minor chords evoked such emotion? It immediately brought back memories of his sister Evie and his dog who died when he was seven. What had brought on this sudden bout of melancholy? Was it when he remembered happier times spent together or perhaps when he acknowledged Jacquie's current desire for independence? It was not the right time to bring up long-term grievances. Instead, he walked into the bedroom and bid Jacquie a safe journey. Off to London for a girls' weekend, she'd reminded him.

'I'm sure I don't have to remind you to have a good time.'

'We'll be spending our time shopping and chatting. You know … doing girlie stuff.' She pulled out a heavy green jumper from her case before she replaced it with a sleeveless ribbed red sweater.

He tried to imagine the sweater accentuating her curves but, like most of her new purchases, he'd never seen her wearing this one. As he glanced at the bed, he saw the new lingerie had been packed into her case. In black designer jeans with a yellow blouse that he'd also never seen before, Jacquie looked smart and sexy, with her thick black hair bobbed in a new style. As he bent to kiss her goodbye, her hand pushed him away and warned him not to smudge her freshly applied lipstick. He caught a whiff of the intoxicating scent she'd sprayed on her neck and wrists, a warm feminine blend of floral and earthy richness, a mix of something sensual and exotic.

'New perfume?' he quizzed. 'What happened to Chanel No 5?'

'I just wanted something different. It's CK One. Do you like it?'

He gave her an approving nod, but it probably wouldn't matter whether he liked the perfume or not. It was yet another example on a long list of changes that had crept into their relationship. Recently she told him she enjoyed the company of her new book club friends as they offered refreshing ideas with original insights. Those in her writers' group were more positive about giving her the emotional support she believed she wasn't getting at home. Last night, when he accidentally swapped the pillows on their bed, she complained. 'Oh no! This is your pillow. I can't sleep on that. It has your smell.' She wrinkled her nose and threw it back at him.

'Is that such an insufferable thing to bear?' He grabbed her hand as she reached out to retrieve her pillow. 'What happened to our mingling of scent-producing pheromones which once triggered such heightened passion at the beginning of our relationship? Has my body odour now been reduced to something distasteful?'

'Two teenage daughters have happened since then and we were newlyweds when I mentioned the pheromones.' She shimmied across the room to retrieve a pair of shoes. 'I need to rush, or I'll miss my train.'

As he stared at her back, he couldn't resist one last retort before he left. He wanted to ask her why all this shopping before she went to London? Wasn't it her main purpose for going there? But a part of him didn't want to hear the answer. A small vulnerable place inside he wanted to protect from fear of hurt or rejection. He was aware of the futility of passing blows and snide comments. Instead, he took a deep breath as he swallowed his pride and mumbled his goodbyes from the doorway.

'Have a good trip.'

As she rummaged through her drawers, she managed an absent-minded word of thanks without stopping to glance at him. She continued what she was doing with the same frantic pace as she rushed from wardrobe to bed, cupboard to bathroom. A pair of stiletto sandals she crammed into her case, then squeezed the lid down and zipped it shut. He took one last glance at her before he walked downstairs and out the front door.

Desperately in need of a jam session with his muso mates, Mike drove to Bob's house. Bob's drum set took pride of place in one corner of his compact living room. He checked the electronic equipment, tweaked the speakers, and made sure their gear was ready to go. While they waited for Steve and Greg, Mike glanced around Bob's small apartment and wondered what it would be like to be a bachelor. One wall was covered in music books and record albums, the other with framed prints of Ringo Starr and Roger Taylor. Bob's bed doubled as a place to throw his clothes and spread his dirty dishes. A thought slowly formed in Mike's mind. *Not having to be accountable to anyone sounds rather appealing.*

His recently reduced status in Jacquie's world had accentuated and confirmed that his own needs hadn't been met for some time. This new realisation also highlighted how much he'd sacrificed in terms of his personal space. *To spread out my musical gear around the house without complaint from wife or kids would have to be a bonus.* He pondered about the anomalies of life, along with the purpose of marriage. Why did couples go to such lengths to cohabit when they were young, only to crave the need for independence as they matured? While producing offspring was a major incentive, once this task was dealt with, what more were they supposed to achieve? *Perhaps there's a period before we get too frail to make our own decisions where we value our freedom. By then, someone else has decided we need to be cared for by others and before we know it, we're in an old people's home.*

He shook his head. *Is it my earlier bout of melancholy or ongoing concerns about Jacquie that's brought on such morbid thoughts?*

When his eyes returned to Bob, he stared back with a furrowed brow.

'So, how are Jacquie and the kids?' Bob's eyebrow rose.

He almost said, 'They're fine,' but changed his mind. This question had opened the door for him to get certain things off his chest.

'I'm worried about Jacquie. She's not the same anymore.' Then he reeled off his many concerns about Jacquie's lack of interest in him and their marriage. Bob listened without comment. Talking about the issues gave him more insight into the situation, and as he prattled on, he revealed some concerns he'd previously kept concealed from everyone, including himself.

'Recently, she's been doing more overtime at the hospital, so with her working the night shift, I see less of her in the evenings, and I don't want to disturb her during the day when she needs to catch up on sleep. Now that the kids are both living away, there's no real sense of family anymore. It's Jacquie leading her life while I fit in where I can. I'm used to spending nights alone, but surely marriage should be more than this?'

Bob nodded without speaking, yet revealed no sign of surprise or shock. It was like he'd heard it all before or, more likely, had experienced it himself. He tried to lighten the mood.

'So, she's bought new G-strings, you say?'

He hesitated, giving Mike time to swear profusely and complain about the price of the underwear, its lack of functionality, transparency, and failure to cover what it was supposed to hide. Before Mike could launch into further recriminations, Bob's mouth split into a mischievous grin. His eyes sparkled with a hint of amusement.

'Those G-strings ... do you think she took the trouble to tune them before she went away?' Bob now doubled over, bellowed from the depth of his chest; he rocked back and forth on the kitchen chair until the legs toppled, the seat flew backwards, and he somersaulted to the floor.

Mike found it hard to keep a straight face. Despite his concerns, he joined Bob in a low-key snigger, and before long, he, too, had doubled up with laughter as he helped lift his mate from the floor.

'I'm sure they'll be finely tuned by the end of this weekend,' he grimaced. 'That's what worries me most. Why would you need sexy underwear to go shopping with the girls?' Mike scowled as he remembered when he'd last hung Jacquie's old underwear on the line – shapeless, threadbare knickers with perished elastic, pegged out in full view of the neighbours.

Perhaps it's about time she bought new lingerie. When they were newly married, he was happy to buy her gifts of intimate apparel but now it was just a fading memory. *Is it the whirl of kids' activities as Jacquie had suggested that has brought on our current state of apathy, or is it the general domestic drudgery of our lives together?*

Like those intimate items designed not to last, Jacquie's underwear had become another passing memory too delicate to reveal. The boredom in their marriage cohabitated with an absence of desire and a lack of determination to make it better. Yet another topic too painful to address. He swallowed, burying the thoughts deeper in his mind where they would remain out of reach until he had the courage to address them.

Once Steve and Greg arrived, they jammed for several hours and the tension in Mike's chest slowly began to unwind. The issues whizzing around in his head thumped along with the loud reverberating music. While he thought he now had a clearer picture of what he faced at home, his problems still drummed in his ears and pumped around in his chest. These issues were discordant, like an ill-tuned note, as they screeched and grated on his nerves. While he was now aware of his problems, he still hadn't found a way to address them.

A Whisper of Love

'There's a monkey on my bed,' Jo's mother had said one day. 'He keeps staring at me. Over there. Look. Can you see him?'

'No,' said Jo, as she'd glanced around the room. 'I can't see anything.' But her mother had insistently repeated the same statement every few minutes, convinced of a simian presence in her room. Finally, Jo snatched a banana from the fruit bowl and had thrust it into her mother's hand. 'Here, give him this,' she'd said. 'He might be hungry.'

The next time Jo visited her mother in her Sydney nursing home, there was more talk of monkeys, but her mother was also agitated by the sight of two new carers, both of African descent.

'Am I in Africa?' she asked. 'Please take me home. I don't want to live in Africa. I want to go home.'

'It's okay, Mum. You're still in Australia. This is your home.'

She had telephoned management beforehand to arrange a meeting and had asked for her eldest daughter, Erin, to attend. Jo's current concern was not only her mother's health but her declining mental faculties. She didn't need to tap into her own nursing experience to recognise the signs. On each of her previous visits her mother had been acting strangely, quite out of character.

'Do you think Gran may have a UTI?' Erin whispered to Jo on the previous visit. They discussed the possibility, based on urinary tract infections sometimes causing delirium.

'It would certainly account for her confusion. I'll discuss this with the doctor.' While some of her earlier delusions appeared to be harmless, her mother's latest revelation had shocked her, which was why she'd come this morning to discuss it with management.

As peak hour traffic slowed to a crawl, Jo McKenzie took the off-ramp towards Parramatta Road and arrived ten minutes later at Easterly Aged Care Home.

Erin stood waiting at the entrance, having finished her shift at Royal Prince Alfred. She waved as Jo walked across the car park. As they entered the admin section of the sprawling red brick building, Mary Saunders, the facility manager ushered them into her office. She offered them tea or coffee but they declined. On her desk, she flicked through charts and medical records with genuine interest.

As she was about to interpret the latest progress charts, Jo interjected. 'Actually, it's a more delicate matter I'd like to discuss with you today.' Jo readjusted the paisley shawl around her shoulders, pausing briefly before slowly enunciating each word. 'My mother is adamant she's having an affair with her male carer, Paul Wilson.'

'Paul? He's a highly respected carer, happily married with a young family.' The administrator took off her cobalt blue glasses, letting them hang from the attached silver chain.

'Yes, I know. I've met him, and he's mentioned his children on several occasions He seems a lovely man.' She lowered her voice and moved in closer. 'However, my mother has been talking about this for some time now. She insists they are in love.'

'You may not be aware of this,' Mary cut in as she placed her glasses firmly on her nose again before glancing from Jo to Erin, 'but elderly people with urinary tract infections often suffer mental confusion.'

'Yes, I'm aware of that,' Jo snapped, not allowing Mary to continue. From her former nursing experience, Jo regarded herself as being well-informed in recognising and managing UTIs. She sucked in a deep breath and let it out again. 'But due to her deafness, my mother is yelling out every intimate detail, revealing to anyone on the ward who's willing to listen. And she's not holding back. I'm sure by now most regular visitors have been shocked by her disclosure. I imagine you don't want this sort of scandal to blemish the reputation of your aged care facility.'

'No. Definitely not!' Mary's eyes widened as she peered over the top of her glasses. 'Our policy is to uphold our excellent reputation while protecting our staff *and* the well-being of our residents. Your mother's welfare is our utmost concern. I can assure you we will take this matter seriously. From here on we will ensure its only female carers who tend to her needs. Paul Wilson will no longer be working on her ward.'

'Well, I think that's a good starting point.' Jo nodded. 'And what about the possibility of UTI? I'm quite concerned as I know it's sometimes overtreated based on nonspecific symptoms.'

'We should be able to get your mother seen by a doctor this afternoon. We'll do some more tests and take it from there.'

Seeing Jo's frown, Erin turned to Mary. 'We are concerned about Gran taking broad-spectrum antibiotics if she doesn't really need them. As you know, functional decline and increased confusion aren't always due to urinary tract infections.' She looked to Jo for confirmation and Jo nodded in agreement.

'Yes, I would appreciate you keeping me informed of any changes to Mum's meds and treatment. Please let me know what the doctor says. I would like to know as soon as possible.'

'Yes, of course … I will keep you advised of any changes.'

Mary Saunders jotted something down in her notebook then, glancing up as an elderly couple hovered outside her door, flashed perfect white teeth at Jo and Erin. The couple peered in through the glass, the man, bent over his walking frame, supported by the woman's grasp on his arm. Mary nodded at the couple and rose from her chair. 'I'm afraid I'll have to go. I have another appointment and I can't keep them waiting. Thank you for coming. We'll talk again soon.'

With another brief nod, she shook their hands and escorted them from her office.

Jo glanced at her wristwatch and remembered how she'd once prided herself on always being punctual, but nowadays she was forever running late. She turned to Erin whose honey-coloured hair and skin shared a look of fatigue. Regular night shifts were taking their toll, despite her love of nursing.

'I feel as if my life is no longer my own. When I'm not driving here to visit Mum, I'm babysitting for Kali or driving the grandkids to preschool. Even my paid work is driving elderly people to shopping centres or doctors' appointments. It's such a downhill slide from my former career.'

'Mum, you've got a lot on your plate right now. But at least your job contacts helped to get Gran into residential care. Otherwise, we may have been a long time on the waiting list.'

A plane flew overhead drowning out the last of her sentence as they walked across the car park. Jo looked up, remembering the years when she'd been a pilot and flew influential people around the world, a time when she'd taken pride in her career.

Ah, those were the days! She recalled the passengers who could afford the luxury of sightseeing or wanted the immediacy of private business flights. Her earlier life now appeared like nothing more than an unbridled imagination. One day, her idyllic life in Brunei was whisked away from her simply because she wasn't paying full attention to what Gareth had been doing. She'd allowed him to sabotage her job security and their marriage with his foolhardy decisions, which had devastating outcomes. He'd focused on fulfilling his personal needs, while hers went unnoticed, swept like dust under a Persian rug.

'Thanks for listening to my complaints. I don't know what I'd do without you, love.' *Indeed, if it wasn't for Erin, I'd probably still be drifting or completely marooned … washed up on a beach like driftwood buried in wet sand. My strong, independent Erin … she's practically raised herself …* She shrugged inwardly. *… though she did spend much of her childhood with her Gran.* When Jo chose to live overseas in Brunei with Gareth, Erin had stayed behind at boarding school. Coaxed into nursing by Jo, Erin had ensured her she had no regrets.

'I'm glad I can help, Mum. Let's go have a coffee.'

They drove to a nearby alfresco café where they ordered double shots of espresso. Not for the first time that morning, Jo inhaled deeply on a cigarette. Erin watched her mother blow smoke in the direction of the road, adding to the pollution of the traffic.

'Mum, do you think you should be …' She heaved a sigh. 'Never mind … you have enough to worry about already.' Instead, she asked, 'So, how do you think it went, Mum? Are you happy with management's decision?'

'I guess so, but I hate it when these managers speak to me as if I know nothing. I probably have more medical knowledge than she will ever have.' She moved her cigarette hand away from Erin to stop the smoke blowing in her daughter's face; noticed that Erin was studying her and gathered her shawl around her.

'You're probably right, Mum,' Erin said, 'but what's important now is the state of Gran's health. Let's get that sorted out first. Then we might need to look at yours, eh? How long is it since you had a proper check-up?' Erin patted Jo's hand.

'Oh, I'm fine.' Jo fobbed her off, then inhaled deeply on her cigarette. Recently she'd found it hard to relax, even the smallest problems festering within her more than they ever did. She now viewed her life as a picture frame, fastening her in place with metal clasps. She felt trapped inside, unable to escape.

'There was a time when I was in control, in charge of other people's lives. I believed I could take people out of their misery, help them to fly above the clouds. What's happened to that competent woman, Erin? I feel so helpless.' Her voice cracked. 'Why am I stuck in the miserable lives of others, powerless to find solutions. Why, Erin, why? I didn't choose this situation.'

Erin reached out, draped an arm around her mother's shoulder. 'You've got a lot on your plate, Mum. There are times for soaring high, but right now your role is here with the family members who need you the most. You also need to take care of your own health. You're only fifty-five, but you are showing signs of aging too soon. Those dark rings under your eyes tell me you are not sleeping, but it's more than that. You are starting to look gaunt and I'm concerned about the colour of your skin. You are not looking healthy.'

Jo dropped her cigarette butt onto the pavement and stubbed it out with her shoe. 'Sorry, I desperately needed that smoke. Unfortunately, it's just one more thing outside my control. And you've no idea how worried I've been about Mum. It was so out of character when she first mentioned her love affair. I must admit I was shocked.'

'Gran has always been such a genteel lady, always so proper. I'm surprised she even knew about such things.' Erin shook her head slowly, trying to come to terms with this new image of her elderly grandmother. 'Some of her details were so explicit I didn't know whether to laugh or cry.'

Jo tilted her cup, swallowing the last of the coffee. When her mother first began bragging about her love affair with the carer, she'd brushed it off, attributing it to functional decline or increased confusion. Her mother's first descriptions had been rather romantic, an innocent rendering of a young woman in the early stages of love. *It's been so long that I can hardly remember such moments of tenderness. And here is Mother, at eighty, with her mind fading rapidly, still able to recall such details of passion.* 'Well, she was fortunate to have the love of Dad, who'd deeply cared for her and had treated her with respect.' Jo shook her head. 'Perhaps I will never know the love of a man like Dad,' she added.

Being an only child, her father had idolised her and she'd spent her childhood trying to please him, to make him proud of her. She became a nurse to take care of him and she'd gained her wings to follow his path in aviation. She wrapped the shawl more tightly around her. 'I miss your grandpa so much.'

'I'm sure you do, Mum.' Since her first revelation, her gran had been adding increasingly explicit details of her professed love affair. 'Grandpa was the epitome of a gentleman; I'm sure he would not have used such crude expressions. Some of Gran's details bordered on erotica, which should have started alarm bells ringing.'

'If it hadn't been for seeing that news item of elderly patients suffering physical and sexual abuse in aged care facilities, I would never have thought to take her disclosure seriously.'

'Mum, it might put your mind at rest knowing Paul Wilson will no longer be caring for Gran. Although, with all your worries, it will take more than that to give you a good night's sleep, I guess. Speaking of which, how's Kali coping these days? How are the grandkids?'

'Kali? Now that's another story for another time.'

A Better Place

Debra slid one hand under her pillow and reached with her other hand towards Alex's warm, familiar body. But after patting the cold empty space on the sheet, reality dawned – he was gone. Wasn't coming back. Gone was the comforting smell of his body, the sound of his wheezing, laboured breath. With the funeral over and the mourners gone, there was plenty of time for pondering the 'what ifs' of Alex's life. But she didn't want to remember or relive this reality right now. She was wide awake, and there was no way she could get back to sleep. She'd make a coffee to distract herself and suspend these thoughts for a few moments.

She threw the duvet aside with such force that her small iPod caught in the bedding and landed on the floor with a thud, its attached earphones a coiled up, tangled mess. She rolled out of bed and picked it up, then hobbled into a fluffy slipper and hunted down the other by kicking aside the pile of bedding and a few magazines scattered at the foot of the bed. The slipper was half hidden under the bed and she slipped into it as she shuffled towards the bathroom, where she groped for her bathrobe behind the door.

Hanging beside it was Alex's white towelling robe. She had a sudden urge to bury her face in the faint ammonia smell of his sweat, to relive the memories. Instead, she plunged her hands into the spacious pockets, but they were empty, except for one tiny foil packet. Registering the empty cavities of the blistered foil, she read the label, knowing she could easily pop the remaining pills into her mouth. All her pain and loss would disappear. But, although she felt sad, she wasn't yet ready to obliterate all her senses in one desperate act. So, she stood there barely breathing.

It could have been worse. Alex could have died when Sam was much younger while we were living in Brunei. Drugged, robbed, left to die in a ditch, Alex had survived his initial trauma. But the drugging had damaged his kidneys. At least they were able to bring him home to a hospital with expert specialist care. There had been much to cry about when the doctors first diagnosed kidney failure. She'd cried when the dialysis tubes were not flushed out correctly and had developed blockages, resulting in his body becoming cold and clammy to touch. But no one noticed her distress, and Alex was too sick to witness the drama unfolding.

She grabbed his large sad robe with the drooping ties and flapping sleeves. Wrapping it around her, she fastened the ties as tightly as she could and slowly slid down the wall to the cold bathroom floor where she sat staring at the cracks in the tiles. The cold seeped through her but she didn't care. She'd spent many hours, day after day, staring at the same insignificant details on hospital walls. Every tiny crack in the ceiling, each observable stain on the floor, became part of her daily checklist.

She thrust her hands deeper into the towelling pockets and remembered the fit, strong man who had once filled out this bathrobe. Sport had been everything to Alex. He couldn't sit and eat dinner at night without first going for a long run. But dialysis had changed all that. It had been distressing to watch him reduced to the frail patient attached to his tubes of support. After his discharge from hospital, he'd returned to work, but as the dialysis regimes became longer and more frequent, he'd had to leave his job.

'What I would give to be out there playing golf,' he'd say, switching off the television whenever images of Greg Norman appeared on the screen. I want to be out in the sunshine or even in the rain. I'm sick of all this.' He'd flick a finger at the wheelchair, a constant reminder of his inability to achieve his dreams.

Eventually, Alex reached a point where his body no longer responded to treatment; he resented his loss of freedom and decided he could no longer cope with living. While she'd been aware of his frustration, she hadn't realised his depth of despair.

Grasping onto the towel rail, she slowly dragged herself up off the bathroom floor; made a coffee and sat on the sofa in the living room, embedded amongst the red and gold cushions he'd once bought her in Brunei. While she thought she'd been helping Alex to heal, it was obvious to her now she'd been mistaken. And despite her best efforts, she'd been powerless to help Sam as well. With all her frantic attempts at finding solutions, she'd failed, dragging Sam to appointments with counsellors he didn't want to see just as futile.

'Walk away,' the counsellor had told her. 'Let him go. Your son is the only person who can change his life … if he chooses to do so.'

She now felt the heaviness of defeat and an emptiness she couldn't have imagined. Pulling out a cushion from behind her, she examined the embroidered dragon motif. Some of the stitching had come undone and a loose thread now dangled. She pulled on the thread, revealing the empty puncture holes in the fabric. Like her own life, the dragon was unravelling.

Her chest tightened. Then came a reluctant trickle of tears. What she needed was a torrent that gushed out, releasing the anger, the hurt, washing away the years of disappointment. She needed to beat at her breasts, tear out her hair, but the apathy had been building for far too long, numbing her mind and body.

She flung the cushion across the room. It hit the standard lampshade, its thud rattling metal against the beaded fringe. Once it had finished shaking, the lampshade eventually righted itself. But she remained inert, staring into space like an angrier version of the smiling Buddha perched on her mantelpiece. It silently watched her from across the room.

The days and weeks following the funeral dragged on in a blur. She'd locked herself away, turned off her phone, and closed her blinds to the outside world. She'd tried to immerse herself in yoga, but no amount of meditating or chanting could soothe her restless mind or soul. Her sister, Liz had insisted on staying with her for a few more days.

'I'll just help sort out a few things,' she'd said. 'It will be easier with two of us doing it.' But they'd found it hard to focus and hadn't achieved many practical tasks; spent most of their time reminiscing about happier times. Liz had glanced around the living room full of reminders of Alex, his wheelchair, and other medical paraphernalia. 'I'll get Simon to take away some of these things. I don't think they are helping you,' she'd said.

'Thanks. I'm glad I have memories of happier times. It's such a far cry from how I feel right now.'

'I'm sure once you've caught up on some sleep, you'll feel stronger emotionally and physically.'

That night, she lay awake as waves of anger crashed over her. Always the same questions. *Why did he have to die?* When she finally managed to fall asleep, she was jolted awake by stabbing pangs of guilt. *I'm still alive. And he isn't.*

Simon called around to mow the lawn and asked Sam to help with the raking. She viewed them through the kitchen window and heard some of their casual conversation. She sighed with relief seeing Sam involved in everyday activities again. Although he often stayed in his bedroom, at least he was living under her roof again and she knew where he was.

Shaggy lay curled in a furry pile at Sam's feet or burrowed her head under his armpits, watching him with her large soulful eyes, waiting for the time he would notice her again. Realising, Debra grabbed the lead and fastened it to her collar, setting the dog barking – she knew she was about to follow one of her favourite trails, paths they once trod with Alex. Previously, if Debra stopped to rest, Shaggy took the opportunity to chase ducks. Now though, as she trudged along, Shaggy didn't falter. When Debra felt too exhausted to go on, Shaggy nuzzled her warm head in closer and circled around her legs.

In earlier times, when Alex was fitter, she'd pushed him around the river trails in his wheelchair. She loved to explore, admiring each plant or tiny creature expressing gratitude for simply being alive. At the time, she assumed Alex shared her zest for life. But in the hotter months, his mood became like the parched riverbank and surrounding bush, crying out for rain to wash away the desolation.

'Don't you just love the wattle in bloom?' she'd asked and he'd give his usual reply.

'Yeah, but it's a shame about the bloody flies.'

With the recent heavy rainfall, the river was now in flood. Summer was almost upon them, yet the cold bleak skies reflected her mood. The nearby billabongs teemed with black swans gliding along the river's edge. As she trudged along the muddy banks, she spied a pair of swans.

I wish I was a swan, mating for life. If one swan dies, the remaining mate dies soon after. Her frozen grief slowly began to thaw, and the tightly wound emotion around her chest started to unwind. As she watched the first swan shake out its sleek wings, she thought of the Hindu scriptures, the lofty flight of the swan, hamsa. Symbolising the soul's effort to attain spiritual freedom, this divine bird was said to carry others beyond life and death.

Oh, Alex, she whispered inwardly, *I hope you're going to a better place.*

She leaned against the smooth trunk of an ancient paperbark; her arms folded tightly around her as she rocked gently from side to side. Breathing deeply, she released the first of the hot, salty tears and felt an indescribable peace wash over her as a torrent of tears gushed from her. She let them flow. Silently, she prayed. *Please grant me peace and an end to all this suffering.*

As she rubbed her back against the smooth white trunk, the paperbark shed a fine sheath onto her shoulder. Lifting the smooth, velvety surface, she brushed it against her cheek and inhaled the woody scent of melaleuca. Shaggy edged her warm body in closer, whimpering and jumping up on her thighs. She patted the warm silky fur and rubbed each soft ear in turn.

'It's okay, Shaggy. It's going to be all right.'

With her tears spent, her breath softened. She unfolded her deflated body and headed back along the muddy trail, knowing an enormous weight had lifted from her shoulders. Her step became lighter as if a lifetime of pent-up emotion had just been released. With Shaggy trotting along beside her, she felt ready to go home and face the life that awaited her.

Yes, I will be fine.

Where Words Fail

Mike woke to the rattle of the key turning in the lock and anticipated the familiar bang of the heavy wooden door. While he'd been expecting her, he felt ambivalent about her arrival. Since Jacquie's leaving two nights ago, he'd thought about nothing else. Possible scenarios festered over and over in his head like a stuck recording. *Shall I confront her with what I suspect, or should I wait and let it unfold?* Although he'd convinced himself their marriage was not good, he wasn't yet ready to pull the plug, to stop the interminable torment.

From his darkened bedroom, he listened for the squeaking stairs and peered at her through the door as she shimmied across the living room. There was a new animated lightness to her step. She sunk into the armchair with her cup of tea in hand and rested her feet on the small coffee table. Deep in thought, she grinned, as if sharing a private joke or perhaps reliving some cherished moment of the last few days.

He pretended to sleep but opened his eyes a fraction every now and then to observe his wife in the other room. Eventually, she turned off the small table lamp before creeping into the bedroom. She undressed in the dark, gently folded back the duvet and slid into her side of the bed. *His mind reeled: shall I question her now, or wait? I need answers.* But he was reluctant to face the truth.

A tiny knot in his chest screwed into larger folds of flesh, eating away his insides. Yet he felt comfort being in denial, being able to continue with the familiar routine. *Maybe this is enough. It's what we've always had. Once the cork is popped, there's no chance of pouring the fizz back into the bottle. It'll be gone for good, the effervescent bubbles replaced with the minutiae of everyday life. Will the flat, lifeless water seep slowly at first, then swamp us in a mudslide of apathy? Maybe I should sleep on it and see how I feel in the morning.* He rolled over onto his side of the bed and pulled the duvet over his head.

***

As the first rays of daylight crept through gaps in the chintz curtains, Mike knew there was no point in prolonging the agony. He reached out and flicked on the bedside lamp, but Jacquie's eyes remained closed. As he sat upright in bed and stared down at her, he sensed her first stirrings as Jacquie squirmed beside him. There was once a time he would have admired the shape of her lips, the curve of her nose, when he would have buried his nose in the womanly scent of her skin. But this morning all he could feel was tension building in every part of his body, like a volcano about to erupt.

Blinking, she opened her eyes and then peered at Mike. 'What? What is it?' she muttered.

He continued to stare at her, sensing her discomfort. Then he looked away briefly before quietly asking the question he'd been dreading. 'Do you want to tell me about him?'

It was obvious he had hit the nail on the head as Jacquie tried to regain her composure, her expression revealing a collision of emotions. For the briefest moment, she arched her brows in disbelief. *About to respond with denial.* She brushed her fingers through her hair. *Gaining time.* His jaw set.

Her gaze flicked up to the left … *trying to find the appropriate response, maybe drum up her alibis.* As she stole a glance at him, she knew that he knew by the stark, hurt look in his eyes.

She inhaled slowly before murmuring, 'You know?'

'So, who is he? How long has it been going on?' Mike secretly hoped she would tell him he'd imagined everything, that there was no problem at all. But the shock of hearing her candid reply tore him apart as the screws tightened in his gut.

'It's Dan Carruthers.' The words tumbled out of her as if she'd been wanting to say them for some time. 'I didn't want to tell you as I knew you'd get angry. We've been working closely together. With all the additional stress at the hospital, I guess it was inevitable.'

'Inevitable? He's a fucking doctor. Doesn't he have a code of ethics, a sense of basic morality? Why is it inevitable? You're both married to other people.'

While he'd suspected it, even rehearsed this hypothetical scenario, he couldn't imagine the pain or the hurt he'd feel. Right now, he felt like he'd swallowed razor blades.

'We've known each other a long time. We worked together when I was doing midwifery,' Jacquie continued, her face now deadpan, revealing nothing.

'So, he's the guy you were smitten with years ago while I was working overseas? … when you came here supposedly to study nursing?' Mike propped himself higher on the pillow as he struggled to deal with the disbelief, the choking anger.

'It's probably when it began. We didn't mean it to happen … like this. We were just really good friends.' Jacquie also sat up, gaining more leverage so Mike was no longer staring down at her.

"Yes! That's what every guilty person says when they try to justify it. It's a poor excuse. But you've had fifteen fucking years to end it. It's hardly a mid-life crisis … not exactly a one-night stand, is it?'

'I've wanted to tell you, but I didn't want to hurt you.' Jacquie snuggled her head into the duvet and wrapped it more tightly around her.

Mike threw back the covers and thrust his legs out of bed. 'Well, you sure as hell have hurt me. You might have saved me fifteen years of hurt if you'd told me back then.' He grabbed his shirt and struggled into his jeans, balancing on each leg as he headed for the door. 'I've got to get out of the house. I need time to think.' He couldn't bear to be around her any longer; he needed space and fresh air; he needed to gulp it down like a drug, hoping it might miraculously change the reality of what had happened.

'We can discuss it later tonight if you like.'

'Is there really any point, Jacquie? Is there any fucking point?' He wanted to ask so many questions but wasn't sure if he was in a suitable state of mind to hear the truth. It was opposite to waking from a nightmare, where you experienced huge relief that the devastating event did not really happen – in this case, he was wide awake, and knew it was true, but he still couldn't believe it.

He slammed the front door as he hurried from the house and leapt into the car, unsure where he was going. Traffic built quickly at this early hour with people rushing to get to work, and horns tooted in frustration as he drove. He spied his guitar lying on the back seat, and thought of Bob's house, ten minutes away. *Bob, with his reclusive habits, is sure to be home. More than anything else right now, I need a good mate to lean on, someone to listen.*

When Bob invited him in, Mike poured out the vitriol and frustration he'd been holding onto for some time. 'A fucking doctor. Fifteen years. Hardly a one-night stand. And I was too stupid to notice.'

As he emptied his final drop of hurt and anger, Bob patiently listened, nodding occasionally at appropriate moments. When Mike stopped to take a breath, Bob said, 'I experienced a similar scenario with my last wife Karen. She left an overnight bag with a plane ticket lying around as if she wanted me to find it. I was concerned about how little she'd packed for a weekend away. A brief bikini, gold stiletto sandals and a mini skirt. She obviously wasn't planning on leaving the hotel room.'

'So, what did you do?'

'I grabbed her bag and threw it into a Salvo's bin. When I told her what I'd done, she was livid as the dumper bin was padlocked. She had to telephone some guy to come out and open it late at night.'

'I bet that pissed her off. Did she make her flight on time?' Mike snickered, wishing he'd had a similar plan for revenge.

'Yes, but she never spoke to me again. I had to console myself with images of her scrambling around in the dumper bin trying to find her stuff.' He reached out and patted Mike on the shoulder. 'Sorry, mate, I shouldn't be telling you all this.'

'I'm glad you did. I sensed that Jacquie also wanted me to know. I think she's been wanting to tell me for a while. What do you think I should do?'

'Only you can decide what to do, Mike. Sorry, I can't help you there, mate. What I'm going to do is listen, without giving advice. What I am not going to do is bad-mouth your wife – who knows, you might stay married to her then things would become awkward. What you want to do right now, though, is focus on some practical strategies to cope with Christmas which is fast approaching. And think about how to tell your kids. How are you going to spend Christmas together with all this hanging over you?'

'Yeah, it's probably not a good time to tell the family about what's been going on. We'll need to keep it quiet until we know exactly what we plan to do.'

After Christmas, hopefully we'll sit down and discuss everything in a rational manner. Right now, though, he felt angry and confused. He dreaded the thought of Christmas and pretending to be one big happy family as they spent a fortune on gifts nobody wanted or needed, as they ate enough food in one meal to feed a third world family for a month. He sure as hell wasn't looking forward to Christmas this year.

The Child Within

At the slamming of the front door, Jo sat bolt upright in bed and squinted at the numbers on the bedside clock: it was barely six am – meaning Kali had been out all night. Jo had agonised over the changes in Kali's behaviour since leaving Brunei twenty years ago. She leapt out of bed to speak to her daughter before the children woke. Kali greeted her through lips smudged from last night's lipstick; a red and green Santa hat balanced on her matted hair.

'Where have you been? I was worried about you.' Jo's chest tightened as she stared at her daughter.

Ignoring her, Kali kicked off her shoes and threw her jacket and handbag over a chair. Finally, she returned her mother's stare.

'Met a guy at the nightclub, crashed at his place. I slept with Santa.'

When Kali told her she was going to pre-Christmas drinks with her girlfriends, Jo wasn't sure whether to be relieved or concerned. Would her twenty-seven-year-old daughter be safer with a group of drunken girls or on the arm of one male partner? Jo had listened to Kali's descriptions of her latest hot dates, and nothing she'd heard so far had convinced her of the latter. It was not as if she wanted to deny her a healthy love life, but some of the sexual attention she'd been getting lately was far from healthy. Each time she went on a blind date, Jo worried when she didn't come home, especially if she was drunk. She was in danger of becoming an easy target for the type of men she attracted. Previously when Jo expressed her concerns to Kali, she'd yelled back at her: 'Why don't you get a life, instead of worrying about me all the time!'

This time Jo tempered her approach to avoid another argument.

'Did you know the guy?' she asked, wrapping the belt of her dressing gown tightly around her.

'No, but the sex was great.' Kali pushed a strand of hair out of her eyes and smirked at no one in particular.

Jo surveyed her daughter, trying to remember the cute, innocent child, the tiny baby she'd cuddled in her arms. As she scanned the wild animal expressions with smeared black panda eyes and matted hair, she bit her bottom lip, knowing better than to criticise Kali if she'd been drinking. She didn't need a violent outburst at this early hour, but it was too late. Kali had already sensed her disapproval and seen the sadness in her eyes.

'What the fuck! You expect me to live the life of a nun? I'm going to crash for a couple of hours. I'm tired. Can you please take the kids to preschool if I don't wake in time?'

'What about me?' Jo wanted to scream. 'I've been living the life of a celibate all these years.' As her shoulders drooped, she tried to prise away the tension in her jaw and neck. She could hear all the reluctant words she'd failed to say over the years drumming in her ears, words that couldn't claw their way out of her throat.

She grabbed her cigarettes and walked into the garden, her place of refuge, and sat quietly on the old wooden bench, admiring the azaleas in varying shades of pink she'd nurtured from tiny plants. Inhaling deeply on her cigarette, she contemplated the monastic life of a nun, the peaceful days spent in silent contemplation, all meals provided, guaranteed restful sleep at night, freedom from family responsibilities. Yes, she could easily choose the life of a nun. And like a nun, she would pray for answers to Kali's vulnerability, the neglect of her children, her poor choices in men. She reflected on Kali's night of rampant sex, and her elderly mother's recent sexual fantasies and it occurred to her she was one of the few people in the family not preoccupied with sex.

'Are you taking us to kindy, Nan?' Adam asked as he and Sarah stumbled barefoot in their pyjamas along the garden path. With their mass of tangled golden curls and chubby faces, they appeared as angels.

'What are you doing up so early?' Jo said, surprised, as she stubbed out her cigarette. She wrapped her arms around the children and ushered them into the kitchen. There, they climbed onto the kitchen stools, and Jo tipped cornflakes into their bowls and poured on the milk.

'Is Mummy tired?' Adam asked, shovelling a spoonful into his mouth.

'Yes, we will let Mummy sleep for a while. She had a late night.'

'Mummy says if her door is closed, she's not to be stirred.' Three-year-old Sarah regarded Jo with her version of Kali's large dark eyes, the eyes and face that had once reflected that same impression of innocence.

Adam laughed. 'It's *disturbed*, silly. Not *stirred*.' At five, he liked to remind his sister of his superiority, and that he knew more than she did. He continued to shovel cornflakes into his mouth.

'I'm not silly. You are,' Sarah goaded, scowling at Adam, who poked his tongue at her.

'Let's not argue now,' Jo warned, not wanting to be reminded of the many times the kids had borne the brunt of Kali's foul moods.

Jo worried about her grandchildren and their life of uncertainty. Sometimes at night, Jo was woken by Kali shouting on the phone, arguing with Jacob about the custody of their children. Jo worried about their vulnerability, but at least they were safe in her house. While she enjoyed having them, supporting them was becoming a financial burden. This week she'd paid for Kali's mechanical repairs and the children's preschool fees. She'd already fed and clothed them. And of course, there was Christmas to get through. She knew from last year's fiasco there would be conflict between Kali, who wanted to spoil her children with presents, and Jacob, who didn't celebrate Christmas. As always Adam and Sarah would be caught in the middle of their parents' battles. Jo just wanted to celebrate Christmas with her extended family and find peace wherever she could. While she loved them dearly, she had been helping Kali and her children for several years now with little thanks in return. When she complained about this to Erin, her oldest daughter reacted the way she usually did.

'You need to think of yourself, Mum. Kali's not going to treat you with respect unless you demand it. You need to let other people know how you want to be treated.'

Erin was right. She needed to set some boundaries for herself and consider her own needs. But where would she begin? She wanted to help them and find solutions to their problems. She was also scared of losing them if she confronted Kali or created any conflict.

Jo crept into the room where Kali was sleeping to tell her she was driving the kids, reminding her of the time and the need to get ready for work. Kali mumbled something nonsensical before tossing the duvet over her head. When Jo tried again, Kali screamed at her, 'Leave me alone.'

Jo swallowed her hurt and focused on grabbing school bags and drink bottles before strapping the kids into her car. As she drove through the early morning traffic, she peered at the angelic faces in her rearview mirror, remembering Kali at the same age. She was once her precious tiny baby, born six weeks premature, fighting for life as all their friends and family prayed for her survival. 'She was a fighter,' they'd said. 'She'll pull through.' When they moved her to a nearby neonatal unit, Jo painfully expressed every drop of milk from her swollen breasts so the ICU nurses could feed her. Gareth had pushed Jo in a wheelchair to the neonatal unit so she could visit their tiny miracle. How relieved they'd been when she'd finally pulled through.

Gareth had taken over the night feeds as Jo struggled to regain her strength. He would snuggle into Kali's tiny body, gently stroke the side of her mouth when she appeared too sleepy to feed. The expression of joy on Gareth's face was enough to make her think it had all been worthwhile. During the many times in recent years, when Kali had tempted fate in every imaginable way, Jo remembered how hard they'd fought to keep her alive. They were the happy times, the special moments they'd shared. She and Gareth cherished every minute spent with their precious little survivor.

After Kali was born, Jo and Gareth enjoyed many happy years living together in Brunei. She would have been content to spend many more had he not found a lover in their fresh-faced Malay gardener. While she hadn't thought of Gareth in many years, had he been around, he may have helped Kali cope with some of her struggles. It would have certainly made a difference to Jo not having to face these problems alone. But he hadn't featured significantly in their recent lives, choosing instead another man in another country.

While nothing had been easy for Kali, every incident involving her had been a challenge for Jo. Of all the many weird incidents, the one that stuck in her mind was "The Night of Leaking Gas". Kali had complained to Jacob about the kids being cold due to a lack of heating in Jo's house. Jacob had come around with what he thought was an immediate solution to her problem, a small gas heater. After he left, Kali obsessed about the smell of leaking gas. 'I'm sure Jacob is trying to asphyxiate us,' she said.

'Why don't you turn off the heater?' Jo couldn't smell anything, and it had been a long day as her mother had recently gone into aged care and was still fretting and ringing her throughout the day. After another long, upsetting phone call, Jo brought her mother home for the weekend.

While settling her mother in the spare room, she assumed Kali was putting the children to bed in their room along the hall. As she collapsed on her bed, exhausted, Jo slipped into a deep rollercoaster of sleep. The deafening wailing of sirens and the red and blue lights flashing through her bedroom window woke her, and a loud banging on the front door forced her to leap out of bed and grab her dressing gown. Two policemen stood at the door with a fireman standing behind them. By this time both the children stood clinging to her legs, frightened at the noise and lights. Jo's mother wandered around the house, disoriented, convinced it was wartime.

'We should all go down to the air raid shelter,' she said.

As the first policeman squinted at the family group, he scanned their stunned expressions. 'Don't tell me this is a prank call.' Slowly he shook his head looking from one to the other. 'A female caller rang to say you had a gas leak which immediately alerts all emergency services.'

'I'm sorry, I know nothing about it.' Jo blinked, trying to clear the sleep from her eyes. She thought there wasn't much that could still shock her these days, but oh, how wrong she'd been.

'Does Kali Robbins live at this address?' The policeman tapped his notebook with the point of his pen.

Jo nodded. 'She's sleeping,' and no amount of sirens or flashing lights was going to wake her.

'Is she of sound mind?'

'No, not really.' Jo fixed her gaze at a spot on the ground. 'I'm sorry,' she said, returning her focus to the policeman. Her pressing need was to get rid of everyone, for them to be gone, out of her house.

'We have to take these calls seriously.' The policeman's voice softened; became less aggressive. 'Do you mind if we check your house? It's routine procedure.'

Jo nodded. If this meant she could get some much-needed sleep, she would agree to anything. All she wanted was a peaceful household with some calm in her life. Throughout the stomping, the banging of doors in each of the rooms, Kali slept soundly, lost in a world of languorous dreams.

Next day, as Jo drove to the nursing home, her mother still rambled on about air raid sirens. Like most of her other thoughts, these too eventually disappeared. At the sight of the nursing care staff, her mother's thoughts returned to her carer, Paul Wilson. She continued with boasts of her all-consuming affair.

'We are in love, you know.'

'Yes, Mum. You've already told me.'

'We're getting married in that church over there.' Her mother pointed at a building across the road. When Jo gazed at the building in question, she read the sign above the door, All Seasons Funerals. *For everything, there is a season.* But this was not the season for a happy marriage, nor a happy ending for her mother.

'Yes, Mum. I'm sure you are, but let's get you into your own room.'

Another World

For the first time since Alex's funeral, Debra relaxed with her siblings in a riverside café, enjoying the tranquil setting. Two canoeists slowly paddled down the river, and a pelican glided onto the water nearby. While Simon went to the counter to order their food, the girls sat admiring the view.

'You said you'd had a letter from Jo,' said Liz.

'Yes, I've got it here somewhere.' Debra rummaged through her handbag and read out snippets of her friend's most recent news. Jo was planning to attend a reunion in Brunei where they'd once lived as neighbours. Twenty years ago, they had no idea what life had in store for them. It was the seventies when they'd lived as expats in large adjoining houses surrounded by tropical jungle.

'When you're ready, why don't you think about joining me there. It might be good for you.' As Debra read Jo's letter, she heard new enthusiasm in her tone at the prospect of reuniting with old friends. *'Please consider coming,'* Jo had urged, *'I'd love to see you again.'*

'So, are you going to join her?' Liz asked.

'I'm thinking about it.' When Jo rang on the day of the funeral, they'd talked mostly about Alex, yet, when Jo first mentioned the reunion, there was a flatness in her voice; it was not the animated Jo she remembered.

'Life can't be easy for Jo taking care of her daughter and grandchildren while also worrying about her aging mother,' Liz said. 'Like you, she probably needs a holiday.'

Yes, it would be nice to see my old friend again. But am I ready to return to the place where I left behind so many memories, Am I ready to revisit painful reminders of a life unlived? Recently, life had sucked the joy from her, like a wringer squeezing out every drop, leaving a flattened sheet of her former self. Her first instinct was to tell Jo she wasn't up to facing the outside world. But she heard the softest whisper, a yearning from deep within telling her to go.

'Something tells me I should … and yet?' She shook her head as memories she thought she'd stuffed out of sight now resurfaced. She remembered a warm, sultry night with Jo squeezed into the back seat of a taxi with Sam and Kali. She recalled the sad song that played on the radio as they cried all the way to the hospital where Alex lay in a coma.

The last image she had of Jo was before she flew home when Jo had handed her Rahim's letter. What a shock that had been. At the thought of Rahim, a warm tingling sensation ran up her spine. She sighed deeply and enjoyed the long-forgotten sensation. She felt like a butterfly slowly pumping fluid into her cocoon, preparing to unfold her wings. Up until now, she'd remained dormant. To survive these last few years, she'd blocked out many emotions; she'd been numb for so long she'd forgotten how to experience love or joy.

'I think Alex would want you to go, Debra. A holiday would be good for you.'

For so long, Debra's focus had been on caring for Alex or worrying about Sam's ongoing problems. This unexpected surge of love and longing was something she hadn't felt in a while. She wanted to recapture it, make it last. She wanted to remember the young woman she once was when she'd shared her emotions with someone who loved her deeply. For the first time in many years, she wondered what became of Rahim. Did he think of her as she was thinking of him now? While she was frightened of the future, there was a part of her that wanted to feel alive again. She was sick of focusing on death and dying.

'I mentioned it to Sam. He seems willing to go to Brunei.'

'That's a good sign,' said Liz.

Simon arrived with the coffee and placed the mugs on the table then returned for the food, while Liz started planning the trip for Debra, reminding her of what she needed to do before she left.

'You might want to try a new hairdo,' Liz suggested. 'Perhaps a bit of leg waxing, too, if you're going to the tropics.'

'I think I've reached my use-by-date. No amount of pampering can transform me now. Dried out skin, woody on the inside, I feel like a vegetable that's been left too long in the soil.'

'Oh, go on. I'm sure there's still some life left in the old girl yet,' Liz laughed.

After leaving the café, Debra followed Liz's advice. Like a gem that needed polishing, she lacked lustre and felt desperately in need of nurturing. She found a nearby beauty salon and booked in for a complete makeover the following day. Exiting the salon, she caught sight of her reflection in the glass. A thin woman with a mass of messy blonde curls stared back at her. She'd been too busy taking care of Alex to have time for pampering herself. She let her fingers wander through her hair, caressing her face and body. By tracing her outline, she hoped to bring her vital essence back to life the way it once used to feel.

Further down the street, she found an op shop and searched the racks for long-sleeved shirts to wear in a Muslim country – something cool enough for the tropics. She read the sign above the shop, *Seafarers Mission*, part of the Flying Angel Club. It was once a haven for lonely sailors who found themselves marooned in ports like Fremantle, far from home. Across the street, an aging limestone chapel bore the name Stella Maris. A star to guide lost seamen, a refuge for those needing prayer or solace. She had a sudden urge to sit in the church and absorb the peace of its tranquil inner sanctum. Maybe after she'd finished her shopping, she would return to this place of lost souls and sit with her own sorrow.

Just inside the entrance to the op shop, a tapestry propped between a blue glass vase and a Wedgewood plate caught her attention. Embroidered on canvas, bordered in silk, the intricately detailed tapestry had exquisite stitching. An attached note explained the artist's work, *Sea of Drowning Men*. It was hard to imagine anyone achieving such precise detail with needle and thread. She held the tapestry to the light and admired the shimmering illusion. A vivid web of colour, the artist had favoured every tone of sunset with touches of aquamarine. She ran her fingers over the knobbly texture, imagining the love and labour involved in bringing these characters to life.

As she gazed at the figures, she discovered not all of them were men. At least one was a woman, another a mere child. What did it mean? She examined the tapestry more closely, fingering a loose thread, and found herself surrounded by death. All the figures appeared to be drowning. While one was alight in crimson flames, another clung to a blackened rope or anchor chain. The woman floated with her hair entangled in seaweed and flowers. Only one appeared to be walking on water. It reminded her of a Leonard Cohen song, and she silently hummed the tune.

Perhaps they, too, were hoping the sea of experience would free them. Like these sailors tossed in the oceans of chance, she understood the risk and uncertainty. Having ventured to a place where she bargained with her soul, she understood entanglement. Like a tapestry, her life consisted of the many threads woven in from past events along the way. She hoped that the warp of her life would be strong enough to allow the weft to untangle.

Moving to the racks of clothing, she chose a shirt suitable for her trip – it was brightly coloured, cheerful, and more importantly, made of cotton. It would brighten her mood, lift her spirits, and keep her cool in the stifling tropical humidity. As she folded the shirt into her bag, she thought about the people going to the reunion. While some had played a major part in her life, Jo was the only person so far that she'd heard from. Her mind wandered to the friends she once knew who she thought would always be a part of her life. But as it turned out, she hadn't kept in touch with any of them.

When Jo mentioned Mike Jasper was going to be at the reunion, she smiled. *Now there's someone sure to provide entertainment on this occasion.* With his dry sense of humour, he'd brightened her days teaching alongside her at the college. In the staffroom, he loved to tease, taking great pleasure as she blushed or cringed. He was the only one who noticed, cautioning her dangerous liaison. *Would I have heeded those warnings if I'd known then what I know now? Probably not.* She wondered if Mike still exuded the same charm and exuberance, or had his bubble been deflated by the prick of an unforeseen pin? That was hard to imagine, but she was keen to find out for herself.

***

The next day, Debra wriggled down onto the narrow bed and eased her head onto the small pillow. She was out of her comfort zone, wrapped in a white towelling gown with her hair pulled back in a headband. She breathed in whiffs of lemongrass and bergamot as it wafted past her nose. During the next sixty minutes, the beautician, Keira, promised to transform her. While extolling the virtues of each beauty product she used, Keira worked her magic on Debra's face and body. Her hands fervently cleansed, moisturised, massaged, and waxed, yet her impassive face showed no sign of emotion.

For the first thirty minutes, Debra listened to what Keira described as a soothing whale song. As she inhaled deeply, she tried to relax despite the humpbacks' squeaking, whistling calls.

'Do you find it soothing?' Keira asked.

I would find it more soothing without the humping whales, she wanted to yell. Instead, she suggested, 'Perhaps the restful sounds of the rainforest you mentioned earlier might be more relaxing.'

Keira switched the music as Debra adjusted her neck once more. She sank deeper into the pillow, letting the cooling alpine snow lotus exfoliate her skin. Keira then applied the green herbal clay mask, a product sourced from Scandinavian cold-water lakes.

Debra tried to focus on a tranquil image of lakes and alpine forests. She could smell the fresh pine and felt the icy cold water, but the sound of her phone ringing pulled her out of her reverie. While Keira muttered about peptide moisturisers working their magic on her face, Debra grabbed her phone and saw it was Sam. He could wait. As Keira massaged moisturiser into her hands, first one then the other, Debra tried to relax her restless legs.

She thought of the many times she'd tried to ring Sam when he wouldn't answer his phone. On his twentieth birthday, she'd been round to his flat to wish him Happy Birthday but couldn't wake him out of his stupor. As her stomach churned with dread, she'd choked back tears and collapsed in a heap on the floor. She'd curled up amongst the discarded cigarette butts and bottles, trying to block out the detritus of his life. She was sick of fighting and cleaning up his mess. 'Walk away, walk away,' the counsellor's voice in her head kept reminding her. With her energy spent, she'd finally dragged herself from the floor and surrendered to the compelling messages in her head.

Now she was aware of a different voice as Keira explained she was wrapping her hands in soft mitts to absorb the moisturiser. Hands that had previously laboured in the sun and dried out like starfish now rose to attention. She remembered running her fingers over a smooth pebble on the beach, stroking a bird's feather, soft and downy. She enjoyed having her hands caressed in a way they hadn't been for some time. The gentle touch to her skin ignited a sensation of comfort and love. She had once known hands that loved her, hands that had waved her goodbye.

As Keira finished the hand massage, Debra placed her left hand on her heart. Even the slightest memory these days was enough to trigger a tear. Grief as deep as a cold-water lake rose inside her and she wiped her eyes with the tissue Keira placed in her hand.

Her phone beeped. She reached for it and saw a text message from Sam. 'Can you ring me ASAP.'

She tried to convince herself it wasn't urgent. He could wait a few more minutes. She needed to concentrate on Keira who had now moved to her legs, and she winced as the first strip of wax ripped hairs from her calf. The strips that followed appeared less invasive as Keira deftly pulled, pressing her flesh with the gentlest touch. She finished waxing then massaged cream into both her legs.

'Are you having a Brazilian,' Keira asked.

Debra nodded, assuming it was yet another exotic beauty treatment. She tried to ignore Sam's message and relax. She imagined herself dancing through the streets of Rio. As Keira moved to an area above her legs, it didn't take long to realise her mistake. Even if she could, she no longer felt like dancing, especially in Rio. Keira had extended one of her legs in the air while the other she bent in a half-lotus position. She'd whisked off the flimsy paper panties and was blowing onto the hot wax blob on her brush. As she spread it onto the soft, delicate area, Debra wanted to leap off the bed. She grabbed her phone and saw another text message from Sam. *Mum, can you take me to the hospital? My jaw is frozen. I can't move my lips.'*

'I have to ring my son,' she yelled, louder than she intended.

'I've almost finished. Just a few more minutes.'

Closing her eyes, she clenched her fists, dreading the next burning contact with her skin. One leg was now wrapped around Keira's neck. The other hovered in sympathy, experiencing every jerking spasm of pain. Peering down at her bald baby appearance, she muttered, 'Wait until I see Liz. I will kill her.' Her face flushed with embarrassment as Keira offered her a glass of dandelion tea, but she declined. 'I've got to rush.'

'Take your time,' Keira said, hurrying out to calculate the bill.

Climbing into her jeans, Debra could feel pieces of wax sticking to the fabric and parts of her body itching like crazy. Her jaw dropped as she read the bill Keira handed her. She was no longer in touch with the outside world. She'd just spent more on beauty treatments than she did on her weekly groceries.

As she clambered into her car, doubts crept into her mind. She was probably kidding herself that Sam could cope with an overseas trip. She remembered birthday celebrations that were sabotaged or abandoned in years gone by. Each year she had dreaded what each latest milestone would bring. With Alex's health deteriorating, it was a painful reminder of the passing of yet another unfulfilled year. The year, Sam turned twenty-one, they'd planned to meet for lunch with family and friends before Sam went to Bali.

The guests arrived bearing gifts, keen to celebrate this rite of passage. Everyone had arrived on time, except Sam. Thirty minutes later, she'd rung to find out where he was. He said he wouldn't be able to make lunch as there were problems collecting his passport. He was conspicuous as the only one missing from his birthday celebration. While everyone tried to laugh it off, it was hardly a joke. She put on a brave face for the guests, brushing it off as just another family occasion to end in disappointment and frustration. But that night she cried herself to sleep.

Today, the traffic was light so she arrived home within ten minutes. Sam was waiting for her outside the front gate, his jaw now firmly locked, his expression frozen, his lips barely moving as he tried to talk. He leapt into the passenger seat, his eyes darting from side to side. Grabbing her handbag from the floor, he forced the leather strap between his teeth.

'I can't open my mouth,' he muttered, squeezing more of the leather strap through his lips.

Hearing the wheezing sounds as he struggled to breathe, she stole a glance at him before veering off at the hospital turnoff. Dropping him off at the emergency entrance, she directed him towards the reception desk before parking her car in the first available space. By the time she ran inside, a nurse had admitted him through doors that flew open, leaving her to fill out the necessary paperwork.

Debra stood fixed to the spot, watching the doors close again, but the clerk pointed to a seat in the waiting area. She felt cold and numb as vivid images from the past flashed through her mind. Her stomach tightened to block out the old gripping terror, but as she sat on the cold chrome seat, gazing at the stark sterile walls, she remembered the same anxiety that had immobilised her several years earlier. How could she possibly forget?

The first time she had raced Sam to a hospital, her heart had raced too, terrified he might die. In her desperate need to purge her inner turmoil, she'd vomited all over the floor, splashing the nurse's shoes. She was in such a state they fetched her water and towels but could do little to calm her anxiety. She'd never imagined then that these terrifying scenes would become the norm in her life. Back then, her fear had eventually turned to anger as she asked herself again and again: 'How could he do this to himself? How could he do this to us?'

Much of Sam's antisocial behaviour she'd kept to herself. Alex had enough of his own daily challenges without taking on Sam's problems as well. Sam's behaviour had become so strange she kept a journal to remind herself these things were real. She was not imagining these weird happenings. One day, he'd pumped air into a series of black garbage bags lined up by the front door. Beside them was a rattan chair that he'd pulled apart.

'What on earth are you doing?' she'd asked.

'I'm building a raft to float down the river.'

She stood there, speechless, her mouth agape. What could she say? No questions would give her the answers she needed. All she could do was quell her fears and convince herself she wasn't going crazy. She was not losing her mind.

She pulled out an old photo of Sam from her wallet, the one with chocolate cream smudged around his mouth as he celebrated his fourth birthday. He had a mischievous grin, and his eyes shone the way they once did before life switched off his inner light. Therapists had been quick to point out his struggles with identity and his lack of purpose in life as possible triggers with addiction. Maybe planning a trip to the place of his childhood might provide him with the answers he needed. It might help him reconnect with his roots.

She'd been waiting almost an hour, lost in bad memories and emotions when a nurse strode towards her.

'We've given him medication to reverse the adverse reaction. He should be fine now, but we will keep him in for a couple of hours of observation. Do you know what he was taking?'

'He mentioned his GP had prescribed a new medication. I'm not sure what else he took …' She threw her hand to her mouth. 'I'm so glad he's okay.

'He's experienced some serious side effects from one of these meds. It's best he stops taking them for now and talks to his doctor about alternatives as soon as possible.'

'Oh, I didn't realise.' She cradled her face in her hands before adding. 'We are hoping to go overseas in a few weeks.'

'Is that a good idea? Anyway, it's not for me to say, but you can discuss that with your doctor.'

She heard the nurse's premonitory tone. She'd heard this tone before with doctors at other times. It wasn't the nurse's concern for Sam's health as much as her doubts regarding his behaviour. She was really asking, *Do you think he might relapse again?* And the answer to that question was as elusive as it had always been. *There are no guarantees.*

'Maybe not but it's a birthday treat. I thought it would be good for him. He's just lost his father.' She tossed her handbag over her shoulder, but a far heavier weight caused her shoulders to slouch. She contemplated saying what the counsellor had said … that it might be therapeutic to revisit his childhood home, a time when he lived a carefree lifestyle, full of promise for a better future.

'No! It's probably not a good idea to take him overseas, but I'm running out of good ideas.' She looked at the nurse's tired expression. She had other patients and other places she'd rather be.

'You can see your son now if you like.'

It's got to get better, she thought as she thanked the nurse before moving towards Sam's room. At least Sam was now willing to travel overseas when previously he'd travelled no further than his bathroom. This time he was doing it cold turkey. This time, he needed to succeed.

When she walked into the ward, Sam was dozing, but the colour of his face had returned to normal. He looked more alive than when she'd seen him an hour ago.

While she waited for him to wake, she tried to focus on happier times, remembering his fun-filled birthdays as a child. This latest birthday had an element of hope. The day before yesterday, he'd sat opposite her at Sizzlers celebrating his birthday, tucking into his grilled Swiss chicken. For someone who hadn't ventured out or dined with other people in several years, it was quite an accomplishment and she wanted to shout it out, to celebrate and feel the joy. But the niggling voice inside her said, *Take it one step at a time.*

As she stared at the stark, sombre walls, Sam's voice woke her from her dreams. Lifting his head from the pillow, he murmured, 'How long have I been here?'

'Not long, but it's a good thing we got here when we did.' She reached across to hold his hand.

'Sorry about your handbag. I tried to force my mouth open.' Sam peered at the leather handbag resting in her lap with the teeth marks still visible on the strap.

'Whatever it takes. At least you're alive.'

'The doctor said the medication would help me,' Sam mumbled, his thoughts elsewhere. 'He didn't tell me about any side effects.'

'Well, at least you know now. Are you hungry? Would you like some water?' She moved the water jug towards him.

'They're bringing me a sandwich.' Sam stared out the window for a moment and then asked, 'Those mango pancakes … do you think they still have them in Brunei?'

'I'm sure they do. If you're still keen to travel, we'll have fun trying out all the local food.' She felt a warm buzz listening to him talk about food. It was a positive sign. For years he'd lived on sugary junk if he ate anything at all. The happy memories from his childhood were worth remembering, whereas many from recent times she wanted to bury forever.

On the way home from the hospital, they stopped at a supermarket, where she tempted him with more food, healthy options but a few treats for comfort. After all, it had been a challenging day.

The Last Supper

This year, Jacquie's mother was to host the annual fiasco and confirm her position as 'she who cooked the best Christmas pudding and cake' in the family.

'Poor Mum wants us all at her house this year,' Jacquie said. 'You know how lonely she's been since Dad died.'

So, the kids gave up more exciting options of spending Christmas with their boyfriends to come and spend a boring day with Nanna. What the girls didn't know was that their parents were now no longer sleeping in the same room, that they were barely speaking to each other.

Jacquie had requested a truce for Christmas Day to keep her mother happy, so they forced their strained faces into grimaces and attempted to be civil to each other, to Nanna, and their daughters. They managed these pleasantries for several hours within the close confines of Nanna's house. Despite their best efforts to distance themselves, Jacquie and Mike squeezed around one another inside the tiny cottage.

Their girls were preoccupied with their busy personal lives, content to talk non-stop about their work, their friends and lovers. They didn't know their parents' love life had been shattered. They didn't notice their father's strained expression or how he sat on his hands to stop himself from throwing one of the willow-patterned plates at his wife sitting opposite. He watched Jacquie laugh at something her mother said, patting her hand as if nothing had changed since last Christmas. He looked at the gaudy tinsel hanging overhead and thought how he'd like to wind a strand tightly around Jacquie's throat to stop her laughing.

Nanna poured more custard onto his pudding despite his protestations. His hand bumped her arm and a yellow blob slithered onto his lap. Jacquie threw back her head laughing, while he attempted to scrape it onto his side plate. She'd been experiencing the same happy Christmases for the last fifteen years while he'd been living a lie not of his creation. He grabbed piles of discarded gift wrappings and rammed them into the bin. He scraped Nanna's precious plate with such vigour it shattered, and tiny pieces of blue willow scattered across the kitchen floor. As he swept up the pieces with his hands, a shard lodged in his finger. He ignored the blood dripping onto his trousers, but this latest pain exacerbated his growing rage.

'Look at all this rubbish going into landfill … wasted food that could feed the starving.'

'Why don't you wrap it and give it to the poor instead of complaining.' Jacquie smirked, tossing back her heavy fringe.

When the charade finally ended and it was time to say goodbye, Jacquie's mother took him aside in the kitchen and suggested in her own version of subtlety that he might want to put more effort into his relationship.

'I've noticed you both seem a bit strained with each other.'

Well, she didn't need to be observant to notice that. Stevie Wonder would have picked up the vibes. But it was what she said next that took every bit of restraint to stop him shouting obscenities in her face.

'Wives need a lot of attention. Sometimes you need to try a little harder to make things work in a relationship,' she said, with more grimace than smile.

He took a few rapid breaths, before glaring at her. He wanted to shout at her, to tell her the home truths about her precious daughter. *Husbands also need attention, you old cow. Not that you would know as your husband probably died to escape from you. Why don't you tell your daughter to try a little harder? In fact, perhaps you should have told her fifteen fucking years ago.*

Instead, he transferred his toxic thoughts to his face, squeezed his brows together, and cursed through his teeth. 'Sod off, Norma. Give it a rest.'

With her mouth agape, she threw her hand to her heart, the royal jubilee tea towel still fluttering in her hand.

Once they were home and Jacquie asked him what her mother had said, he released the last of his pent-up rage. 'She's trying to blame me for our disastrous relationship. Telling me I should be trying harder. Why didn't you tell your mother you'd been playing Doctors and Nurses these last fifteen years?' Slamming the door behind him, he stormed out of the room.

As he walked into his girls' bedroom, it was like entering Toys 'R Us. Occupying the shelves were families of Cabbage Patch dolls, My Little Ponies and Care Bears of every persuasion. Covering the walls were framed pieces of amateur art and photos. He looked at a baby photo of Amanda, their firstborn. In it, he was holding this precious bundle in his arms, and his eyes sparkled as he gazed at Jacquie with affection. They looked so young, no doubt believing this joyful state would last forever.

He remembered singing to Amanda the old Temptations song, *My Girl*. He looked at the next frame of Amanda at two with her baby sister, Alison, in her arms, he and Jacquie supporting her on either side. He recalled how helpless and soft those tiny babies felt. He'd had an urge to wrap them tightly in his arms to protect them from the world. He could no longer do that. He now felt as vulnerable as a newborn and had no idea how to protect himself, let alone his children. The guilt at what he was doing to his daughters churned in his gut. They were tearing their family apart.

More alcohol was probably the last thing he needed right now but he grabbed the keys and drove to Tesco. He had to get away from this house with its sad memories and walls that were closing in on him. When Mike returned with six bottles of wine, Jacquie took out two glasses and placed them on the table next to the wine.

'I just bumped into Hugh at Tesco, and he barely spoke. In fact, he looked as if he was going to avoid me.' Mike opened a bottle of Shiraz and poured two glasses.

'Well, he and Jan are my friends. They're obviously embarrassed about our situation.'

'They were my friends when they asked me to help install their new TV. They were my friends when they wanted me to pick them up from the airport last month.'

'Friends don't like to choose sides when couples break up. It's very awkward for them.'

'Well, Hugh made it clear who he was siding with just now. You've obviously given them your version of our situation.'

'I told them we've grown apart and decided to go our own ways.'

How could we have grown apart when I made the decision to return to the UK to make this marriage work. When Jacquie wanted our daughters to have a traditional English upbringing, with good schools, their grandparents nearby and them pursuing their careers in England, I agreed. While I was devoting my life to growing towards her, it seems Jacquie had other ideas. Maybe it is time for us to move on, to go our own ways in life. Jacquie seemed to be reading his mind.

'We need to sit down and make a few rational decisions, Mike.'

'Yes, I think you're right. We don't seem to have much left to salvage.'

***

Jacquie had chosen *The Rose and Crown* to meet for drinks after work. While it was close to the hospital where she worked, she also knew it would be rowdy. Intimate surroundings would mean long drawn-out silences and awkward conversation. Why they had to have this meeting at all was beyond Mike, but Jacquie thought they could discuss all they needed to in a safe neutral setting.

As Mike walked in the side entrance of the pub, a young couple drunk with love and numerous bottles of cider were singing a discordant version of *Nothing Compares 2U*. With their arms wrapped around each other, it was difficult to see who was supporting who. He walked towards the bar and spotted her long legs dangling from a bar stool. She was sharing a joke with the barman. After all this time, he still found Jacquie attractive but the loving feeling he once enjoyed was now replaced by an icy shiver.

The bar was full of young couples throbbing with lust. He could smell the pheromones emanating from their nubile bodies as they rubbed against each other. Everywhere he looked lovers moved in closer to share their lewd plans for the evening. A red-booted girl was wrapping her feet around the veloured legs of a track-suited hairy male, his soporific eyes and grin fixed firmly on her breasts.

Jacquie greeted him with a brief peck on the cheek, a habit she had perfected over twenty years. After grabbing a drink, he suggested they move to a quieter table at the back of the lounge bar. As he scanned the room for an empty table, he remembered a similar bar to this, where he'd first met Jacquie.

While he was playing in The Banned, she and two friends had danced close to the stage. She knew all the lyrics and had sung along to a song they were playing. Twisting provocatively with her hips, she'd really turned him on. He was mesmerised. With her long black hair parted in the middle, her hair swayed in time with her body. By the end of the night, he thought she was his. It was only in recent years she confessed it was the drummer and not him she'd fancied that night.

They sat at a table and there was an awkward silence before he turned to her.

'Do you remember the first night we met at The Plough? You were dancing, singing along to the song we were playing? What was that song? Do you remember?' No sooner had he asked the question the answer immediately came to him.

'Smoke on the water.' They both spluttered, laughing, at the same time.

'We joked about it always being our theme song like in the movies. What do you think your theme song would be now?' he joked, but his eyes were not smiling.

She paused before giving him her answer. 'Probably Tina Turner. "I don't want to Fight." She studied her drink closely before glancing up to gauge his reaction.

'You always loved a good fight.' He attempted another joke but saw the slight quiver of her lips, sensed her discomfort. Perhaps her desire for freedom didn't have the same appeal now that it was within her reach. He too had a hint of fear at leaving behind the familiarity of those he'd come to know so well.

She didn't react immediately but instead asked him the same question. 'And your song. What would it be?'

Mike tried to lighten the mood, but it was noisy, and the atmosphere had become heavy. He twirled the glass in his hand as if trying to find some inspiration. *Disappear.* 'Right now, I'd like to follow INXS and simply disappear. Maybe sometime in the future, we will refer to this night as the last supper.'

She didn't laugh at his joke. Instead, her eyes moistened as she focused again on her drink. 'It doesn't have to be this awkward, Mike. I don't know why you're making it so difficult.'

He moved in closer to avoid sharing the state of their disastrous marriage with the barman or anyone else who happened to be walking by.

'I've lost fifteen years of a marriage I thought I had invested in for life. You think I'm making it difficult.' He thumped his glass down more loudly than he intended.

Jacquie forgot her momentary remorse and launched into attack. 'It's not as if you were always faithful. What about Debra? I'm sure you slept with her.'

His jaw dropped and he was momentarily stuck for words. 'Debra? You've got to be joking. There was never anything between us.'

'Well, you always raved about her … how amazing she was.'

It had been a while since Mike had thought about Debra, but he wasn't being completely honest. The fact there was nothing between them wasn't from lack of desire. The reality was he didn't stand a chance, not with Rahim around. He couldn't possibly compete with him. That was a match he could never win. Since Jacquie had sought to resurrect Debra from the past, he found himself thinking about her. *What has become of her? Where is she now? Will she be going to the reunion?* There was only one way to find out.

When the waiter brought a Caesar salad for Jacquie and a chicken parmigiana for him, Mike asked him to refresh their drinks. After they finished their mediocre meals with several bottles of wine, they managed to discuss the necessary business details. They planned to sell the family home in Worthing and their holiday place in the Dordogne. From the proceeds, they would both purchase smaller, separate dwellings. Their daughters could choose to visit each of their parents whenever they wanted.

Initially, their girls had complained about them selling both houses. 'Where will we go for our holidays?' they asked. 'Where can we store our things if you sell the house?'

'I think it's time you began storing your own things, time to let go of the past,' said Mike. It was a time for culling anything they no longer needed in their lives. It crossed his mind that perhaps the good doctor had a holiday house on the Riviera where the girls could spend their holidays. But it was still way too painful to think about right now. With the paperwork out of the way, Mike started to unwind and ordered another bottle of wine.

Jacquie, too, was experiencing the effects of the alcohol, relaxing her body and loosening her tongue. She reminded him of the time he was late for the birth of their first child. Previously she would have retold the tale with added recrimination. Now with the help of the wine, she laughed as she shared the joke with him. He, too, was willing to admit the excuse he'd always given was a lie. Instead of his car running out of petrol, he'd actually stayed for a few more beers after he got the call to say she was in labour. His mates thought he should at least wet the baby's head before he went to the hospital.

'What about when you kept me waiting twenty minutes at the altar?'

She conceded it wasn't because of a faulty zipper in her bridal gown. It was because of last-minute nerves. 'Mum had to practically drag me into the limousine.'

This latest revelation came as a shock. It was like a punch to the ribs. As he hadn't prepared himself for the blow, he felt the full impact. He was disappointed to think she was having second thoughts at a time when he was totally committed to their relationship. But there was also a sense of relief that this charade was now over. After all these years they could choose to see the funny side. He'd probably been sensing the unease for some years but wasn't ready to confront the consequences. Now the wound had been opened, he wanted to heal and move on.

They walked towards the exit where the young couple from earlier in the evening were still singing the same tuneless lyrics of Sinead O'Connor.

'Do you think they will remember this one day, recalling it as their theme song?' Jacquie laughed at him with bleary eyes.

'I bloody well hope not.' He playfully bumped her shoulder.

As they staggered along the cobblestone lane, they became aware of someone following them. They quickened their pace, but the man ran faster. He yelled as he chased after them. Mike grabbed Jacquie's hand and pulled her around the corner. The man followed in hot pursuit until he was upon them.

'What the fuck?' Mike spun around with his fists raised ready.

The man doubled over, his hands resting on his knees. In between breaths, he gasped, 'The boss says you have to go back … pay your bill.'

Mike spluttered as Jacquie shrieked and threw her arms around his neck. He grabbed her around the waist, as they hugged and laughed. It had been one of those unbelievable nights.

Revelations

Jo left the aged care home after visiting her mother and walked to her GP's private practice. Conveniently located merely one block away, Jo could no longer put off a visit she'd been dreading for some time. Since planning her trip to Brunei, she'd undergone a long overdue medical check-up. Today she was awaiting the results of the tests.

As she sat in the doctor's reception area, she clenched her jaw, dreading what the doctor was about to tell her. While she massaged the tension in her neck, she forced her focus to her upcoming holiday instead of her impending test results. The trip would be a great opportunity to reconnect with old friends. After talking to Debra on the phone recently she acknowledged how much she missed her dear friend. She was everything Jo had hoped for in a next-door neighbour.

One of her current neighbours, Robyn Jamieson walked through the door and waved to her. 'I need to have my hearing tested,' she shouted across the waiting room.

Jo nodded, moving her handbag from the seat so Robyn could sit next to her. She was an affable woman but, as she refused to wear a hearing aid, it was impossible to engage in lengthy conversations with her. Fortunately, due to her deafness, Robyn was spared from Kali's frequent aggressive outbursts.

'I've just seen our neighbours Ralph and Aiden taking Mimi for a walk. They were bringing in your bins.'

'That's sweet of them.' The grandkids adored Mimi, their Chihuahua, and despite her initial hurt of discovering Gareth's secret gay lover, she had nothing against Ralph and Aidan. She couldn't have asked for better neighbours.

Lately, she'd been thinking about Gareth and could at least remember some of his positive qualities. When they were living next door to Debra and Alex, there was always time for a coffee or a chat. And she remembered Debra … *since Alex's death, it's been tough for Debra. Sacrificing the love of her life to nurse Alex through his worst years can't have been easy.* While speaking with her on the phone recently, Debra had asked her, 'Do you remember the letter you gave me before you left Manila?'

Debra mentioned the name of her past secret lover, but Jo couldn't remember it now. He'd asked her to deliver a letter to Debra. *What on earth was his name?* She rolled a few names around on her tongue, but none appeared to fit. Rama, Roman? Finally, it came to her. *Rahim.* She remembered steaming open the letter and resealing it after reading the eloquent prose, the words of pent-up love and longing. It was the type of old-fashioned love letter people wrote when separated by distance or circumstance.

'Why did you keep it from me for so long?' Debra had asked.

'I don't remember,' she'd said when Debra had recently asked her. She remembered it contained a yearning for love so intense it stayed with her long after she'd handed it over. An outpouring of passion that could not be covered nowadays by a simple text message or email. She knew it was wrong to pry but she wanted to discover the secret language of people in love, to know how it felt. An intimate missive to be read in private by the recipient of the sender's desire. By opening the letter, she had breached their privacy. She wondered if she would ever experience anything quite as precious.

'Would you like to come through now?' the doctor's words jolted her out of her reverie. The dread tightened in her chest once more as she heard her doctor's words. 'I have the results of your tests. I'm afraid it's not good news.'

She closed her eyes as she sank into the doctor's chair dreading another challenge she would have to face alone. She thought of the stress she had stored in her body which was once full of comfort, providing nurture for the family she loved. Was this to be her reward? Poor health? More stress? Those same receptacles of nurture now transformed into organs of disappointment, regret, riddled with disease.

By the time Jo arrived home, she was determined to tell Kali about her latest health concerns. Once she would have shielded Kali from her bad news, believing she had enough challenges of her own. But this latest news had shown her the importance of acting now while she could still make clear decisions. It had reinforced the need to make the most of what precious time remained. From now on she would be putting her own needs first. While Kali didn't react immediately to her mother's health news, she was interested in her plans to take a holiday in Brunei.

'I'll come with you to the reunion, Mum.' Kali pulled out her mobile phone. 'When are you going?'

'In two weeks. But what about your kids, Kali? Where will you get the money?'

'I'll ask Erin to lend me the money. Jacob can mind the kids.' She scanned her diary, checking various dates.

'Do you think that's fair? Erin is saving for a new car. Jacob will have to take time off work.' She took a deep breath and tried to relax the tension in her jaw and neck.

'Mum, I can take care of you over there. Besides, it's the place where I spent my childhood. I'd like to go back.' Kali had made her decision and, putting her own plans into place, was about to ring Erin and Jacob.

Jo sighed and shrugged her shoulders. Once more, she gave into her daughter's demands. 'I'll give you the money for the trip if Erin agrees to mind the kids for a couple of weeks,' she said.

'Thanks, Mum, I'll pay you back.'

'Yes, Kali. I'm sure you will.'

A Flight of Fancy

Debra sat nervously in the departure lounge, alternating glances at their carry-on bags and checking her wristwatch. Occasionally she peered at the flight departure times in case the electronic numbers had clicked over again. *Ten minutes to boarding time. Twenty minutes since Sam took off and there's still no sign of him. Perhaps he's panicked and done a runner. It wouldn't be the first time.* He'd gone for a wander around the shops, but she suspected more likely he had ducked outside for a last-minute cigarette.

Unaware of how long she'd been clicking the handle on her carry-on bag, she noticed the bald man sitting next to her staring down his nose at her. She fanned herself with her boarding pass, slowly at first, then gathering speed until the same man glared over the top of his newspaper. Shoving the boarding pass into her handbag, she checked her passport was still there then once more peered at the departure board. When she looked back, Sam stood in front of her.

'I got some Nicorette and sweets.' He showed her the packets in his hand.

'We'd better get in the boarding queue,' she said and, rising, pushed her case toward the line of passengers.

Waiting in the long queue, she shot a glance at Sam and noted the slight twitch to his mouth that appeared when he was agitated. She reminded herself that it had been many years since he'd been on a flight and a long time since he'd been in this proximity with so many people.

As they squeezed into their seats, she touched his hand. 'How are you feeling?' then reminded herself to give him the emotional space he needed. It would take time for him to heal.

'Okay. I'm just going to watch a few movies.'

Later, she stole another glance, pleased to see him picking at the food on his tray and laughing at the movie. In this comfortable silence, she sank against the headrest and closed her eyes.

When her chin fell onto her chest, she jolted and blinked, trying to remember where she was. She wasn't sure how long she'd been asleep, but it was the best sleep she'd had in a while. Leaning towards the window, she squinted at the glare but saw nothing but clouds.

'We're almost at Kinabalu,' Sam said without taking his eyes off the flight map on the screen. The cabin was abuzz as people adjusted their seats and strained to look out the window. The pilot announced they would soon be flying over the highest mountain in Southeast Asia. Sam rested his forehead on the glass and peered into the mist, searching for the momentous spectacle his mother had promised him.

'I hope this is worth waiting for,' he mumbled, one corner of his mouth twitching. He had mountains of regret at the many holidays he couldn't share with his father, and since he'd been on this aircraft, he'd been wrestling with his guilt.

'I hope you won't be disappointed.'

'I hope so too.' He continued to gaze out the window. 'The clouds are so thick I can hardly see anything at all.' It was like the fog of not knowing how to please his father, mixed with the shame of disappointing him. Despite his regrets and the loss of his father, there was a feeling of lightness around his neck and shoulders, but he couldn't explain this sense of relief to his mother.

'Hopefully, they will pass soon, and you'll get a clearer view.' But when the long-awaited vision finally appeared, he was hunched over, stuffing his iPod into the seat pocket. 'Sam, there, look!' She pointed at craggy peaks rising mysteriously out of the mist. It reminded her of the old Kadazan legend, the peak shaped like the profile of an old woman, waiting for her Chinese lover who never returned.

Sam turned around in his seat long enough to take in the wondrous sight before the flimsy stage curtains obscured his vision. Debra continued to gaze at the window hoping for another glimpse, but it wasn't to be.

'Wasn't it worth waiting for?'

'I guess so, but I was expecting ... I don't know ...' Returning to his iPod, he adjusted the dial. It was yet another disappointment, something which didn't meet his expectations.

'You might get to climb it one day. I don't think you're ready right now. It would mean getting fit, giving up cigarettes.' She immediately bit her lip, regretting her tone of reproval. She'd promised to give him some slack and he now scowled at her.

She mouthed the word 'sorry', the thought suddenly embedding that he was almost the age she was when she first brought him here as a three-year-old. He flicked a mop of dark hair from his face, his curtain of hair separating him from the outside world as he closed his eyes. How much he had changed since then.

He sensed her observing him and opened his eyes. 'Are we there yet?' A faint glimmer appeared in his eyes as he attempted an old childhood joke.

'Not long now.' Up until recently, the thought of returning to Brunei had been too painful to consider. She hoped she was strong enough to face it. Glancing at Sam's hunched lean frame, she hoped she was making the right decision.

'We should be landing soon.' He grinned.

She sensed a silent truce between them and scanned his face again, a habit she couldn't shake off easily. His eyes were distressingly blank, but at least the whites were no longer red. Nor were his pupils dilated – all comforting signs when crazy doubts competed for space in her head. This time, there would be no Alex waiting to greet them – and *no Rahim*.

An unexpected rush of blood sent her pulse racing. She silently rolled his name on her tongue. Twirling the beads at her throat, she felt the knots tighten and took a few deep breaths.

'Are you all right, Mum?' Sam patted her thigh and moved in closer.

'Yeh, I'm fine. Just tired.' While there was no point dwelling on the past, there had been times when her life choices had led to exciting unpredictable outcomes. But the stress of taking care of Alex had led her to seek out the permanency of safer paths and dependable outcomes. She hoped they were now on the right path to finding the peace they both so desperately needed.

Sam, who'd been fiddling with the buttons on his armrest, wrenched off his headset and tapped his fingers on the food tray. 'I need another Coke.'

He peered around in his seat, searching for a flight attendant. But the attendants were busy collecting empty cups and getting ready for landing. Debra signalled to a shy Malay girl hovering nearby. She nodded obligingly and brought Sam his drink. After sculling the Coca-Cola, he anxiously fiddled with the empty cup. Then he asked about when she had climbed the mountain many years ago.

'Was it cold? Were you dizzy?'

It had been cold at the summit. She'd wanted to climb quickly, but the scenery was breathtaking. She remembered the cold seeping through her sweaty T-shirt as she stopped to take in the spectacular views. Whenever they rested, she was aware of the dark shadow hovering above her, but the cold wind speared through her, forcing her to move on.

'I suffered from altitude sickness. My head was throbbing. I had to keep resting. But when I reached the summit, it was so well worth it. Sometimes you need to keep pushing on through the tough stages. It's definitely worth it in the end.'

'Dad climbed it in record time, didn't he?' he said, thrusting his thumb into his mouth and starting to bite his nail.

'Yes, he climbed it several months before me. Apparently, he did it in four hours.' She peered at Sam. 'You miss your dad, don't you?'

'Yeah,' Sam nodded and then fumbled with the in-flight magazine and started flicking through the pages, his hands trembling. He popped a piece of nicotine gum into his mouth and waited for it to quell the cramping in his stomach. The beginning of a headache was not helping his nausea as he wiped more sweat from his brow. He chewed slowly until he could taste the nicotine, followed by a tingling sensation in his mouth. After a few minutes, when the tingling was gone, he began chewing again. He pointed to a photo in the flight magazine of the base camp at Mount Kinabalu showing orchids and pitcher plants. 'Do you remember the pitcher plant I had as a kid?'

'Yes, you were upset by the trapped insects. You wanted to help them escape.'

'I felt sorry for them. They didn't know the risks they were taking,' Sam muttered.

'Perhaps they thought the risk was worth it. The lure of temptation is often stronger than anything else.' She thought of the risks she'd taken in her own life, pursuing forbidden love. An enticing prospect was always hard to resist. She also thought of the risks Sam had taken, but when she saw him scowling, she changed the subject.

'Look at those glorious orchids. Such beautiful colours.' When she'd climbed Mt Kinabalu, she'd had no way of knowing there would be far greater mountains ahead. It had taken her many years to learn how to climb the insurmountable and many more to navigate rocky paths. The first time she had peered over the edge she was breathless, terrified by what she saw. After this more recent glimpse of the summit, she resolved to make the most of each precious moment and not dwell on her fears.

For years, she'd suffered along with Sam in his agonising, slow waltz with death. When she woke in the middle of the night, drenched in sweat, always her first thought was, is he still alive? Her head abuzz with hideous, self-inflicted torture, she'd worried day and night about what her child was enduring. Why would this perfect child, whom she lovingly nurtured, be so intent on self-destruction? It took a long time for her to learn there were no rational answers to such irrational behaviour. But now she needed to move on.

She watched Sam eat the last of his salted peanuts and seeing him eating was a joy she couldn't describe. To see him sitting next to her on this aircraft was beyond her wildest dreams. Without warning, her eyes moistened again, and she quickly wiped at the tears.

After Sam's most recent admission to hospital, she knew she wasn't ready to abandon him. They had a stronger need to cling to each other, to keep their heads above the eddy that threatened to suck them into its depths. Together they would get through the loss of Alex.

The flight attendant took Sam's empty cup and proceeded with her round, ensuring the seat backs were upright and the food trays stowed before landing. Shoving his iPod into his bag, Sam zipped the outer pocket as the landing wheels clanked into position. With engines humming, the fuselage creaking in protest, the captain pulled back on the throttle and jolted them onto the runway. As they taxied towards the terminal, Debra caught glimpses of the ocean and palm trees outlining the airport perimeter of Kota Kinabalu.

The shuttle bus took them to their hotel on the waterfront; it overlooked a grandiose 18-hole golf course of verdant green mounds and a marina where itinerant yachties moored their luxury craft of extravagant sizes. She chose Sabah to begin their journey so Sam could visit the orangutans in Sepilok. His love of animals had helped him survive some of the toughest periods in his life. Hopefully it would help him deal with the next step of his journey. Despite the fear piercing through her, she also felt a pressing need to return to this strange land with its poignant memories. She had returned to make her peace with what she'd left behind. Kota Kinabalu was the last place she'd spent a few nights with Rahim, and she had shed many tears since then.

Kota Kinabalu

They settled in the hotel room and unpacked before taking an organised tour around the base of Mount Kinabalu. For about an hour, the coach driver travelled towards the mountain along a bumpy, winding road. Each bend provided a different vista of craggy peaks peeping through thick white clouds. Debra peered through the window at each changing view.

Stepping out of the coach, she inhaled deeply, filling her lungs with the invigorating freshness. She couldn't remember the last time she'd felt this relaxed. Sam replayed the video he'd filmed but handed her the camera and pulled out his pack of cigarettes. She ignored his planned assault on the fresh mountain air. When the tour guide asked for a volunteer to lead the walking group, she foolishly raised her hand, forgetting she was now fifty and not exactly fit.

As they set off along a rocky path of gentle inclines, Sam panted as he stubbed out his third cigarette, taking regular breaks to catch his breath. For a young man, he was not in good shape.

His emaciated frame and unsteady step reminded her of Alex after he'd been in hospital for several weeks. When Alex was finally discharged from the first hospital overseas, she'd been a mess of mixed emotions. While relieved he was well enough to go home, she felt nervous about the flight and worried about how they would cope with their new life challenges. In Australia, Alex's hospital stay was much longer than they'd expected, with regular sessions of dialysis.

Eventually, some semblance of normal family life trickled into their otherwise organised chaos.

She reassured herself that Sam would get better, especially now that he was eating again. Unlike his father, he had a chance to improve his health and regain his fitness.

She checked again on Sam, who now walked without complaint, managing to keep pace with the group. While they were merely at the base of a mountain, they were making progress one step at a time, ready to face each challenge as it presented itself. On a bamboo suspension bridge swinging gently with the breeze, she rested a moment to catch her breath. Everywhere she looked a show of vibrant flowers peeked out amongst ferns trailing over giant palms, helping her to focus on the present instead of the past. As she weaved her way across the swaying bridge, she wiped away the sweat dripping from her brow and running into her eyes. Her damp, clinging T-shirt and trousers concealed the stinging heat rash gathering under her breasts and between her thighs.

When they reached the Poring Hot Springs, a cleaner cold-water pool beckoned, and they wasted no time jumping into the freezing water. In response to her shrieks of protest, Sam laughed and splashed water on her face. Rolling around in the water, he resembled a large hairy walrus, shaking his dark sodden fur. When she commented on his likeness, he launched into a discourse on the life of a walrus.

'Did you know walruses are amongst the most gregarious of animals? They haul together in herds. You rarely see one alone.' He dived, then emerged once again and shook out his hair.

'Is that so?' She playfully splashed water on his face. 'So, they take care of one another?' She thought of his own reclusive lifestyle. While he enjoyed his pets, he no longer sought out the company of friends.

'Yes, unlike many humans who don't give a shit about anyone else.' He completed another cycle of rolling over and over, and when he resurfaced, she tried to tap into what he'd just said.

'I'm sorry if I haven't always been there for you, Sam. I was often busy taking care of your father. You know he would have liked to share your activities, but wasn't always capable. We both loved you very much. I still do. And I'll try to be a better mother.' She watched him bite on his thumbnail before diving deeply again.

The coach driver took them to a restaurant with magnificent views of the mountain, where Sam tucked into a plate of mee goreng; she ordered a samosa with coffee. By the time the coach dropped them at their hotel, Debra felt exhausted. For the first time in many years, she slept soundly. The next morning, she woke refreshed, ready to tackle whatever lay ahead.

After a taxi ride to the airport, it was a relatively short flight from Kota Kinabalu to Sepilok, where a coach took them to the orangutan sanctuary. Stepping out of the coach, Sam keenly videoed the wildlife. She sighed as she glimpsed the rehabilitation centre, a sanctuary to protect endangered orangutans.

The jungle's familiar smells elicited many vivid images. The stilted wooden buildings with traditional shingled roofing and wooden shutters still held the dank, musty smell of years gone by. Her friend Mike had lived in an older house of similar design in Brunei, and she'd become accustomed to the sounds of wooden floorboards creaking, while noisy ceiling fans clicked and whirred in the humid air. A forgotten moth fluttered in her chest as she remembered the room in Mike's house where she last spent precious moments with Rahim, where wooden shutters opened onto a garden courtyard providing spectacular views of Mike's fishpond, replete with large golden koi.

Another image flashed to her mind of the same fishpond where dragonflies hovered and whirled. Chinese paper lanterns hung around a fragrant garden of frangipani where Rahim placed a single blossom in the palm of her hand before folding her fingers around the delicate flower. She remembered his smell of musk and citrus, his warm, sultry skin as he leaned in closer, and Jo, who had been observing them, described it as 'a token of love' while Debra tried to justify it as simply a flower. With good neighbourly sensibility, Jo had warned her of the risky path she was treading. As a concerned friend, she could foresee, long before Debra, the entangled web of love and deceit, unimaginably sublime yet so dramatic as to change her life forever.

They walked along the elevated wooden planks of the sanctuary, with its many jungle sights and sounds. A long-tailed macaque swung from a vine overhead and crashed clumsily into a clump of bamboo, Sam deftly zooming in with the camera, laughing as he captured the monkey's antics. Despite the stifling humidity, it was a joy to see him laughing again. After he declared he was hungry, they sat outside a nearby café and ordered iced lemon tea, with curry puffs for Sam.

While they waited for their food and drinks, a busload of tourists clambered down the steps and walked towards them. Debra watched the men wipe their brows with handkerchiefs while the women shook their bamboo fans. *Welcome to the tropics*, she thought, smiling to herself.

Sam quickly devoured his curry puffs before racing back to the viewing platform to wait for the orangutans' arrival. Slowly stirring the slices of lemon, she clunked the ice blocks against her glass. As she lifted the straw to take a sip, a tall, bearded man strode towards her. There was something familiar about the slouching shoulders and gangly swinging arms. As he stared at her, his face split open in a wide grin.

Increasing his stride, he drew nearer, until he stood in front of her, laughing loudly. 'Debra. Oh my god! I saw you from the coach window. I had no idea it was you. I didn't expect you to be here.' As he took off his sunglasses, his blue eyes brightened. He didn't admit that, for the last ten minutes, he'd been watching her, the way she moved along the elevated walkway had caught his eye, as if she was dancing or lightly skipping each step. The sunlight shining through her flimsy skirt revealed those long slender legs. It had to be her. Twenty years may have aged her but there was still a girlish bounce in her step as she balanced along the wooden planks.

'Mike Jasper! My God. It's been a while. You haven't changed a bit.' Grinning like a teenager, she stood to greet him.

Tall, tanned, and lean, his arms seemed to wrap around her several times as they hugged. At this unexpected gesture, the surprise at seeing him elicited more tears, and she wiped them with her hand. How much she needed to be embraced, to be loved by a dear friend.

'It must have been hard parting with all those curls.' He released her from the hug so he could inspect her more closely, then he ruffled her newly cropped hair.

'So much easier to manage.' The chic style the hairdresser created was now a mass of shorter sweaty curls. 'This is the new me,' she said, twirling on the spot in front of him.

'Well, I like what I see. You appear more …'

'Sophisticated?' She raised her eyebrows, waiting for his response.

'Wiser, I was going to say.' He nodded, confirming his choice of words.

'That sounds like a polite way of saying older. But yes, I certainly hope I'm wiser. Sit down, I'll get you a drink. Are you going to the reunion?'

'Yeah. I thought I'd break the journey in KK before going on to Brunei. I've spent the last couple of days climbing the mountain. Oh my God, my knees are still groaning. Twenty years ago, it was a cinch. It's no fun getting older. While your memory thinks you can do it, your body sure as hell lets you know you can't.' He looked at her iced lemon tea. 'I hope you've brought plenty of duty-free booze. Apparently, you can't even get beer in teapots these days. Things have really changed in Brunei.'

'I grabbed a bottle of gin in Duty-Free. It should be enough for me. Sam's no longer drinking. Here he is now.'

Sam eased away from a group of Japanese tourists and their clicking cameras, hurried up to his mother, and noticed Mike. He frowned slightly before blurting out his news.

'They're about to open the nursery for viewing the young orangutans. Do you want to see them?'

'I'll follow you in a minute. Sam, this is Mike. He and I taught together at the college in Brunei. He's also going to the reunion.'

'Hi, how are you?' Sam said, slowly thrusting his hand out towards Mike.

Grabbing Sam's hand in both of his, Mike shook it like he was mixing a cocktail. 'Holy shit. When I saw you last time you were a little ankle-biter. Now you're nearly as tall as me.'

'Yeah, right. Have you seen the orangutans yet?' Sam relaxed, hearing Mike's friendly banter.

'No, but I'm about to. I thought it was a great opportunity while I'm here. Setting ourselves these gruelling itineraries, we obviously forget how draining the humidity can be. I can't believe we lived in the tropics for six years. No doubt we eventually acclimatised, but I'm finding it tough now.' Mike took a handkerchief from his pocket and wiped the sweat from his face.

'We didn't live here that long but I know what you mean,' Debra agreed.

Sam pulled at his clinging t-shirt. 'Yeah, right. Anyway, I'll see you later.' He darted back to where the rangers were about to feed the orangutans. Another reddish-brown hairy form performed somersaults on a rope and Sam laughed, pointing to his mother. Debra waved back at him before turning to Mike.

'It's such a relief to see him laughing,' she said. 'He's been through hell these last few years.'

'And you also, no doubt. I was sorry to hear about Alex. It must have been bloody tough on you.' He stroked his grey-flecked beard and leaned back against his chair, staring at her. 'I wasn't sure you'd come.'

'I wasn't going to, but thought it might be good for Sam.' She immediately felt at ease with him. 'Let's walk over to the nursery. I hope I did the right thing bringing him here.'

While Alex's death was only one of her many challenges, she wasn't ready to disclose anything to Mike.

'I'm sure it will be good for him. I'm glad you decided to come. It was one of the reasons I came.' He sauntered towards the glass enclosure and Debra followed.

'Really?' Her mouth opened but she was momentarily stuck for words.

He probed her with never-ending questions. When he asked how she was coping, she told him it was harder than she thought but her lower lip trembled, and he reached out for her hand.

'Facing our worst fears is always difficult. Moving on can be daunting.' He gazed at the orphaned animals through the glass. Many had been injured and rescued from logging sites or plantations. 'It's also tough when you're forced to face the regrets and hopes of what might have been.'

Faced with an unexpected opportunity to offload, Debra reneged on her earlier decision not to disclose all to Mike. Instead, she told him how she thought death was her worst fear but discovered the hardest part was letting go. 'I found there's a certain comfort in suffering. Letting go means having to release the source of the pain, but also the love, the memories you want to hold onto.' The challenges she faced, the times she tried to let go had never been easy.

'Yes, it's about finding the right balance of knowing when to hold on and when to let go.' He glanced around the glass enclosure, the towering jungle canopy of overhanging trees and vines. 'At least the animals are safe in this ideal environment,' he added, but his face fixed in a frown.

'I'm sorry, Mike. I haven't asked about you and your family.' She placed her hand over his. Visible signs of tiredness had formed around his eyes.

'We all have our own brand of pain. Mine was divorce, so I can relate to some of what you're going through. At least your sense of loss.' He moved his hand to his beard, stroked it with his fingers. 'I had no idea what was going on in my marriage. Although I probably could have seen the signs if I'd really wanted to.'

'And how are your girls coping?' Debra asked. In front of her, rangers spread out food bowls of milk and bananas for the young ones who couldn't forage for themselves.

'They're survivors like me. They'll be fine.'

'But still a terrible loss. Marriage is never easy, is it? Even when we think we're preparing for what's about to come, it's still hard to let go,' she said.

He lifted his sunglasses to read a brochure he'd picked up at the visitor's centre. 'Did you know we share similarities in DNA? These orangutans are susceptible to our diseases.'

'Yes, I read that somewhere. I'm happy to view them from a distance if it keeps them safe.' She looked at Mike whose face had always been full of fun and laughter. His unfailing sense of humour had helped to put her at ease in many difficult situations. Now she sensed the heaviness surrounding him, a sensation she knew too well.

Sam walked over to join them. 'Hopefully, it won't be long before they can be released. With their natural habitat shrinking, we want them to survive.' Like the sunlight, Sam's expression was bright and full of hope.

'Does this bring back any memories, Sam?' At the sight of Sam interacting with life and nature, she felt a pleasant flush as welcome as the sunlight between the trees.

'I thought we'd been able to get in closer before. I remember touching them.'

'Yes, many things have changed since our last visit.' She placed her hand on his shoulder as they climbed the steps to the elevated viewing platform.

Although she'd only spent several hours with these animals, she had the same positive emotions she remembered playing with her own babies. She felt a sense of elation but regret at the thought of leaving them, saying her goodbyes, and walking away. Sam lingered longer, wanting to capture these precious memories on camera.

'I'm sorry I didn't keep in touch with you or any of my old friends, Mike. But when your child is struggling there's often no good news to share.' She brushed back her hair and wiped sweat from her forehead.

'I'm sure there will be plenty of opportunity at the reunion to reminisce with old friends.' He grinned. 'Hopefully, you and

I can spend more time together. I'd better join my tour group, though, before they leave without me.'

When she stole a peek at him; there was a new sparkle in his eyes, as if he was preparing to laugh or cry at the same time. They exchanged phone numbers, and agreed to meet in Brunei, where they were staying at the same hotel.

'It's been amazing bumping into you like this.' He hugged her before kissing her on the cheek.

'Yes, it's been lovely. I'm looking forward to catching up in Brunei.'

As he strode off, she thought how much she'd missed the company of good friends in recent times. And Mike had been the first one to welcome her to Brunei. With his clever wit, he'd created a fun-filled atmosphere at the college. Otherwise, she may have been uncomfortable teaching in a Muslim country, surrounded by men of a different culture.

***

They left the orangutans to visit the next destination on their tour, the house of writer, Agnes Keith, who had lived in Sandakan during the war. In her diary, she described the anguish of raising a young son within the confines of a prisoner of war camp. Her son, George, had been two years old when they'd first entered the camp and five years old by the time the Japanese released them.

Debra empathised with the mother and child who had endured such suffering. She knew too well the sensation of being powerless to help her son. She understood why a mother would starve herself to feed her child, but she could only imagine the punishment inflicted upon them. While George's playground had been a cramped, rat-infested camp lacking basic sanitation, at a similar age Sam's life had been comparatively comfortable.

She felt extremely grateful that Sam had survived his life of misadventure and was still here for her to love and nurture. If Agnes and her son had lacked space in the camp, she hoped Agnes had curled in close to her child and was soft enough to serve as a pillow for him. She hoped she was strong enough to move heaven and earth when he needed her most.

Outside the house, Sam stared at a large mango tree, its branches weighed down with ripened fruit. 'This is like the tree Kali and I used to climb.'

Kali, his childhood friend, daughter of Jo and Gareth McKenzie, had been his constant companion. Throughout the day the children had wandered between the two gardens which had adjoined their houses. Kali's life had not been without its challenges, and Debra was looking forward to seeing the little girl she remembered and the young woman she'd become. She was also keen to catch up with her caring neighbour, Jo, who had supported her through many trials. Debra, in turn, had helped Jo through the scandal with Gareth and his secret lover. At the time, she'd tried to console her, but Jo's thoughts had been muddled, her words incoherent. Sleepless nights hadn't helped her to make sense of what was happening.

'Life has a way of handing us thorns when all we want is roses,' Jo had said. 'Gareth had no regard for the love and labour I put into our relationship.'

Debra had listened to her friend at the time and nodded, 'People are often not what they seem, Jo.'

Debra and Sam made their way to the coach for the return journey to the airport. As it wended its way around the many bends in the road, she found herself nodding with the motion of the wheels. After boarding the aircraft, she was not aware of anything until the aircraft bumped onto the runway and Sam touched her arm.

'Mum, we need to get off.' He grabbed the small bag and helped her descend the aircraft steps. When they reached their hotel, she barely managed to shower and order room service. That night she slept soundly and didn't wake until Sam told her they would miss breakfast if she didn't hurry. Exhausted from the humidity and sightseeing, she'd been dreaming about people from her past, including Jo, Gareth and of course, Alex. In a recent recurring dream, Alex had always appeared larger than life and everyone was acting as if he hadn't died. There was the briefest moment when reality overtook the dream, and she buried her disappointment in the bedding and pulled the sheet over her head. It wouldn't bring him back to life but at least it would help cover the huge hole of emptiness inside. She checked her wristwatch against the time for their flight to Brunei.

It was easy enough to flag down a taxi to the airport, and to check in their baggage. After boarding, she checked the number on their seats close to the wings. *What did Alex tell me? The wings are the safest place to sit or is it one of the places I should avoid?* If the aircraft crashed, she would have little time to debate the consequences of such insignificant matters.

A flight attendant pushed a trolley of soft drinks past them – no longer serving alcohol – which reminded her it was a Muslim country and she settled for a Coco Colada, a sweet sickly coconut juice garnished with a wedge of fresh pineapple and maraschino cherry. What she wouldn't give for a shot of rum to perfect the drink and calm her nerves.

As the landing wheels clanged into position, her stomach lurched with a mixture of dread and excitement as they approached the country she'd left so abruptly twenty years ago. She peered through the window at the number of aircraft waiting on the tarmac. *I must tell Alex when I get home; let him know how much it has all changed,* she thought.

A jarring realisation reminded her she couldn't tell him. He was no longer there. Manoeuvring her way through the crowd, she viewed the flashing arrival board and the armada of aircraft now arriving in what was once a tiny sleepy hollow. *And I can't tell Alex about any of these changes. Not the modern terminal building, nor the new aircraft. I can't share any of it with him.*

Bandar Seri Begawan

Driving from the airport to their hotel, along a street named after the Sultan, the bird-boned Malay taxi driver chatted happily. He told them about some of the evident changes and some of which they were unaware. Gone were the bustling market stalls once offering fresh fish, prawns and dried curry paste in the centre of town.

He laughed, impressed with his well-rehearsed repartee, 'Moved out further. Making room for progress. More cars, more highways.' He closed all the windows and turned the air conditioner to its highest setting.

A circular highway led out of town, coping with the influx of faster, modern cars. Through the window, Debra scanned the new high-rise buildings that had risen in the town. Sam pointed out a large, multi-storey shopping centre, its glass and chrome glistening above the others.

'Take a look at that. Talk about skyscrapers.'

'I think I preferred the old markets and small Chinese shops. Hen Long stocked everything from sacks of rice to outboard motors. He used to give you curry-flavoured Twisties whenever we went in his shop. Then he'd surprise your dad by pulling out bottles of beer he'd hidden behind the soy sauce. These modern buildings are stark and soulless.'

Aware of the flat tone creeping into her voice, she tried a lighter approach. 'It's good to see the town is flourishing though. You can't stop progress.'

Revisiting any place is never the same the second time around, but I didn't expect it to have changed so much. Gone were the malodorous monsoon drains encircling the old markets. While she didn't miss those odours, the exotic smells of fish and spices evoked memories from long ago, stored away in olfactory receptor cells but now triggered into life.

Her strongest memories were of the people who'd helped sculpt her enigmatic life in Brunei – most of them now gone, leaving only the ghosts of the past. Her first impression of Bandar Seri Begawan had been a tiny backwater, isolated from the outside world. Now this quaint town appeared to be racing ahead at an alarming rate. *Although some buildings haven't changed.* She pointed out to Sam the mosque, the old Chinese temple, the iconic water village unaffected by the blustering winds of time. Thrusting above these tireless icons, towering billboards tempted consumers with mobile phone and computer hotlink options.

'There's plenty of cheap WIFI deals.' Sam turned in his seat, dwelling on the signs longer. For Sam, these were important details to keep him connected to the outside world. Merely a child when he first arrived, he had little memory of the town or its buildings. Sam now gazed at these ultra-modern monoliths displaying the opulence of their wealthy owners.

'Where do they get their money?'

'The Sultan is from one of the oldest continuing monarchies. A very rich and ancient history.'

The taxi driver confirmed, 'Thirteenth century. Merchants from Persia, Arabia, and India brought Islam to this area.'

Sam nodded politely before sighting the entrance to a luxurious hotel looming in front of them. The driver slowed down before parking outside a salubrious five-star resort set among coastal acres of tropical rainforest. Sam's goggling eyes widened to take it all in.

'You didn't tell me about this,' he waved his hand in a circular motion, taking in the views of sparkling blue ocean and surrounding palm trees.

'I wanted to surprise you. I hoped you'd be impressed.' Debra inspected the sloping roofline of ornate traditional architecture, the imposing entrance of towering glass flanked by Travellers' palms. 'Wait until you see inside.'

While she'd previously only seen images in brochures, she too felt speechless when viewing it at close range.

'Oh my God! It's awesome,' Sam spluttered, rushing to get out of the taxi.

He gawked at the marbled pillars reaching to the high, sloping ceiling, to the sparkling chandeliers catching the light, everywhere he looked, he saw an unashamed display of wealth.

'I'm glad you like it.' She wrapped her arm around his shoulder.

'Wow!' He continued to scan the light-filled lobby, everything flashing with gold. As his grin grew increasingly wider, she laughed at his childlike expression.

A polite young porter showed them to their room which had a balcony overlooking ornamental ponds, a sandy beach, and a Jack Nicklaus signature golf course.

Sam dashed about the room, swearing at the sight of the gold taps on the spa bath, the size of the beds. Despite the air-conditioning, Debra's shirt clung to her back, and she smiled and nodded when he suggested a dip in one of the five pools. She agreed to try out at least one today. They quickly changed into swimsuits before covering themselves in respectable attire to meet hotel standards.

They chose a large pool with a fountain in the centre, where elevated tiled slabs invited them to sunbathe or simply laze around the edge. They sat, dangling their feet to test the water before sliding their bodies into the water. While not refreshingly cold, the water was a relief from the suffocating humidity. Sam explored every corner of the vast pool network while Debra floated on her back, allowing the water to caress her skin. As she gazed up at the cloudy blue sky, an involuntary smile crept across her face. She was here at last. They'd arrived in this surreal place, and so far, none of her dreams had been dashed. Right now, everything in her world felt perfect and she sighed as a tingle of excitement spread through her body.

She eventually lost track of time until a hungry Sam reminded her it must be time to eat. They dried themselves and changed into clothes before sitting at the poolside café. With so many tempting snacks to choose from, they took their time scanning the menu. Sam ordered spring rolls to take him through lunch while Debra settled for a coffee. She laughed as his eyes lit up when he spied yet another favourite on the menu.

'Mango pancakes! I'll try those for breakfast tomorrow. When can we go and search for our old house?' Sam asked as they waited for their food to arrive.

'Maybe tomorrow. Some of the older houses have been demolished. I'm not sure if our house will still be there.' She watched Sam's expression fade. 'But we can certainly try to find it.'

After breakfast the next day, when Sam had tried everything in the buffet, including the pancakes, she hired a car. Then they drove around town as she tried to get her bearings. Some of the old streets had now been blocked off or rerouted to make way for the new highways. For the first few minutes, it was as if she had driven around in circles. Finally, she discovered one of the new roads was a shortcut to the one on which they used to live.

She appreciated that a long, deep concrete canal had been built alongside the low-lying road replacing the smaller monsoon drains. Notorious during monsoonal weather, she remembered when her car had skidded across the road and plunged into a flooded drain. She had thought at the time she was going to die. If she had, she wouldn't be here now with Sam enjoying this holiday. Sam twisted in his seat, straining his neck as he stared out the window.

'Mum, do you remember the street number? Do you think you'll be able to find our house?'

She wasn't sure, given the complicated system of house lot numbers that included the number of crossroads along a main road. She was about to tell Sam she had no idea when a series of numbers flashed into her head.

'*Simpang 226*,' she spluttered. 'It's just come to me.' She stared ahead at the crest of a hill where the road veered left in a sharp bend. 'It's starting to look familiar. I think it might be over that hill.'

'There's *224*,' he yelled, echoing her excitement.

Rising in front of them on the other side of the crest was their old home. From its exterior, the house appeared the same as she remembered, but the paintwork had faded from the relentless sun. The lane once separating the house from the local *kampong*, had become so overgrown the house now blended in with the Malay village.

Newly built for them to move into, the house had appeared modern and stark rising out of the jungle in isolation. As newly arrived expatriates, they too had stood out as strangers in this exotic land. She had no idea then how enmeshed she would become in this home with its tropical surroundings. Nor did she know how this country would wrap its tendrils around her, pulling her in closer until the moment it was suddenly wrenched away from her.

Jungle had been cleared to build the house, and the newly planted garden had been sparse, except for the fully grown mango tree. The Chinese landlord had used some foresight in planting bananas, papayas and pineapples before the house was completed and they never grew tired of indulging in the fruit of his labour. She scanned the garden for signs of the fruit trees and the once-familiar sunflowers that followed the path of the sun.

After pulling into the laneway, Sam grabbed the video camera and dashed around the perimeter of the fence. All at once, he was a child again squealing with excitement as he pointed out how tall the mango tree had grown, and that the rope swing still hung from its branches. They heard someone shouting from behind the house and a woman's face appeared at the window, staring out at them.

'We can always return here. Now we know the house is still here, you might like to come back to explore on your own when you have more time.' She waved at a small boy who appeared at the front door. Sam finished filming and packed the camera away in the bag.

At the sight of the boy, who looked about four years old, she remembered Sam at a similar age and felt a lump in her throat. She remembered squeals of delight from the lower end of this same garden, a small, brown, puppy rushing past, followed by Sam on unsteady legs. Kali's wig of long red hair sliding off his blonde curls as Kali, dressed as an angel, ran after him. She could still remember the children dancing with joined hands, as a languid sun cast off another day. *Yes, I remember the happy times when Alex was well, and we appeared to have everything we needed in life. It was a happy home yet a house concealing secrets and desires.*

'Yes, I'll come another day. I'm hungry right now. Where can we go for lunch? Is there somewhere near here?'

'I saw a small café by the river. Let's try there.'

As they drove along the lane, a Malay man on the front verge slashed long grass with a parang. The rhythmical sound of the large metallic blade slashing the grass reminded her of the first time she'd arrived in this country with Alex. He'd been keen to show her their garden, but they'd arrived late at night. When she awoke the next morning, eager to explore her surroundings, she discovered her new contact lens had scratched her cornea. Barely able to see anything at all, she had to visit the local hospital.

This time, she would embrace everything. She would keep her eyes wide open and enjoy exploring everything anew. She would also try to forget the painful past and focus on enjoying each precious moment.

The Joker

After lunch at their hotel, they tried out an infinity pool that overlooked the golf course. As Sam frolicked, she relaxed in the soothing water. Later, when she walked through the lobby, she saw a familiar lanky form standing at the reception desk about to check-in. She'd spied him earlier getting out of his taxi, but she'd hesitated, not wanting to appear too eager. She'd been expecting him and felt relieved to see he'd finally arrived. Since their recent meeting in Sepilok, thoughts of him had crept into her mind when she'd least expected them. She blushed now at the thought and tried to distract herself.

Edging her way over to him, she took time to admire a gold-framed photograph on the wall: an aerial view of the water village of Kampong Ayer. She peered closer, admiring the stilted wooden houses and the mosque in the background, then took a deep breath before approaching the reception desk.

'I'm glad you arrived safely,' she said, tapping Mike on the shoulder.

'So am I. My flight was delayed an hour, but it gave me a chance to buy more duty-free.' He pointed to a large plastic shopping bag on the floor. If you'd like to come to my room for a sundowner, I'm happy to share.' He squinted at his room key, deciphering the engraved numbers. 'Room 506'.

'That sounds great. We'll come up about six o'clock. I'll let you get settled first.'

She took the lift to her room on the third floor and found Sam stretched out on his bed. When he saw her, he lifted his head from the pillow and rubbed his eyes.

'Can't believe I fell asleep. Must be the humidity and all the exercise.' He wandered onto the balcony and lit a cigarette, inhaled deeply and gazed out over the sparkling ocean and shoreline rimmed with palm trees strung with fairy lights. These would soon light up the vast stretch of sandy beach. 'Can I order room service? I just need a snack before dinner.'

'Sure. I'll jump in the shower.' Last night she'd relaxed in the spa bath, taking her time, lighting the perfumed candles positioned around the rim. Tonight, she wanted to take more time to get dressed. It was so long since she had a special occasion to prepare for, she wanted to enjoy every moment. She had missed the thrill of anticipating, choosing what to wear and looking the best she possibly could. *But how should I act and how should I feel?* She was so out of practice at experiencing joy that her nerves weren't sure whether they were ready to fire or if they needed recharging.

She hesitated before telling Sam about Mike's invitation for drinks. Would he be uncomfortable around alcohol or socialising with someone he didn't know well? While she wanted Sam to be at ease, she felt excited at the prospect of spending time with an old friend, though felt a little surprised at Mike's show of affection when she'd seen him earlier. Her hands fumbled as she unbuttoned her shirt before throwing it on the back of a chair. When was the last time she dressed for a man?

She took her time in the shower, pampering herself with the hotel's fragrant soaps and lotions. Wrapping herself in the largest, fluffiest towel she could find, she redirected a few stray curls with the blow dryer, scrunching the rest into shape with her fingers.

Glimpsing the silver cocktail dress hanging in her wardrobe, she pulled it out and held it against her. *No! it's too formal*, and she didn't want to look as if she was trying too hard. Settling for a cooler, long cotton dress, she fastened a string of pearls around her throat before pulling them off again. *No, too classy.* Her locally made beads looked more casual, as if she'd thrown it all together without much effort. She fingered the colourful Malaysian necklace of threaded beads with the matching bracelet. Traditional motifs painted on each bead depicted part of a cultural legend involving a hero, his weapon, and a mythical venomous snake. This last revelation did nothing to calm her nerves and she broke out in a sweat.

Pressing her lips together, she grinned at her image in the mirror. *Who'd have thought I'd be preening myself for a man? Has it really been twenty years?* Grabbing her purse and door key from the dressing table, she waved to Sam, who frantically surfed channels on the television.

'Will you be okay here? Have you ordered some food?' She hovered at the door.

'You've already asked me that. I'll see you later. Room 506, right?'

When Mike opened his door, he appeared relaxed in an open-necked blue polo shirt. An ice bucket with a dish of lemon slices sat next to the gin bottle on the small balcony table. After filling the glasses with a generous serving of alcohol, he added tonic, handed her a glass, and then raised a toast.

'Here's to us. We came back.'

'Yes! And we survived.' She leant against the wrought iron railing and gazed out at the darkening sky and the shimmering ocean. 'So, Mike, are you still beating out rock 'n roll songs?'

'My band has recently landed a few small gigs so you might say I'm on the road again. What about you? Are you still trying to change the world quoting the words of The Prophet?'

'It was Rumi actually. And yes, I still love poetry. No longer erotic but occasionally romantic. Mainly inspirational prose. I'm still trying to bring peace to the world, mostly through yoga and meditation. I think there's a greater need for peace today than there was in the seventies.'

'That sounds like a description of my life. No longer erotic but occasionally romantic.' He threw his hands in the air and they both laughed.

'Do you ever regret the decisions you made – think you'd have done things differently?'

'There are things I regret not having said.'

She waited for him to elaborate but he remained silent. 'After Alex died, there were many things I regretted – things I wish I'd told him. But would it have made any difference? I think he'd already chosen the way he wanted to live.' She took another sip of her drink. 'And the way he wanted to die.'

'Alex always appeared so self-assured. As if he knew exactly what he wanted and he was going to go after it. I'm surprised he didn't survive longer.'

'Yes, and yet, at other times, inside the large, confident man, I glimpsed a scared little boy.'

'I can relate to that.'

'You, Mike? Never!'

'I'm a sensitive soul when you get to know me. Like I said, Debra, there are things I regret not having said ...'

'Do you want to talk about it?' She stared out to where he was gazing over the sandy beach below.

'I'm not sure I'm ready to tell you yet. Maybe later.'

'You never called me Debra before. It was always Ms De Bra or Grainger, but never Debra.'

'I was always nervous around you. Somehow it felt too intimate to call you Debra. You know we jokers like to hide our real emotions. We use comedy to mask our vulnerability.'

Glancing at him, she checked if he was about to share another joke, but the lines around his mouth showed an unexpected childlike expression. She'd thought the nicknames he gave her were part of his thrill of playing around with words, but now she started to view him in a new light.

Mike continued to stare past the myriad of ornamental lights. After finishing their drinks in silence, he refilled the glasses, spilling tonic onto the table. He quickly mopped at it with his handkerchief.

'Perhaps we should have a toast to absent friends.' She raised her glass.

'Not yet. Maybe later.' He lifted his glass and drained the contents. 'Let it be just the two of us for now.'

She was not used to this serious man who had replaced the once fun-loving person she used to know. She was about to tell him so when the doorbell drowned out her words. Sam was late as usual, but she chose not to comment.

Although she knew Mike was keen to eat, he didn't rush Sam. Instead, he tried to bring him into the conversation, asking him what music he was into, who was his favourite band.

'So, you're a Springsteen fan,' Mike read the print on Sam's T-shirt. '*Born to Run*. Is that your favourite song?'

'Hard not to love The Boss. He's written some great songs.' Sam spent a lot of time listening to music on his headphones, and admired the man who empathised with the destitute and downtrodden.

'I'm surprised you're not an Acker Dacker fan. Ozzie rock legends closer to home.'

'Yeah, I get ACDC. *Highway to Hell. TNT.*'

An appropriate anthem for Sam's life, Debra mused as they finished their drinks. In the past, his explosive lifestyle always heading in a downward direction, was indeed a highway to hell. The rocky road was his choice, though, and nobody was going to slow him down.

Mike held the lift door open to take them down to the restaurant where an air of grandeur reflected the overall opulence of the resort. The menu included many local dishes and Debra pointed out a dish she thought Sam might enjoy. The popular Chinese steamboat allowed them to cook their own food.

She felt easier now Mike, the serious, had disappeared and re-emerged in a persona she remembered well, the guise of the joker. He delighted in amusing Sam with stories about a modest restaurant that used to specialise in this same dish but lacked modern conveniences. Forever the consummate storyteller, Mike described the long black extension cords snaking their way across the restaurant floor from the kitchen to the electric cookers on each table. He mused about the times he'd also tripped on many of the cords.

'Depending on the amount of alcohol we consumed,' Mike assured Sam, 'it could be quite treacherous. On most occasions, I managed to manoeuvre my way through the meandering minefield, but I had a few mishaps.'

Sam's grin widened as he listened to each new amusing tale. Mike was now on a roll, each of his stories becoming more ridiculous than the preceding one.

Debra couldn't remember a time when she heard Sam or herself laughing like this. The heavy weight that had anchored her to the floor seemed to have lifted. She had a strange lightness around her shoulders and, when she left to visit the toilet, she felt she could simply float away. *Is this how it feels to let go?* she wondered.

Mike dropped an assortment of raw meat, seafood and vegetable pieces into the bubbling broth, tempting them both with each tiny morsel. He spent several minutes trying to rescue a slippery quail's egg with wobbling chopsticks but, as he got it closer to her mouth, the egg slipped off the table and onto the floor. Sam laughed, gripping his stomach with both hands. He toppled and almost fell off his chair.

'That's it,' Mike declared, laying aside his chopsticks. I know when I'm defeated.'

He returned to entertaining Sam with more of his tales from the past and spoke of dining on similar humid nights when they were entertained by rats scuttling across the trellis and peering at them as they ate. Debra, too, remembered being mesmerised by these rodents, terrified that they would suddenly appear on her plate.

'We kept our hands hovering above our plates, scared they would drop onto our food.' Mike circled his hands in a frantic combative motion.

'Bullshit! You're pulling my leg.' Sam laughed, then stood and pushed in his chair. 'I'm going out for a smoke.'

'Thanks for entertaining, Sam. He obviously enjoys your company. I haven't seen him relax like this in ages. I keep reminding myself to find the joy in every moment. But often the past gets in the way.'

'I won't argue with you there, Debra. Do you think you're capable of making a new start?' Mike stared at her with brows arched. He had turned on his serious face again.

'I need to give it a try, so long as my body is not permanently frozen. I feel like the Ice Queen. Maybe this humidity will thaw me out. Hopefully, there's a whole load of joy hidden inside.'

'I hope so too.'

When Sam returned, he told them about the flying ants he saw outside, the discarded pile of wings. 'It shows they've recently mated. When it's time to reproduce, the young queen grows wings, flies off to mate and starts a new colony.' His face brightened, and his chatter became more exuberant. 'Once the males have mated, that's it. Their role is over. The queens chew off their own wings and begin searching for a suitable nest. That's the pile out there. Keep an eye open for large, winged females joined together with smaller males.' He nodded. 'It's the nuptial flight.'

Debra's jaw dropped. She couldn't believe the enthusiasm in Sam's voice as he waxed lyrical – her laconic son now full of fervour as he expressed his passion for low-ranking insects far down the food chain.

'Bloody hell. You know a lot about mating, Sam. Thank God, you didn't tell me the females eat their males. That would put me off copulation for life.'

In recent times mating had not rated highly on her agenda, but Debra now considered the plight of a flying ant. While it clearly meant a nasty end for the males, it was not exactly a pleasant task for the females chewing off their own wings. She hoped she could grow new wings and embrace her new freedom. It might take a while, but she sensed the beginning of what it would be like to explore new horizons with endless possibilities.

With an interested audience, Sam told Mike about reptiles he was interested in and those he was keen to see. After reading books on Borneo wildlife, he hoped to see a Sunda pangolin.

'They're endangered,' Mike told him. 'You have more chance of viewing the stuffed version in a museum than seeing them alive. They are very rare. One of the world's most trafficked animals. They don't do well in captivity, so you don't get too many in zoos either.'

'That's a shame. I thought Brunei was one of the places we might be lucky enough to spot one. When can we go to the museum, Mum?'

Sam had asked this question several times since they'd arrived in Brunei, and she hesitated before answering.

'One day soon.' The words caught in her throat, and she felt the same tightening in her chest each time someone mentioned that place. Before too long she would have to confront her demons. She knew she couldn't keep putting it off.

Several *cicaks*, transparent in the light, ran across the ceiling in search of insects. She changed the subject, reminding Sam of his earlier fascination with these small geckos. How upset he was when they met their fate in the hinges of a door or by falling into a kettle or toaster. Sam's eyes glazed over as if remembering, but he didn't comment.

Mike offered more amusing anecdotes to accompany hers. But it was the tale of Mike's wife being stung by a jellyfish that brought Sam the most laughter. It was not the thought of her pain or discomfort that amused him, but the image of Mike offering to pee on her chest.

Letting Go

Long after Sam had gone to bed, they returned to Mike's balcony to continue reminiscing. The stories grew funnier with each additional drink. As the talk turned to the upcoming Yacht Club reunion, many of the jokes revolved around sailing disasters or drunken yacht club parties.

'I'm so glad I have all those precious memories. It's what sustained me through the tough times,' Debra said.

'It couldn't have been easy coping with Alex's illness.'

It was as if he were reading her thoughts, and something about his affable manner made her want to confide in him. The weight she'd carried for too long cried out to be lifted, to be offloaded onto someone willing to listen.

'There was an incident,' she confided. 'Apart from Jo, no one knows about it.' She strummed the beads at her throat. 'It had nothing to do with Alex. But it's shattered my trust in men, possibly tarnished my love life forever.'

'My God. What happened?' Mike's jaw dropped as she told him about the night she was due to fly out of Brunei.

'I wanted to say goodbye to Rahim before I left. We'd arranged to meet at our secret place. While I waited for him, two men who'd obviously been watching me, waited for the right moment to pounce.' She closed her eyes, supporting her head in her hand. The memory still had the power to churn her stomach and sour her mouth, but she continued. 'I didn't have a chance with two of them. They were brutal with no concern for my well-being. I fought them off, but my body was bruised, my spirit crushed, my resolve weakened forever.'

'Bloody hell! I'm speechless. And you didn't tell anyone about this?'

'Apart from Rahim. Jo was waiting for me when I got home. But I was numb. It took a while before I was able to talk about it. She flew with me to Manila where Alex was in a coma.'

Once she started to offload, she wanted to rid herself of the burden that had been weighing her down for so long. 'Alex was too ill to notice my bruises or ask any questions. I was so concerned about his pain I didn't tell him about mine. You can see why I was reluctant to come back here. I can still smell the fear, as if it's lurking, waiting for me.'

'Gosh. And all I had to cope with was a bloody divorce.'

'Everyone has their own version of pain, Mike. You're entitled to yours. What I felt was shame and guilt. No matter how much I washed, I felt as if I'd never be clean again.'

'I can imagine.' Mike stretched out his long arms, inviting her into his fold. The silence that followed was more healing than any words. As he held her, she felt warm and safe with her face snuggled into his neck. Mike slowly released his grip but continued to search her face. 'A drink is probably not the answer but it's all I can offer you right now. Anything I said would fade into oblivion after what you've just disclosed.'

'You've given me more than you know. For the first time in ages, I feel almost human.' She glanced out beyond the gardens to the spectacular lights of the *Istana Nurul Iman*, the Sultan's palace. Illuminated like a Christmas tree, it was a magical scene, like something usually witnessed during the festive season.

'There's enough bloody power out there to light up the streets of London,' she said

Mike followed her gaze. He also tried to lighten the mood that threatened to suffocate them like a London fog. 'All that wealth and power. But does it make him happy?'

She remembered when they first came to Brunei with nothing but a few basic possessions. How quickly they began to accumulate the trappings of life, a larger house, a luxurious car. It didn't take long for her to understand that these material objects failed to bring her the happiness she'd been seeking. 'While I sometimes envied the Sultan who had so much, I also admired those who led a simple life yet appeared to be happy.'

'Like Rahim?' he said.

Her pulse quickened at the mention of his name. There'd been a time when that name could trigger a response in her as swift as a flaming bushfire. Now there was a huge empty space where his presence once occupied every cell in her body. The same sinking emotions washed over her as they did when he sadly disappeared from her life.

'He didn't always have a happy life. During his teens, when he went to live in KL, it was difficult for him.'

'Before you knew him?' Mike's eyes clouded over, and the mood shifted once more, the air becoming heavier. 'Meeting you changed his life. I could see that. He was a different person with you.'

'He didn't always have me.' The precious time she shared with Rahim had been much too brief. The fairytale had ended soon after it began. She observed Mike, and while there was a hint of the carefree person she remembered, the serious persona seemed to be competing for space. She wanted to learn more about this enigmatic man but was not sure how long it would take. 'And what about you, Mike? Have you moved on with your life? Found another love?'

'No, I still need to convince the right woman.' As he grinned, his face took on some of his familiar comical expressions.

'The old Mike Jasper had no trouble convincing any woman.'

'You never really knew me, Debra.'

'I admit I should have got to know you better. There were so many other things competing for my time.'

'And other people. But there's still time. I'm here now.' Mike chose this moment for a rare disclosure. 'I've lost my confidence with women. It seems Jacquie didn't care as much for me as I did for her. It was a relief when the split finally came. Our relationship had become like a well-orchestrated song. I guess it had reached its natural cadence.'

He failed to mention that his fear of becoming involved with another woman was churning his insides, causing him to break out in a sweat. He poured them both another drink and in no time it was as if there'd been no gap and they'd been chatting every day of their lives.

'Fifteen years she was unfaithful to me … leading a double life. I must have been an idiot not to notice. If I ever sleep with another woman, I'll be paranoid thinking they, too, are faking it.'

After swallowing her wine, Debra's tongue softened. She rearranged her mouth into shape and thought about her past life of deceit. So many regrets and so much left unsaid. Aware of the hurt and disappointments involved in any relationship, she was no longer sure if she was willing to commit, but at least she could test the water.

'I'm worried that all my working parts have rusted out from misuse. I might have to fake it too. That's if I ever have sex again.' The alcohol was now talking, emboldening her to continue, to take a chance.

'That's easily fixed,' Mike laughed. 'I can get you some engine lube. WD40. It removes rust in car engines; I'm sure it would do the trick for you.'

'Oh, Mike, at least we can laugh about it, which is better than the alternative. My emotions are such a mess. I find myself happy one minute and sad the next. Hopefully, the happy times will soon outweigh the sad. Then I can experience real joy.'

While slurring their speech and unsteady on their feet, they'd captured the past and believed they'd solved many of the world's problems. They were both yawning but when they kissed goodnight, it was cosy, like a warm cup of tea. Later that night when she dozed, she dreamt of strong arms wrapped around her, comforting her, and blue eyes twinkling like the stars.

Nodding Donkeys

Debra and Sam joined Mike for breakfast in the courtyard next to a pond replete with well-fed koi and whirling dragonflies. Debra followed Mike's gaze, mesmerised by the flash of darting red and gold, or occasional silver and white.

'They're not a patch on the koi you used to keep, Mike.'

'They wouldn't have thrived had it not been for Rahim,' he laughed. 'He had the golden touch.'

Again, the flush rose to her cheeks at the mention of his name. She fingered each bead at her throat, each one fastened with a knot, matching those in her stomach. She hesitated before asking the question she'd been dying to ask. 'Do you ever hear from him?'

Mike paused and slowly shook his head. 'No. We lost touch.' Tiny wrinkles spread to the corners of his eyes as he searched for an appropriate response. 'I tried to keep in contact. Don't know what happened. Not sure where he went.'

'I heard he went back to KL.'

'Maybe.' Mike moved towards the breakfast foods spread along tables beside windows with magnificent views of the South China Sea.

She'd been holding her breath but now let it go with a sigh of disappointment. While food was a poor substitute, she needed comfort and followed Mike to the buffet table. Sam woo-hooed at the array of food on display and wanted to try most of the dishes. Debra smiled as she watched him savour the boundless feast. *It's so good to see him eating again.*

Mike laughed, and shook his head at the sight of Sam's plate piled high with food. 'Sam, if you keep eating like that, you'll outdo the pangolin. What was it you said he ate? 20,000 ants a day.'

'200,000.' Sam laughed and almost choked on a piece of fresh pineapple.

After breakfast, they hired a driver for the day. When Johari asked if they were interested in an itinerary he'd designed for tourists, they initially declined, but later decided they might need one. So much had changed and they were keen to visit new places as well as old haunts.

At Sam's request, Johari took them to the other end of the State. He wanted to see the 'nodding donkeys' pumping oil out of the ground along the sandy coast, and insisted on taking a photo of Debra and Mike leaning against one of the mechanical pump jacks. Mike's initial response was 'sod off', but he dutifully posed for Sam, wrapping his arm around Debra and pulling her in closer. As she edged over to peer at Sam's screen image, Mike kept his hand on her shoulder. Sam wanted to add the caption, "old nodding donkeys, hard at work."

'You little prat!' Mike tussled Sam's hair as Sam focused on the photo. It showed he'd accidentally cut off their heads.

'Too much nodding,' Sam laughed. 'I'll have to change the caption.'

Debra gazed out to sea where a crude oil tanker was being loaded beside the LNG tanks and semi-submersible drilling rigs. Sunlight glistened on the water as Mike brushed his fingers along her arm.

'What are you thinking, Debra?'

'I think Sam's probably right. We are a couple of old donkeys with our heads chopped off, well past our use-by-date.'

'I don't know about that. I'm still got a lot of life in me yet.'

She smiled as Sam moved on elsewhere to capture another image.

'What about all those storage drums,' Sam exclaimed. 'Imagine if there was a fire!'

Mike now reverted to his teacher role and gave Sam a quick history lesson about WWII when Brunei was occupied by the Japanese before being liberated by Australian troops.

'As they retreated,' he said, 'the Japanese sabotaged it all setting fire to 38 wells.'

'Holy crap! Imagine the heat and flames.'

'Yeah. Apparently, it was ablaze from end to end. Took months until the last blazing well was brought under control.'

The terrors of war were soon forgotten as they drove through white silica sands that sparkled like snowfields. She gazed out the window at the changing landscape, noting the inevitable changes that had taken place over the years.

Glimpsing her appearance in the rear-view mirror, she acknowledged the changes that had affected them all. She was no longer a young vibrant woman, and Sam was no longer a child. She was not sure yet how much Mike had changed but she would enjoy trying to work it out.

Even though afternoon shadows were lengthening, the temperature inside the taxi felt stifling. Johari apologised as his sweaty arms and hands wrestled with the air conditioning knobs. She wiped her brow, aware of Mike watching her every move.

'You appear to be deep in thought. Always the philosopher, Debra. Do you still have an answer to all life's mysteries?'

'I never professed to have all the answers.'

'And now?'

'I'm still searching.'

Out of the swamp and beyond, kampongs appeared alongside the road with villagers in conical hats hunched over watery, green paddy fields. Plastic bag scarecrows waved in the breeze, and she stole a glance at Mike, who was still watching her. He turned to the driver.

'Can you take us to the Royal Regalia Museum?' Mike flicked through a glossy tourist brochure. 'That's one we haven't seen yet.'

Johari nodded. 'Yes, I know the place.'

They arrived at a large domed building with a gold mosaic design. On the marble floor inside the entrance sat a huge, gilded chariot that had carried the Sultan through the streets during his silver jubilee. But it was the exhibit of a golden forearm that caused Sam to grip his sides laughing. It was a prop the Sultan used during his coronation city tour.

'I can't believe it.' Sam stifled giggles with his hand. 'In case he got tired of waving?'

'He was only a boy when he came to the throne … younger than you, Sam. Not surprising his arm got tired.'

Royal family pictures, including photos of his late father's funeral, spread around the walls, depicting important events in the current Sultan's life.

'I don't know how we endured that period of mourning when the old Sultan died. No TV or radio for a month, and only then mournful dirges.' Within a few days, melancholy music had replaced it, then less sorrowful laments as the weeks passed by. 'Our dog used to howl and even the lighter Baroque was enough to make him whine.' Finally, strains of Mozart's *Requiem* and Bach's *Come Sweet Death* had flowed through the speakers. No music had ever sounded sweeter.

'And those white armbands we had to wear,' Mike added. 'One day I forgot mine. I tore off paper from an adding machine at work and stapled it around my sleeve.'

Debra sighed. At least there'd been certain protocols to follow, a specific time laid aside for grieving. Everyone knew how to behave. She thought of her own recent mourning. With no idea what was expected of her, she lived each day not knowing how long this grieving would last or how she should deal with it – so many unknown rules and expectations.

As they drove past the town square, Sam pointed out a tall monument, commemorating Brunei's independence. 'Welcome to Brunei Darussalam. Abode of Peace. Did they change their name in 1984?'

'Yeah. It was the best excuse for a piss-up we ever had. Social functions at every foreign embassy in town.'

'Now why doesn't that surprise me, Mike?'

While she wasn't in Brunei to witness the auspicious event, she could imagine what independence meant to these people. And now, she was only beginning to discover what independence represented for her. Without a partner to discuss possibilities and outcomes, the responsibility of making major decisions was now hers alone. She was the one who would choose what was best for her and how she could move forward.

Still laughing, Mike recalled the stunt he'd pulled during the Independence celebrations, turning to Sam who sat in the front next to Johari. 'All the teachers took the students to the square to join in the flag waving. But once we got there, I left the students with Rahim to duck into the Sheraton across the road. While I was enjoying a quiet drink, Rahim was left to cope with the rowdy students.'

Debra watched Mike laughing but suddenly twitched at the mention of that name again. 'Did Rahim return to Brunei?'

'Yes. It was a whole load of bollocks. But they got their independence.'

'So, Rahim came back to Brunei? I thought he was in KL.'

'Yes, he came back. My God, it was funny.'

She could no longer focus on what Mike was saying.

'I show you where the old sultans are buried,' Johari suggested.

'No!' she screamed.

Johari turned, startled at her reaction. The others both stared at her, their eyes questioning before Mike spoke.

'Are you okay?'

'I've got a headache. I think I need a drink.' It wasn't the tombs of the old sultans that had upset her – their ancient resting place lay next to the museum overlooking the car park where she'd waited that fateful night. When Johari suggested a diversion, she sighed with relief.

'I take you to nice restaurant. You have cold drink.'

'That sounds like a great idea.' Mike reached out and patted her hand.

Johari chose one of the newer shopping complexes and parked outside an ultra-modern high-rise. He waited as they walked towards the foyer where an enormous crystal chandelier sparkled from the ceiling. But the vast shopping space was devoid of shoppers. When Sam went off for a cigarette, Debra took the opportunity to quiz Mike about some of the events that had happened after she'd left Brunei.

He told her about a woman who'd survived a car accident but stepped out onto the road to get help for her injured husband. The driver coming towards her failed to see her and knocked her down, killing her instantly. 'That's why Rahim left Brunei,' Mike said. 'His daughter was also hit by a car, in KL. That's why he left in a hurry … to be with her.'

'Oh, my God. I never knew that. Was she okay?' All at once she had goosebumps, wishing she could have comforted him, been there for him. *If only I'd known.*

'She survived but the accident damaged her legs.'

'Poor Rahim. When did this happen?'

'Not long after you left.'

'And no one told me. He came back to Brunei. I didn't know. Yet you don't know where he is now?'

'That's right. We lost touch. Like your rapid departure, I heard about it on the grapevine. It was a terrible time for tragedy. I didn't want to pass on any more bad news.'

Her eyes moistened as she recalled that time when she'd been preoccupied with her own problems. She'd had no idea Rahim too had experienced family trauma. There'd been many times in her life when she didn't want to share her own personal dramas. Perhaps he, too, had cut himself off from the outside world.

Sam joined them before racing up the elevator to check out the food hall. Following him at a more sedate pace, Mike turned to Debra.

'Didn't you have an incident once with some guy in a lift?'

'Yes, I'm sure you've heard it all before. At the time, I felt vulnerable and violated. I couldn't believe a stranger would grab me like that.' She'd been holding Sam's hand, clutching a large cake in the other, and didn't have a chance to fight back. The cake was spoiled, and her spirits crushed.

'You should have kicked him in the goolies.'

'I was young and scared. Now I wouldn't hesitate. Had I known what fate awaited me on the last night at the museum, I would probably have done far worse. I was in the wrong place at the wrong time.'

'It happened at the museum?' Wide-eyed, Mike leaned in closer so he could hear.

'In the car park. Not far from the old sultans' tombs. That's why I didn't want Johari to take us there.'

'Holy shit! I can understand why.'

'I will return there one day, though. When I'm ready.' There was a time when visiting the museum had filled her with unimaginable joy. 'You know it was also our secret meeting place? We exchanged our letters there. Hid them in one of the old bronze canons.' As a natural barricade, several cannons had been mounted upon the museum wall as if guarding the area below.

Debra gazed around the food hall, empty except for a handful of cleaners. 'Do you remember the steep stone steps leading to a secluded garden concealed from the road? That's where we used to meet.' Well-maintained lawns sloped down to the banks of the Brunei River where encroaching jungle hid a solitary wooden bench.

'God knows it couldn't have been easy. Finding somewhere to hide in such a small town as this. Plenty of eyes always watching you. With your mass of blonde hair, you were always capable of turning a few heads. Even now, look over there.' His gaze lingered on a young, skinny man wiping the tables nearby. 'That guy hasn't taken his eyes off you.'

She laughed at his compliment. *A rarity these days, but I'll accept any praise that's offered.* Mike confirmed it by pointing to a second bearded man in a white tunic who followed her with his gaze. It reminded her of that last night. While she didn't see their faces, she could still recall their threatening shouts, their offensive smell. One of them had a bristly beard that scratched her face.

She rubbed the side of her cheek and focused on pleasant images of the museum. It had been exciting to dive her hand into the canon's hidden recess and find Rahim's letters waiting for her. She had no trouble recalling the comfort she felt from reading his words.

'In the beginning, he used to leave me notes in our pigeon-holes at work. Then it became too risky.'

'Oh! shit yeah. There wasn't much privacy in our staff room. I'm surprised you guys didn't get caught.'

'Well, I'm sure people began to talk. The trouble is you believe you're invincible. You think no one will notice. But I'm sure they do.'

'There was an amazing energy between the two of you. If I could see it, I'm sure others did too. He was a great guy.'

'Yes, he was one of a kind. And we'll probably never know what happened to him.' While his presence brought her immense joy, it wasn't meant to last. She'd come to accept, like most moments of happiness in her life, it was only ever meant to be ephemeral.

In the food hall, brightly coloured signs advertised a weird mixture of European and Asian food. Highly amused, Sam wanted to photograph some of them. He held the video camera zooming in on an advertisement for avocado and sweet corn ice cream. 'Yuk,' he laughed. 'Can you hold the camera? Quick, I need the loo.'

'Careful you don't fall in. Yell out if you need help.'

'And you'd come running?'

'Not likely.' With her handbag slung around her neck, she'd previously waded through floors awash with water where people preferred to sluice rather than wipe. Despite the sparkling chandeliers in the foyer, some things hadn't changed.

On the way back to the hotel, at Sam's request, they turned off at the entrance to an amusement park. Rumoured to be a smaller version of Disneyland, it had only opened a few months earlier and was said to have cost the Sultan billions of dollars to build. When Sam asked the price of admission, his jaw dropped.

'Free,' the short dark man grinned as he swept around the entrance. 'You come here next month. See Michael Jackson for

Sultan's birthday. Also, free.' He smiled through crooked teeth as he picked up a discarded can from the ground.

'A free concert. Can you imagine how much it would cost for Michael Jackson to perform here?'

'I'm guessing millions of dollars. But then money, it seems, is no object.'

As they entered the park, two young girls in pink flouncy dresses sat erect on their horses as they circumnavigated the double-decker carousel. A matronly woman stood next to them, keeping one hand on each child's shoulder should they lose their grip on the reins.

'I've never seen a two-storey merry-go-round. That's real luxury.'

'Perhaps they get double the fun or twice the ride,' Mike mused as he headed for the roller coaster. No sooner had they fastened their seat belts than the ride began. There didn't appear to be anyone controlling the equipment, and most of the rides lay dormant waiting for people to fill the seats. Apart from identical twin boys on a gilded pirate ship and a ponytailed girl on a painted pedal boat, there was a distinctive lack of patrons.

In any overcrowded third-world country, children would gladly clamber onto these seats. They would welcome the spin zones, laser mazes, and two-storey carousels. They would embrace anything to transform their drab lives into this world of fantasy. Yet this free amusement park, fully equipped with all the rides money could buy remained empty, like a vacuous giant ghost train.

'Perhaps we could go to Jerudong Park and see the polo ponies. It's not far from here.' Specially designed for the Sultan to house his numerous polo ponies, the park had hosted international polo matches with Prince Charles and the Sultan of Pahang. When Sam was young, she and Jo used to sit in the café while the grooms let Kali and Sam pat the ponies as they exercised the horses along the beach. While Mike directed Sam to the stables, Debra ordered coffee from the same nearby café. Looking out at the manicured lawns stretching to the edge of the sandy beach below, she thought of Jo and Kali. She was meeting them tomorrow at the water village. So much to talk about. So many memories to share.

Kampong Ayer

While Debra waited for Jo and Kali outside the mosque, Sam wandered around the perimeter with his video camera. Built in the centre of the capital, the iconic landmark was named for the sultan's late father. By the seventies, when they'd first arrived there, the current sultan at twenty-one had already inherited the throne.

Sam returned with a brochure and read about this creation of visible opulence constructed from the best materials the world had to offer. 'Exterior walls built of Shanghai granite, floors of Italian marble, stained glass from England, carpets from Saudi Arabia. Its golden dome is covered by three million pieces of Venetian mosaic. Can you believe that?'

'Yes.' She'd heard it all before, but as she gazed at the magnificent architecture, she pondered the expensive gold leaf used to create the huge dome.

As Sam strode towards her with the video camera, he asked the same question she'd been asking herself. 'How much do you think it cost?'

'Squillions of dollars. If you climb to the top of the minaret, you get fantastic views across the water village.'

'No way.' He gazed up at the dome, shielding his eyes. 'It's too bloody hot.'

Even at this early hour, the humidity clung to her like a wet sheet and her underwear felt drenched. Debra moved towards the shade of the tall palms encircling the mosque.

Outside the mosque entrance, an elderly Malay man handed out black shapeless gowns to conceal the naked arms and legs of scantily dressed tourists. A perturbed young woman argued with him, objecting to wearing the specified standard of dress to enter. After a last attempt to convince the young woman, the man threw his hands in the air. A European tourist, like them, she was more noticeable with razor-cut hair streaked with highlights of pink. Something about her agitated manner and emaciated form caused Debra to instinctively steer Sam away from her.

The pink-haired woman strode away from the mosque, her flimsy T-shirt falling about her shoulders.

'Kali, it's okay.'

Staggering up the marble steps in front of the mosque, a woman in her fifties yelled at her daughter to stop; she waved her hands in the direction of the holy man and the mosque. While the daughter looked vastly different and was no longer a child, Debra had no trouble recognising her mother. Despite her thinning hair and frame, Jo still bore the same mien, the same commanding tone.

'Jo, oh, my God!'

As they moved in closer to embrace, she noted Jo's eyes had lost their sparkle, but her face broke into a grin.

'Debra, after all these years. How good is this!'

'It's great to see you, Jo.' She moved in closer to Kali. 'I didn't recognise you. You're all grown up.'

Sam stood awkwardly to one side staring at Kali as Debra raced in to hug her. Kali's jewelled nose stud caught the light as her tattooed arms wrapped around Debra's. Her face looked strained, but she and Jo both moved in closer to hug Sam.

Apart from Sam, who remained deadpan, tears fell all round and it was an age before anyone said anything. Finally, Jo broke the silence.

'It's been too long. The last time we all hugged like this was when we were leaving you in Manila. Alex was being transferred to a hospital in Australia and we had to return to Sydney so Kali could start school.'

'Sam is keen to look around the water village. Are you happy with that?'

Jo started coughing and Kali handed her a tissue from her handbag. 'Mum, are you okay to walk around?' Kali placed her arm on Jo's shoulder.

'I can manage a short distance.'

Debra looked at Jo's face where a greyish tinge had replaced her once healthy glow. 'Let's find somewhere to sit,' she said.

They followed the maze of wooden boardwalks spread around Kampong Ayer and the mosque. Sam walked across to a nearby jetty where fishermen weighed fish on ancient scales before bundling them in newspaper. Kali pinched her nose and moved away while Jo sat on a wooden plank mopping her face with a tissue. Local women in brightly patterned sarongs and head scarves lowered woven baskets on string to the small boats below. Vegetable sellers filled their baskets with dried red chillies or ripe green jackfruit and the women hauled them up onto the jetty with ease, before balancing them on their heads.

'Kali, can you bring me my pills.' Jo's words were drowned out by a small water taxi's outboard engine as it zipped across the choppy wake.

'Are you sure you're okay, Mum?' Kali moved closer and handed her mother a small plastic container and a bottle of water.

'Yes, I'll be fine in a minute.'

Debra sat next to Jo on the rickety wooden bench. Nearby was a power box where tangled electrical and telephone cables snaked their way around the walkways, wrapping the village in wires. Next to this formidable mass of power, Jo looked far from robust.

'Are you okay, Jo? You're not too tired to continue.'

'I'll be fine. What about you, Debra? How are things with you?'

'Pretty good so far. I'm obviously much stronger than I thought. Sam is making good progress too.'

'I'm so glad. You have been through hell. It must have been awful.

'We're getting there.'

Intrigued by the many stray cats without tails, Sam bent down to pat them. *He's always loved cats.* When he was in rehab, she had agreed to feed Tiger and Elvis who both shared key aspects of Sam's personality. While Tiger was depressed and spent most of his day sleeping, Elvis was demanding and liked to wander about at night. Unlike Elvis, Tiger would brush against her legs, meowing without making a sound. Perhaps the trauma of living with Sam had made him mute. She had not let herself become attached to his cats. If she could keep her distance, she would feel no guilt at their abandonment. Remaining detached helped her survive.

The cats at Kampong Ayer sunned themselves along the planked walkways. They lazed outside quaint wooden houses propped on stilts or beside the fishermen, lured in by the smell of fish. In the river below, Sam pointed out small turtles stranded in the mud by the outgoing tide. He zoomed in with the camera to capture the scene while the rest of them navigated their way around this amazing wooden labyrinth.

Sam and Kali gazed out at the small water taxis ferrying families across the river with children sheltering under their mothers' brightly coloured umbrellas. Sam flagged down a larger boat and Kali helped her mother descend the wooden ladder. As they zipped around the water village, they were dwarfed by modern high-rise department stores rising above the skyline. On one bank of the river, Sam pointed out a paved parking area where residents of the water village parked their latest model BMWs, Mercedes, and 4-wheel drives. As their boatman swerved to miss another boat, water sprayed up from the wake, drenching them all. The passing fishermen in conical-shaped hats waved at them before casting their nets.

A megaphonic sound reverberated across the water as the muezzin called the Muslim faithful to noon prayer. Five times a day they answered the call. Kali blocked her ears at the distorted echo and Sam grimaced. Finally, peace reigned again, except for the droning of the outboard motor and the gentle lapping of the waves.

Debra ducked as a turquoise-breasted kingfisher swooped down for a fish. Jo placed her hand on Debra's arm.

'Do you remember the sea eagles the last time we flew?'

'When you took me in the Cessna? Yes, I remember the eagles and their mating rituals. The way they clung to each other mid-air.'

'They were willing to risk everything for love.'

'They were tempting fate,' mused Debra. *Yes! How easy it was to believe nothing could stop us or stand in our way.* She, too, had been prepared to risk everything for Rahim, but that was another lifetime.

'It was my last flight … after Gareth flew those illegal immigrants across the border.' Jo's eyes glazed over as she gazed across the water. She took a cigarette from her bag but after several attempts with the lighter, she gave up. 'He put our lives at risk. I was terrified of what would happen.'

'I think you made the right decision leaving him. He betrayed you.' Debra placed her arm around Jo's shoulders.

'And yet I still miss him. I dreaded the thought of being on my own. I still do now. Don't judge me, Debra.'

'I would be the last one to judge.' She looked out at the river, which today appeared a dark milky green. 'Do you still fly, Jo?'

'No, I have a few health issues.'

'Anything you want to talk about?'

'No… it's nothing.' Jo nodded towards Kali who was already climbing out of the boat. 'I'll be fine.'

The boatman tied the boat to a wooden bollard and Sam steadied it, holding onto the rope as Kali leapt onto the step. With his other hand, he helped Jo climb onto the ladder. Debra took Jo's other elbow supporting her as she climbed. Kali leant down from above to help her mother step off the last rung.

As they walked back along the boardwalk, the mosque's outline seemed to dominate the surrounding skyline. Its golden dome and minarets caught the rays of sunlight off the white granite walls, reflecting every hue of sunset. Jo looked up and tripped on a loose board, and Debra reached out to grab her arm.

'My God, I'd forgotten how beautiful this place could be,' Jo said, scrambling to get her camera out of its bag.

'There is beauty everywhere, but we don't always see it.'

'A bit like happiness. We need to remember the fleeting moments. It may be all we ever get.'

Debra turned to Jo, who looked older than her fifty-five years. 'I have a surprise for you. I've seen Mike Jasper and he wants to meet us for dinner.'

'Oh! how lovely. How is he?'

'He's far more interesting than I remembered. Perhaps that's because he's the only man I've met in many years. I've had several conversations with him. He's changed somewhat, but he's still the same Mike you would remember.'

'That sounds rather mysterious. Is there something you're not telling me?'

'No, but you can find out for yourself when you see him.'

'I shall enjoy that.'

'This village is said to be one of the largest of its kind in the world,' Kali read from the tourist brochure. 'Apparently, the government offered them houses in the city, but they preferred to stay here.'

'You think they would want to live in clean modern houses,' Sam suggested.

Debra gasped, remembering some of the dreadful places Sam chose to live in. One crumbling old house had an assortment of junk collected from kerbside rubbish piled near his front door. The mess inside was worse. An orange vinyl barstool from the seventies, a red pleated lampshade, and a rusty biscuit tin overflowing with cigarette butts greeted her the last time she'd visited him. She'd ploughed through mountains of dirty clothes and mouldy food remains to help him find his driver's licence and health care card. Her stomach had protested at the nauseating stench.

She listened to him espousing the benefits of clean, modern living and placed her arm around his shoulder. He stared at her from under his fringe, flicking it back from his face.

'What is it, Mum?'

'Nothing. Everything is great.'

***

Kali wandered around the village of quaint wooden schools, clinics, and small shops full of people and life itself. She stared at the residents peering out of shuttered windows in these houses propped on stilts above the river, and turned to her mother. 'They seem happy living together like this. I reckon it gives them a sense of belonging. A real community. They care about each other.'

Kali looked at the friendly, smiling faces and sensed that they knew who they were and where they needed to be. Perhaps that was enough. 'It would be great to know where you really belong.'

Jo welcomed the friendly faces beckoning her into their homes but worried she might be intruding, peeping into their lives. An old man, staring out at the water, sat so still it was hard to believe he was alive. Before Jo's father died, his speech deteriorated to the point where she could barely understand what he said. She grew impatient waiting for him to retrieve the correct words to answer her questions. The long pauses between sentences became gaps between words as he searched in his mind for lost data. As Jo had focused on the silent spaces between the words, she'd eventually learned the importance of those powerful pauses. In a world of constant noise and clamour, it had given her time to choose how to respond, to give the best answer she could rather than reacting with an answer she might later regret.

Something drew her in closer to this silent old man. Sitting before her on the deck, he sensed her presence and turned his face to her. She smiled at him, and he continued to sit enjoying the sunshine and the nourishment his family were bringing him. If she could wish for anything right now, she would like a touch of his presence and a hint of his peaceful state of mind.

***

'I want to show you something.'

Sam took Debra's hand and led her to a house constructed of odd pieces of timber tentatively tacked together. Faded pink net curtains hung across small glassless window frames where small curious faces gazed out at them. Sam turned to his mother.

'You want to retire to a home with river views? This is it! You wouldn't have to drive to the supermarket. Your food would be delivered fresh each day. Fish and turtle burgers.'

'That's gross, Sam.' Kali grimaced.

'You can't get rid of me that easily.' Debra squeezed his shoulder, delighted he had considered her future welfare and was taking an interest in the lives of others. Previously he'd had little interaction with the outside world, and she welcomed this touch of levity.

Jo looked on, fascinated by the old grandmothers smiling through missing teeth as they jiggled babies on their laps, while toddlers with soulful brown eyes played at their feet. There was a companionable connection between the elders and their grandchildren. A younger woman offered a bowl of food to the old woman, touching her gently on the shoulder. Jo wanted to capture this scene of domesticity. She needed this reminder of how blissful family life could be, of how a mother's life should be, surrounded by family who cared for her – not confined to an aged care home fantasising about erotic love scenes with her male carer.

The Other Side of Life

With the reunion dinner only a few nights away, Debra and Jo arranged to meet Mike and other members for a busy bee at the yacht club. As some of the refurbishments to the new clubhouse had not yet been completed, they were all lending a hand. For many years there'd been talk about a reunion, but it had taken long-term residents Dick and Beth Worthington to finally organise it.

Jo hired a rental car, but Kali insisted on driving them to the Yacht Club.

'Are you sure you don't want me to drive?' Jo offered. 'It would make more sense. I know where I'm going.'

'I know how to drive,' Kali insisted, but despite Jo's instructions, she kept missing turnoffs and speeding around bends.

'Kali, please slow down.'

'Stop telling me what to do. It doesn't help.'

Debra clutched the edge of the seat as Kali swerved once more, barely missing an oncoming car. They approached a small shop, for the second time, having already driven past it several minutes earlier.

'How about I go in and get some cold drinks,' Sam offered.

Kali followed him in while Jo and Debra discussed the direction they needed to be heading. Sam took a turn behind the wheel and Kali sat next to him in the front, one minute fiddling with her phone, the next minute tapping her fingers on her thigh.

'Come on, Sam, put your foot down. It may have been

quicker if we'd sailed there.'

Jo frowned at Kali, but Debra patted her hand and winked.

'Do you still sail, Kali?' she asked.

'No. Not since I left school. The last time was when we were in Broome. This is what I bought.' She twirled a solitary pearl hanging at her throat on a delicate thread of wire. Unlike the pearl, Kali appeared to lack lustre for someone so young. Once a pretty girl, her shining layers had become tarnished with time. 'I haven't had much fun in recent years. Work and kids occupy most of my time.'

Jo opened her mouth to reply but instead cleared her throat, promptly changing the subject. 'Wow, check out the swimming pool. That's a new addition.'

It seemed to be one of many visible changes that had occurred since their last visit to the yacht club. Two men were staining the pool decking, their shorts and T-shirts splashed with splotches of red that matched their sunburnt faces. Another man in gardening boots shovelled mulch around the poolside garden. An expanse of sand and sparse trees had been transformed. It now looked like an image from a gardening magazine. Debra scanned the workers' faces, searching for Mike, but he was probably inside, closer to the bar.

As they climbed the stairs to the bar and lounge, several women were stringing party lights around the balcony railings. Behind the bar, one fixture hadn't changed. The stooped Chinese barman, now missing a few more teeth, still had the same welcoming smile. Despite the many characters he'd seen pass through these doors, Chang Lee greeted them like old friends. Sam and Kali quickly escaped the amusing stories from the past and took their drinks to the balcony.

'When we were kids, I used to love sitting here. I imagined I was overlooking my own secret kingdom. I was the mermaid queen.'

'Didn't you have a T-shirt with those words printed on it?'

'Yes, I used to let you wear it sometimes. You loved wearing my clothes and my red wig.'

'So, it's your fault I'm so screwed up. Dressing me up in your clothes. No wonder I have an identity crisis.'

'But the tiara was mine. Nobody else was allowed to wear the tiara or the angel costume.'

'Yeah, you loved wearing those wings. Once you were hiding under the stairs. Everyone thought you were lost but I found you there still dressed in your tiara and angel wings.'

'Yeah, I think I remember that. I often felt like hiding away. I still do.'

'I always saw you as an angel, Kali. For many years I hid myself from the world. I wouldn't have come on this trip if it hadn't been for Mum.'

'Yeah, I came for Mum,' said Kali. 'And I needed a holiday.'

As Debra stood at the bar waiting for their drinks, Mike appeared at her shoulder.

'Great timing, Debra! Now the work's been done.' He brushed back his hair, still damp from showering.

'You smell nice.' She moved in closer to sniff his spicy musk aftershave. 'I'm sorry we're late but Jo needed to rest, and we got lost.'

'Is Jo OK? I was talking to her earlier. I thought she looked terrible.'

'Yes. She appears to have lost her zing. I miss the old energetic Jo.'

He moved in closer and whispered in her ear, 'And I've missed you.'

'It's only been twenty-four hours, Mike.'

'I know. But it's been a long day.'

Workers finishing for the day laid aside their tools, shook off the grime of their labour, and traipsed inside for a shower, and the bar soon began to buzz. A larger woman with home-dyed brown hair sorted through items of memorabilia from a box to decorate the bar. She yelled out to Mike in a broad Aussie twang.

'Do you reckon it'll be ready for tomorrow night?'

'I bloody well hope so. We've been at it all day.' Mike placed his hand on Debra's shoulder pointing at the other woman with his head. 'Do you remember Rosa Lyons? This is Debra. She was also with the airline.'

'Well, it was Alex who worked for them. But I got to enjoy the free flights.'

Rosa spun around, searching Debra's face for familiarity, then threw her hand to her mouth. 'Of course, I do. Oh, Debra! And your poor husband! How are you coping?'

'I'm here with my son, Sam. We're doing okay, thanks. I'm waiting for Jo. I'm sure you remember Jo and Gareth McKenzie.' Debra watched Rosa's eyes widen.

'I think you shared the same gardener, didn't you? What was his name?' There was a hint of mirth in Mike's voice.

'That one! I could tell you a few stories about him. Did you know he and Gareth were …' Rosa threw her hand to her mouth.

'And here's Jo now.' Mike interjected. 'Jo, this is Rosa Lyons.'

While Jo exchanged the expected social pleasantries with Rosa, she showed no sign of recognition. It was as if she'd forgotten any significant connections with Rosa or her gardener.

'Anyone for another drink,' Mike asked.

Sensing the uncomfortable silence, Debra swapped to a safer topic, hoping to catch Jo's attention. 'Did I tell you we stopped at the war memorial in Sandakan before we came here? We were in KK, so it was a good opportunity.'

'Yes, we've been there. And the one in Thailand,' Rosa chipped in. 'It's rather confronting, isn't it.'

'It's a far cry from the manicured gardens and graves at Labuan.' Jo's voice was barely audible. 'All those young men dying before their time. Incomprehensible.'

'All this talk of death and dying. Perhaps we should talk about something more pleasant.' Rosa scanned Debra's face for support.

'Unfortunately, death is a reality. It's what helps us appreciate life,' Debra said. 'We wouldn't be here for this reunion if we weren't celebrating life.'

A balding man with a large beer gut struggled up a ladder in the centre of the room. Rosa called to him and offered her help attaching streamers to the ceiling. Jim Lyons threw a packet of balloons at her, which she opened and handed to those around her.

They all grabbed a couple and began to blow, including Sam, who blew with such gusto, one burst with a loud bang. Kali, who was fidgeting with the beer mats, pushed away the balloon and whispered something to her mother. Jo spun around on her stool.

'Kali's upset about something. I think we'd better go. You stay, Debra.'

'Yeah, stay a bit longer. I'll drive you home.' Mike waited until Jo had left the room before turning to Debra. 'What's going on there?'

'I'm not sure exactly. Kali has been very agitated today. But then I don't think Jo is well either. She says she is, but she appears quite vague.'

'If she doesn't want to tell you about it, there's not much you can do.' Mike signalled to Chang Lee and ordered another round. 'Debra, do you remember Dick and Beth Worthington? It was them who organised the reunion. They've also booked a helicopter ride to visit a longhouse if you're interested. I also invited Jo and Kali.'

'That sounds great. I'm sure Sam would love it. Did Dick and Beth used to live on the air force base? He was mad on cricket. Always yelling on the pitch?'

'That's the guy. They are now living at Labuan. Set up a business selling swimming pools.'

'Swimming pools? Who would have thought there'd be a demand for those here? And they're still here after all this time? I guess they came here chasing the sun and couldn't face the cold back in England.'

'Yes. Like so many of us. Anyway, they've invited me to stay with them for a night before I fly back to the UK.'

'Oh!' She stopped mid-sentence, unable to finish.

'Why don't you come with me? I'm thinking of going over on Sunday.'

'Labuan? I'll have to check with Sam … see what he wants to do.' She was still not used to this life of independence and automatically included him in any of her plans. But she felt a sense of freedom slowly emerging. She stole a quick glimpse in the mirror above the bar to see if any of these changes were obvious and smiled back at her pleasing image.

When Mike drove them back to their hotel along one of the newer roads, he discovered a shortcut to one they knew well. High above on a hillside, a large colonial-style wooden building extended out over the river.

'There's the old British High Commission,' he said, pointing ahead. 'We had some good piss-ups there on many occasions.'

'I'm sure Sam doesn't need to hear about those.'

'Yes, I do. I want to know how people behaved in the seventies.'

'Rather badly, I'm afraid.' She remembered inebriated people dancing through steamy parties any night of the week.

It didn't matter whether they had to work the next day; they partied regardless. The seventies were a time of grasping everything wild and exciting before conventional mandates got in the way. It was a time of contradictions. They'd gained the freedom to vote yet were forced to fight. All they wanted was to make peace and love.

'The Sultan's birthday was the best event on the ex-pat social calendar. Plenty of food and free booze,' said Mike.

'Yes, it wasn't simply the cocktails and frippery though. You can't forget the small talk and snobbery. It was always, "What does your husband do?" No one was interested in what the wives did. It used to infuriate Jo and me.'

'Poor Rahim was never invited so I sneaked him in once to see what would happen.'

'I remember that night. Alex drank far too much and insulted Rahim in front of the High Commissioner's wife. I was so embarrassed.'

'I'm sure Rahim forgave you.'

'I never had a chance to find out.'

When she'd left Brunei, she'd thought it was for a short term. Once Alex's health improved, she assumed he would return to his job in Brunei. But then everything changed so rapidly. Alex was too sick to return to his job and they chose to live in Australia to access the specialist care he needed. All the questions she wanted to ask Rahim were left unsaid.

'There's a lack of communication here – no decent radio stations.' Sam leaned over her shoulder, trying to adjust the radio. 'How did you survive without a choice of radio or TV stations?'

There'd always been a lack of communication and it had continued after she left. She had no way of knowing whether Rahim survived. Rahim's father believed the ex-pat lifestyle provided too many temptations away from his family and culture. He wanted him back in KL.

'Sam, you will see a different side of Brunei tomorrow when we go to the longhouse,' Mike said. 'Life here wasn't always about ex-pat debauchery. We were fortunate to climb the mountains, travel into the jungle and explore the rivers. We saw the magic of rural life in its raw state before it was polluted by commercialism and greed. Hopefully, you will still see some beautiful scenery. Make sure you bring your video camera. There will be lots for you to film.'

'I hope I get to see some interesting wildlife. Are you sure we will all fit in the helicopter?'

'I'm sure we will. They're military helicopters. Quite large, and used for moving troops. They take about twelve people I think.' Mike pulled up at their hotel and they climbed out as a hotel valet took the car keys.

'Couldn't we go by boat? Going up the river sounds like fun.'

'It would take too long. The rivers can be treacherous with many rapids. You would have to get out and carry your boat some of the way.'

'No way!'

'You might even have to carry it on your head.' Mike ruffled Sam's hair before hugging Debra and planting a kiss on her lips. 'Well, it's a very early start in the morning. I think we should call it a night.'

As they stepped into the lift, Debra sighed as it raced up through each floor. It would have been nice to have a nightcap, but then … there was always tomorrow.

The Longhouse

At the air force base the next day, Beth and Dick directed them to the Bell Iroquois medevac helicopter that squatted on the tarmac ready to take off. It accommodated seven easily, including the pilot and the two medics who were flying to this isolated district to treat sick residents in several longhouses. Beth and Dick had visited this Iban longhouse several times before and were keen to show it to their guests.

Soon after climbing into the helicopter, Jo quizzed the pilot. 'How many flights have you done?' She also asked about the safety of the aircraft.

'Just relax, Mum. Let the pilot fly the helicopter. Sit and enjoy the scenery.'

Once airborne, Kali scanned the meandering river below and pointed to a barefooted woman carrying a basket on her head. Like a tightrope walker, she moved with grace as she crossed a fallen log bridge.

'Oh! how cute!' Kali gasped at the sight of two women carrying babies wrapped in sarongs on their backs.

Sam laughed as he pointed out a man carrying a canoe on his head as he scrambled across rocks. He gestured to Mike. 'I thought you were joking about carrying boats on our heads.'

'No. I wasn't joking.'

Where the river widened, Debra saw young boys fishing by casting out a conical-shaped net.

The helicopter flew over isolated huts and longhouses where smaller streams and tributaries flowed into a larger river, the main source of transport for the residents living there.

The pilot hovered with rotor blades almost touching tall tree canopies before skillfully dodging overhanging vines to land in a clearing close to the longhouse. Specks of grass and dirt flew into the air as children rushed out from the nearby longhouse holding their hands to their ears. The older residents followed more sedately, warning the children to stay back. Sam and Kali leapt out of the helicopter first and scrambled along the muddy bank.

'I'll race you to the jetty,' Kali yelled as three young boys jumped into the river stark naked. A young girl wrapped a sodden sarong around her hips before jumping from the jetty where several small boats were tied. Debra lingered, waiting for Jo who struggled to climb out of the helicopter.

'Here, grab my hand,' she said, but one of the medics took Jo's elbow and helped her to the ground. They followed the laughing children who beckoned them towards the longhouse at the edge of the river.

Perched on tall timber poles five metres above the ground the Iban longhouse had an entrance at either end. Mangy dogs and scruffy cats lazed around the perimeter while squealing pigs rooted in the mud under the house. A rooster crowed, competing with the buzz of cicadas.

A small Iban girl sat on a log outside the first entrance feeding figs to a young hornbill perched on the arm of an older man. The bird remained still, its huge black and white tail feathers inert as the girl popped wild figs into its large yellow beak. The bird watched them as they approached, its large dark eyes, ringed with vivid blue.

'Oh, my God!' Keen to film the bird, Sam ripped open the camera bag, dropping the lens cap in his haste. The older man, Abang, told him they were treating the injured bird as it was now illegal to keep these protected species as pets. As Sam edged in closer to video the brightly coloured bird, the man asked if he'd like to hold him so Debra took over the camera, zooming in on the giant yellow beak opening and closing as Sam handed him another fig. She also captured the joyous expression on Sam's face, his mouth spreading into a wide grin.

'I bet you'd like one as a pet,' Mike teased.

'It would be awesome. It's amazing to see it up close. I can't believe my luck.'

'These *Kenyalan* birds were once sought after by the early Chinese.' Joining them, Dick gave them the benefit of his knowledge. 'The ivory from their beak was carved into ornaments.'

'That's gross. I'm so pleased they stopped doing that. We need to protect them,' said Kali.

'It's sad they were at the mercy of poachers. So cruel.'

Sam stole another glance at the huge exotic bird perched on his arm. Through the camera lens, Debra saw his strained face and heard his concern. Recently she'd observed Sam's self-appointed role as defender of the weaker species. Maybe, like the Ibans, he saw the spirits who were said to be everywhere and in everything. What would the spirits of these huge birds have to say? According to Dick, placating the spirits was a way of bringing harmony into their daily lives and birds were a symbol of their mysticism.

The old man now held the bird and said the hornbill symbolised the spirit of God. If one was seen flying over your house, it was said to bring good luck. 'Should not be locked in cages.' He told them omens could be read into the sound of bird calls or the direction of their flight path across the sky.

'Because they mate for life, hornbills are also regarded as a symbol of eternal love and fidelity,' Dick added. 'Apparently, when the male hornbill begins courting, he brings the female food for a month before mating. The female lays her eggs in a hollow tree and remains trapped inside while the male plasters the hole with the female's droppings. The male delivers food to the female and chicks through a small hole in the trunk.'

'I knew you were a naturalist but didn't realise you were such a romantic, Dick.' Mike winked at Jo.

'Oh, to be waited on with such devotion! Wouldn't that be great!' Jo sidled over to the log seat to catch her breath.

'I'm not so sure I'd want to be locked up or plastered with bird droppings,' said Debra.

'Don't you girls go getting any ideas. Don't expect us guys to wait on you like that.' Mike nudged Dick who shared his joke.

'Yes, I tried to convince Dick it might be something he could use to stimulate foreplay. But he warned me to be careful, or he'd lock me in my nest forever.' Beth fluttered around in her brightly coloured feathers of orange shirt, green trousers, and red straw hat, her ears and throat shimmering with gold and diamonds.

'The female hornbill finally breaks out of her chamber,' Dick continued. 'Once the babies have their feathers, she joins her mate and provides food for their young.' He took a navy kerchief from his neck and wiped the sweat from his brow and upper lip.

'At least he returns for her. I'd hate to think she was stuck in there forever waiting for him to return.' Debra turned to Sam. 'That was something worth seeing, wasn't it? Perhaps not as spectacular as a Sunda pangolin but a rare opportunity to experience a hornbill up close and personal.'

'I'd still like to see a pangolin.' Sam turned to Kali. 'Mike says I might have to settle for a stuffed one in the museum.'

'Pangolins always look scary to me. All those scales and sharp claws.' Kali shuddered, cringing as she curled her fingers.

'Those scales are made from keratin, the same protein as your hair, skin, and nails. That's why there is so much illegal hunting. Even a lion can't bite through. They're so tough.'

'I've seen footage of them,' said Jo. 'They curl up in a defensive ball whenever they are threatened. They look so sad and vulnerable.'

'That's how they get their name. The Malay word *pengguling* means to roll.' Mike remembered an argument with Jacquie when he'd accused her of 'rolling' around in the hay. At the time he was joking, but she'd objected vehemently. His accusations seemed to have been accurate. 'Pangolins are quite elusive and very rare.' *Not at all like Jacquie, with her need for an audience.*

'Elusive? Rare? Sounds like you, Sam.' Kali laughed.

Sam gave her the finger and Mike interjected. 'Keep your eyes open for butterflies. You might see some Red Harlequins or maybe even a Rajah Brooke Birdwing.' He scanned the surrounding jungle where a heavy stand of bananas was ripening beside the longhouse. 'Was that a flash of red?'

The *Iban* headman welcomed them and gestured towards the entrance. Beth greeted him as *Bapa* so the rest of them used the same term of endearment. Small in stature, his earlobes had been stretched with heavy brass weights. Tied around his head was a dark red cloth patterned with flower motifs, like those tattooed on his arms and shoulders. He directed the visitors to where they could climb steps notched into a log ladder.

'Grab the roped handrails. It's incredibly slippery,' Beth said as she scrambled up the muddy incline.

After ducking through a low-lying doorway, they were greeted by women and children huddling in a corner of a larger communal living room. Shy in their movements, their soulful eyes were warm and welcoming as they watched the group shuffle across the bamboo pole flooring. Loosely held together with cross straps, the bamboo clicked and rattled in musical accord. A row of doors in the main living room led to smaller sleeping rooms on either side. Roughly hewn tree trunks propped up the side walls and thatched roof where woven baskets hung from the rafters. High in the ceiling, a lofty storage space also held fishing nets and an assortment of everyday necessities.

Torn pages from Western magazines adorned some of the walls, revealing faces of European celebrities from the past as they stared out at people from an earlier pristine culture. On a communal veranda, a small dinghy sat next to a large Chinese water jar. Wet clothes dripped from a clothesline propped on long bamboo poles. Mike pointed to the huge porcelain water jar, eye-catching with its distinctive blue glaze.

'Before Ibans became reliant on a cash society, their medium of exchange was household items such as these jars. Each had an agreed value based on its size. But they also had a value based on their sound as water was poured into them.'

'So, their business transactions were not only based on the functional but also the aesthetic.'

'Yeah. I love the way they find musical resonance in their day-to-day lives.'

'That's amazing. I guess because they rely so heavily on the river, the Ibans would be finely tuned into its many sounds. Not surprising when water determines the rhythm of their lives.'

Through the open window, Debra heard playful splashes accompanying the gleeful squeals of children, the sound of lapping waves against the hull of a small boat, and the whoosh of a fishing net thrown across the surface of water. She imagined the pitter-patter of rain, the gentle trickle of water running over rocks in low tide, and the surging rush after heavy rain. Water and what it represented formed an important part of the mystical Iban lifestyle.

Several young girls collected water in gourds and hauled them up the steps from the river below. Dick had already explained how the women cooked rice inside bamboo poles on the fire before fermenting it into alcohol. When a young man passed around drinks in halved coconut shells, they assumed it was the infamous rice wine. Kali tried it first, taking a cautious sip; she grimaced then passed the coconut shell to Sam. He shut his eyes as the bitter cloudy liquid slid down his throat.

'Be careful with the *tuak*,' Beth warned. 'One sip and you'll be off your face.'

By the time the drink had gone through a few rounds, they were all convinced it was not harmless rice wine. They felt the burning in the pit of their stomachs, the heat as it flushed their faces, and the fuzzy effect on their brains.

'Do you think we could have some water?' Jo asked. She was now coughing as she sat with her back propped against the wall, her face flushed and sweaty. Beth handed her a bottle from the insulated bag she carried.

A young Iban man, who Kali referred to as Sonny, continued to tempt her with more tuak, laughing at her grimaces each time she swallowed. She was now spluttering and laughing along with him. As the wine drizzled out the corner of her mouth, some of the grainy sediment remained on her chin and she licked it with her tongue.

Debra had been stealing glances at Sam, noting his droopy eyelids and flushed face. She was pleased he refused the drink on the third round, and leant over to whisper in his ear. 'The rice wine contains river water. You should warn Kali. It might make her sick.'

Kali's speech now slurred as she waved her arms in the air and insisted on reciting numbers in Malay to the young men surrounding her.

'That's all I remember from school,' she said. While Bahasa Malay was not their native tongue, Kali was too inebriated to care, and they were too polite to tell her. Besides, they appeared to enjoy her theatrical antics and playful games and made no attempt to stop her. She had now established the ages of at least half the people in the longhouse, and everyone now knew she was twenty-seven.

Jo dozed in the corner, occasionally glancing towards Kali and the crowd of young men gathering around her, but said nothing.

An older, almost toothless Iban woman brought out a blackened cooking pot of rice. On the top rested a large bony fish with eyes and teeth still intact. As it floated on a dish of curry sauce, its large glassy eyes stared back at them. Mike laughed at Kali, her eyes widening at the sight of the fish, but her expression softened as a younger woman brought out a plate of steamed jungle ferns.

'They must have known you were Vegan.' Sam joshed, elbowing Kali in the ribs. He doubted they understood her dietary preferences, but when he tasted the *midin* greens, he admitted they were quite palatable.

Jo refused the main meal but was happy to eat the fruit that followed. Debra passed her slices of sweet jackfruit, which tasted like a cross between apples and bananas.

After they finished eating, it was time for gift-giving. They had brought consumables, such as whisky for the headman and sweets for the children. Beth had brought a huge basket full of biscuits and cakes, which she shared with the women of the longhouse.

As they handed out sweets, the children's faces glowed with pure joy. One small girl no more than three years old took a fistful of sweets from the bag and promptly hid them behind her back. After Debra smiled at her, she changed her mind and opened her palm, offering to share them. As Debra blew her a kiss, she snuggled herself in closer then gave Debra the warmest smile, capable of melting any frozen heart.

Scattered across a patchwork of woven mats, they sat in a drowsy circle, lulled into their soporific state by the rice wine and food. Despite the humidity, there was an air of excitement as most of the Iban men disappeared from the room then reappeared dressed to perform their traditional dance. In headgear of hornbill feathers and clad in loincloths, they converged as warriors bearing swords and shields. As the Iban women beat out a rousing rhythm on a row of brass gongs, the men lifted their feet and waved their weapons.

When the dancing was finished, it was time for the younger men to demonstrate how to shoot their blowpipes. The young man known as Sonny asked Mike if he would like to have the first turn at shooting the bamboo darts. He assured Mike these ones didn't have poisonous tips, but Mike inspected the blowpipe shaped from a piece of strait-grained wood about two metres long. He checked out the metal spear tied with rattan at one end before offering it to Sam.

'Here, Sam, you want to be a Jedi knight. This is better than any light sabre.'

Tripping on the woven mat in his haste, Sam asked for reassurance, 'Are you sure these darts aren't poisonous?'

Several of the Iban men shook their heads.

Debra grabbed the video camera to capture this unique cultural exchange of a tech-savvy young man who could still be impressed by a rare ancient craft from another era.

Dick told them it used to take the Ibans about three to four months to make the blowpipes when using their primitive methods. With a long metal rod and chisel-shaped bit they bored out the centre for the darts to pass through.

'Sometimes they even built a hut to stay in while they did it, preferring to work in solitude.'

Debra thought about the dedication involved and the importance of silence. While they honed their craft, they were no doubt mindful of the spirits who disliked idle chatter. Nowadays, a factory could produce a blowpipe in a matter of hours … *but imagine the noise.* The finished product would be missing the love and dedication that only the craftsmen alone in his hut could create. She looked at the blowpipe and imagined the craftsman pouring water into the hole to float out any remaining wood chips, before rubbing the outside with a slightly waxy leaf.

The headman placed one hand on his heart. 'This one made from here always the best.'

Debra nodded as he told them the original darts had a metal tip coated with the poisonous sap of a tree and the venom of a snake. He faltered, asking his son to interpret for him.

'Ipoh tree,' Didi said, 'and the poison from cobra. Once hit, a monkey will be dead in seconds. We make different sizes, long ones for wild boar, small ones for squirrels.'

'Yes, we have one of your blow pipes hanging on our wall at home,' Beth told him. 'I'm always threatening Dick if he misbehaves, I will use it on him.'

'You are all talk, Beth. Besides your aim is skewed.' He turned to Debra and whispered, 'I guess you've heard about the Iban's past practice of head-hunting … fortunately, eliminated long ago. They believed the spirit resided in the head. Their interest in collecting human skulls was not about violence as people assumed. It was more about having faith in the spiritual power of renewal.'

Debra gazed around at these gentle, peace-loving people, trying to imagine bloodthirsty warriors with a fearsome reputation. She was about to ask when the practice was banned when Jo joined in their conversation.

'Apparently, during the Japanese occupation, the custom of taking heads was not exactly discouraged.' She raised her eyebrows with a knowing nod of the head. 'According to my father, who was based here during the war, the government was willing to turn a blind eye. Some of the heads hanging on longhouse walls were still wearing round horn-rimmed spectacles.'

The headman now passed around what looked like tobacco wrapped in banana leaves. Sam and Kali took the home-made cigarettes, happy to try them, but Jo said she'd stick with her own brand. 'I know my own poison,' she said.

'I'll have one just to be sociable.' Mike accepted the hand-made reefer and the lighted stick that a young man offered him. He coughed as a plume of smoke blew into his eyes and throat. After inhaling deeply, he offered it to Debra.

'No thanks. I think I've already inhaled enough passive smoke.' She looked at the enlarged pupils and soporific grins of Sam and Kali. It was an interesting blend of tobacco. She squinted at Sam.

He saw her frown of concern and gave her the thumbs up. 'No worries, Mum.'

He'll be fine. I shouldn't worry.

Several teenage boys invited Sam to join them in the river where they jumped from rope swings. As the headman handed out another round of the potent rice wine, Debra encouraged Sam to go with the boys. Judging by their lithe lean bodies, swimming was a far healthier option. From the open window, she watched and heard him laughing as he ran with the boys towards the jetty.

***

One of the Iban boys, Hari, tossed Sam the rope beckoning him to jump but he hesitated. Right now, he needed to get it together. He heard his father's voice in his head. *'Try harder, Sam. You've got to get it right.'* The other boys were waiting for him, and he started to panic. Would he let them down? But they were enjoying themselves, smiling as they dived under the water. They didn't care if he got it right. They only wanted him to be their friend.

As he clasped the rope in his hands, he knew there was an element of trust involved but he needed to first trust himself. If he took one small step at a time, he'd be fine. He needed to hold on long enough, balancing on the slippery bamboo railing before he leapt off. He must also trust the strength of the rope the boys had tied to a nearby tree. Why was he worrying? The boys knew what they were doing. They had done it many times before. Like them, he would get better with practice.

Even at a distance Debra could see from his body language he was nervous as he took his time climbing onto the railing. As he tried to balance, he toppled but leapt off quickly, grasping the rope with both hands. At the last second, he let go of the rope and landed in the water.

Seeing the grin on his face, she felt proud, knowing he'd succeeded. He'd gone outside his comfort zone and managed to let go. Delighted, the boys cheered loudly as they swam towards him and patted him on the back.

Before too long, Kali joined the boys jumping off the jetty. She removed her jeans but was still wearing a pink T-shirt and lacy black underwear. Her bright pink hair bobbed above the water, and her wet T-shirt clung to her bra. She sat on the jetty and lifted her T-shirt to show her dolphin tattoo to the young man Sonny. His mature body and sleek dark hair concealed the innocent eyes of a child. He reacted as if he hadn't yet seen a tempting side of life as the one Kali was offering him. He moved in closer, his eyes widening at the sight of the image tattooed on her smooth shapely hip. She pointed to his back, asking him about the fish he had tattooed near his shoulder.

'No drowning,' Sonny said.

'You will never drown because you always swim with the fishes.' She laughed and they both dived to the bottom.

Jo walked over to the window to join Debra and watched Kali leap from Sonny's shoulders into the water. Previously, she'd asked the headman about the significance of the tattoos seen on many of the young men.

'Apparently, it's a totem to protect the children who spend much of their days in the river,' she said. 'I hope Kali's dolphin tattoo offers the same protection for her.'

'Kali is a survivor. You said so yourself, Jo.'

Balancing precariously, Kali now wobbled on the railing, ready to jump in again. Mike joined the kids, peeling off his shirt and shorts to reveal blue Lycra briefs. Posing for Beth's camera, he flexed his muscles, which were still in good shape. As Debra stared at his lean, muscled frame, she noticed Beth also gazed at him with interest. She yelled at him through the open window, 'One of the boatmen is taking me upriver to see those glorious orchids. Will you come with me, Mike? Dick doesn't want to go?'

'OK. Let me cool off for a minute. I'm so bloody hot.'

As he dived in, Debra gasped.

Beth walked down to the jetty and wrapped a towel around Mike as he climbed out of the water. Debra's lower lip twisted, as if she had a grip on something but it was about to slip out of her grasp. She watched Beth standing with her legs and lips slightly parted, pressing her body against Mike.

'You might want to keep your manhood covered,' Beth said. 'We don't want to frighten the young girls.'

Mike accepted the towel but didn't flinch when Beth kept her hands on his shoulders.

'Who cares what he looks like? This is a time to be carefree, a place where you can be yourself.' Kali had discarded her T-shirt, which was now being worn by her favourite boy with the fish tattoo.

Sam had also swapped his 'Born to Run' T-shirt for a handmade batik shirt. The owner of this shirt now showed him how to make traditional woven fish traps from split rattan for catching small river fish. While Sam had sacrificed a T-shirt that had cost him his birthday money, he willingly exchanged it for the experience he'd gained. He couldn't estimate in monetary value the lessons these boys had taught him about finding contentment in the smallest things in life. While they didn't appear to own much, it was enough, and they were happy to share whatever they had.

Weaving from the Heart

Gazing around the longhouse, Jo admired the unique style of community living – a village under one roof, a central visible symbol of the Iban way of life. Fun-loving people, with a good sense of humour, they didn't appear to resent this group of strangers who'd landed on their doorstep. Instead, they welcomed and trusted them with their babies as they passed them around the room. She liked the way bare-breasted young women nursed their babies before passing them on without concern or judgment. How could these children not be happy, receiving an entire village of love in such a relaxed atmosphere?

Jo reflected on her own grandchildren, who were often awake at night fretful and anxious. How comforting it must be to have that level of support when raising children; not being left alone with the undivided guilt or overwhelming sense of failure. For the Ibans, family responsibility was something they shared along with their labour, love, and lives.

'Did you see how easily the baby went to sleep when she put him in the hammock?' Jo pointed to a makeshift cradle where a sarong had been strung between two upright poles in the corner.

'Yeah. Imagine being able to sleep through all this noise.' Debra glanced at the older women sitting on woven mats, their faces and arms weathered from the sun. One old lady chewing betel leaf spat out the masticated red liquid through the open window. Her mouth and remaining teeth were stained red but, like many of the women, their lack of teeth didn't stop them smiling each time they stole a glance at their guests.

Debra scanned the living area, admiring the traditional blankets lying in a pile on the floor. One young woman, Mimpi, offered to show her how they wove traditional motifs into the warp.

'Jo, do you want to come and see this?' Debra waited for Jo to open her eyes and raise her drooping head from the wall where she'd been napping. When she sauntered over to join them, her face looked ashen. 'Are you feeling okay, Jo?' Debra asked again.

'I'm fine,' came the response, Jo's face brightening slightly as she watched Mimpi's hands weave hidden messages of love into the blankets, binding them to those she loved.

'You like to buy?' Mimpi asked.

'How much?' Jo asked.

Mimpi lowered her eyes and shook her head. She wanted them to make an offer. But how could they calculate the true value of this artist's unique work? It was a labour of love involving hours of intensive toil. A young man fluent in English told them it was the role of the older women to create these totemic designs. The older women were well-versed in the Iban ritual and the esoteric elements of their craft. Younger women, like Mimpi, learnt the craft from their elders.

'I saw something similar in a shop in town. Let's offer her more than what the shops are charging.' Jo chose several pieces of woven fabric dyed in earthy colours of ochre and brown.

'Yes, I'm sure the retailers don't pay them well. But it's such exquisite work. I don't want to offend her.' Debra picked up cloth in shades of eggplant and maroon reflecting the same flower motif seen tattooed on some of the men. Delighted with her purchases, she listened keenly to learn more about this beautiful artwork. 'Your raw materials … where do you get them?'

'Come,' Mimpi motioned for her to follow. 'I take you, show you where rattan grows. We weave it into hats.'

Debra and Jo followed her along the muddy river path, in parts lined with bamboo poles but in other places oozing slippery mud. Mimpi pointed out the rattan, a climbing palm snaking its way around the huge trees that formed the jungle canopy. She took them past a shophouse on stilts further along the riverbank, its small shopfront crammed with a multifarious collection of goods, including weaving tools, wooden shuttles beautifully carved with plant and animal motifs.

'We trade our *getah*,' she said – their rubber crop in exchange for any of these other much-needed items.

Spilling out of the shopfront, an assortment of outboard motors lay dormant beside woven baskets overflowing with dried red chillies, purple eggplant, and bright orange turmeric. Bunches of bananas and pineapples dangled from the rafters above, tied with yellow plastic string.

Mimpi took them to a bamboo grove, where she sliced and stripped the stems of ratan with a sharp-bladed parang. As Debra stretched her arms, a flash of dazzling iridescent blue landed on her finger, and then it was gone. A wizened old woman sitting on a nearby log muttered something to Mimpi in her native tongue, and Mimpi translated for them.

'If dragonfly land on you, bring you good luck.' Mimpi smiled before adding, 'Maybe bring you love.'

'It's more likely attracted to your sweat,' said Jo, wiping her forehead with the sleeve of her shirt. 'From my experience, love and luck are both a fallacy. In the real world, there is no such thing. Everything comes at a cost.'

'That may be so, but I'd like to believe the old woman. I won't refuse good luck when it's offered, or love for that matter.' Sweat ran down her back, under her breasts and she fanned her wet T-shirt against her bra. She peered towards the hilly rice fields where stooped women in conical hats were slashing the crops. *How do they find the energy in this humidity?*

Debra scrambled back along the slippery path towards the longhouse, but Jo struggled and stopped to lean against a tall shady tree.

'Do you want to rest for a bit longer? I can get you some more water.'

'No. I'd rather keep going. It can't be much longer before the helicopter arrives.'

When they arrived at the longhouse, Dick told them Mike and Beth had gone upriver on a small boat with an Iban boatman. Beth wanted to photograph the beautiful butterflies and orchids. Debra forced herself to take a deep breath. He hadn't said goodbye or invited her to go with him. If she was honest, she wouldn't have gone if it meant sharing their time together with Beth. Beth had assured Dick it was to be a quick trip. They'd be back soon so she shouldn't worry.

An hour later, the helicopter landed outside the longhouse. Mike and Beth had not returned and Debra began to worry. Despite the humidity, she paced up and down, listening for the sound of an outboard. But all she heard was the clicking of cicadas and the swooping of fruit bats as they carried out their daily feeding ritual before the sun went down.

'Can we wait a bit longer for them?' She looked at the pilot who shook his head at Dick.

'He's keen to get going before it gets dark.'

'Perhaps I could stay behind and wait for them. The others can go on the helicopter.'

'There's nothing much you can do, Debra. I'll go with the headman and several younger men to search for them before it gets dark. The pilot needs to return to the longhouse tomorrow with medical supplies. Beth and Mike should be back by then. They will come home tomorrow with me.'

Debra bit her lip, wishing she shared Dick's enthusiasm. He seemed confident they would be found and would stay the night at the longhouse. As they'd waited, Dick distracted them with tales about the natural habitat of Borneo with its 200,000 square miles of rainforest. Despite his knowledge of the inhospitable terrain, he didn't seem concerned by his wife's disappearance. Perhaps he had faith in her survival skills or maybe he'd witnessed similar incidents on other occasions.

As they climbed into the helicopter for the return journey, Jo looked unsteady on her feet and one of the medics assisted her into her seat. She appeared anxious, her eyes darting back and forth to the fuel gauge.

'The indicator's low. I hope there's enough fuel to get home.' She cringed at the pilot's jerky movements. 'I hope he knows what he's doing.'

'Let it go, Mum. You're freaking me out. He's the fuckin' pilot. He knows what he's doing. Chill out.' Kali threw her hands to her face, then turned to Sam, whispering. 'Why does she always have to take control?'

'It's OK, Jo. We'll be fine. We're nearly home.' Debra reached out to pat Jo's hand, but a wave of nausea crept into her throat. It wasn't just the humidity and exhaustion of the day, but the fact the day was coming to an end without Mike. *What if they can't find him and I never see him again?*

Back in her hotel room, she collapsed on her bed. While she desperately needed sleep, conflicting thoughts competed for space in her head. *I shouldn't have left him in the jungle. What if he's seriously injured?* She tried to reassure herself he was strong and fit. *Surely, he's capable of walking out of the jungle and back to the longhouse. At least their Iban boatman will know his way back.* A barrage of more alarming questions squeezed their way into her mind. *What if he doesn't want to leave the jungle? What if he and Beth are having such a good time, they've forgotten about everyone else?*

***

The next morning, Debra rubbed her heavy eyelids and felt disoriented as she scanned the strange yet opulent surroundings. It took a while for her to remember the luxurious bedding and the lavish light fittings, to recognise the paintings on the wall of the room. As she forced herself more awake, her pulse quickened, and she realised all was not well. Then she remembered Mike. *Were they able to find him in the jungle? Did the helicopter pilot return to collect him?*

Glancing at her watch, she realised she'd slept in. She pulled aside the soft white duvet to climb out of bed, but her lower back and hips felt stiff. She thought of the gruelling hours she'd spent sitting on the hard floor of the longhouse, and climbing up and down the log steps. Her mind quickly returned to Mike. *Did he have to spend the night sleeping on a hard bamboo floor?* She thought of the hours the Iban women spent sitting, bending, climbing, and then sleeping on those hard unforgiving floors without soft pillows or mattresses for comfort. Perhaps it was the secret to their firm slender bodies.

She unrolled the pieces of cloth she'd purchased at the longhouse, woven by those strong, versatile women; she ran her hands across the grainy texture before holding the cloth to her nose. She inhaled traces of smoke and spice but also a musty hint of history, a whiff of sweat from hard-working women weaving their lives into the mesmerising motifs of their creations. The first piece she pulled out was a woven ceremonial blanket, Mimpi had explained, used in many Iban rituals.

165

As she uncurled the edges, she gathered it around her shoulders, recalling how it protected the wearer from evil by demarcating sacred space, by honouring the Iban gods and ancestors. She examined the auspicious motif patterns inspired by their dreams. In comparison, her own dreams were often fraught with fear. She lacked the insight of these people who communicated with the spirits to guide them through all stages of the textile process.

When she gazed more intently at the motifs, she remembered the Iban men with similar motifs tattooed on their bodies. Didi, the headman's son had explained the significance of tattoos for depicting different stages in their lives. *Rope of Life,*' he'd said, pointing at the eggplant flower with a spiral at the centre. Resembling the underside of a tadpole, it symbolised the beginning of a new life. When the young men left home, the eggplant flower was tattooed onto their shoulders marking the passage of a boy into manhood. 'A journey of knowledge and wisdom,' Didi had said, 'when they leave their longhouse to experience the outside world.'

What a pity Western culture didn't provide specific rites of passage. How much easier it would have been for Sam without the lack of direction and the confusion of not knowing where to go. A set path with prescribed ritual and steps to follow would have been so much easier for him. A village full of people to support and guide him would have eased his difficult transition.

Yesterday, when she and Jo observed the Iban women weaving, they'd discussed the significance of recording family histories into artwork.

'It's so important to keep a visual record to acknowledge the many milestones in a family's life,' Jo had said. 'I think it provides continuity and inspiration for the generations that follow.'

Debra told Jo about her grandmother's family quilt, sewn by stitching together samples of fabric taken from different events in her life.

'She saved a remnant of silk from her wedding gown, a piece of embroidered satin from her daughter's christening gown. Each of these tiny samples she embroidered together with love.' Inspired by her grandmother, Debra, too, had saved remnants of fabric from her own wedding gown, the christening gown worn by Sam but not Mala. Like many aspects of her life, she'd locked them away in a cupboard until such time as she was ready to face them again. *Perhaps this is a project I will revisit when I return home. But am I ready to face it yet? … The wedding gown maybe, but the christening gown?* She wasn't sure.

Then her thoughts jolted back to Mike and his return journey from the jungle; she hoped the Ibans had taken him back to the longhouse, and the helicopter was bringing him home. She forced back her worrying thoughts by remembering the conversations she'd had in the longhouse with Jo and the Iban women.

Jo mentioned how the First Nations people in Australia also acknowledged and celebrated the rites of passage of each tribal member and stitched together kangaroo skins depicting different stages in a child's journey through life. 'Later they present it to him as a cloak when he comes of age,' she'd said. 'They, too, have significant motifs that represent rivers, animals, reptiles, or plants. Their designs have special meaning for the wearer and are often incised onto the skin using a sharpened mussel shell.'

As they'd spoken of it yesterday, Kali's eyes had moistened. 'How cool. To have a sense of identity and know exactly who you were and where you belonged,' she'd said. 'I'd like to have been told more about my origins.'

'Well, I did try to tell you,' Jo had reminded her bluntly.

Visiting the longhouse had been an emotional and insightful experience. While imbibing rice wine and homemade cigarettes may have heightened Sam and Kali's receptive state, they were visibly moved by the transformative encounter. Exhausted from such a tiring day, each of them had also felt the added stress of worrying about Mike and Beth failing to return from the jungle. Sam, though, had tried to reassure them.

'I'm sure Mike will be safe. He knows how to look after himself.'

But the same questions now kept spinning around in Debra's head. *Why didn't he return on time as he'd promised? Where was he and what was he doing now?* Her anger soon faded, replaced with a shiver of remorse. She hoped he was safe, and she could enjoy more of this man whose presence had become a familiar and important part of her life in such a short space of time.

Demons and Dragons

When Debra arrived downstairs for breakfast, Sam was nowhere to be seen. However, from where she sat in the garden café, she could hear his voice coming from above. Turning her head, she picked up snatches of his conversation with Kali as they stood on the balcony above and to the right of where she sat, concealed behind the yellow hibiscus hedge.

If Sam strained his neck, he could possibly see glimpses of her favourite table near the fishpond in the garden café where she now ate a late breakfast. As she sat watching flashes of gold and red in the water, mesmerised by the darting movement of koi as they morphed into a shining mass of silvery white, an iridescent blue dragonfly hovered above the water, its wings almost transparent against the shining, watery surface.

Through the clumps of hibiscus, Sam might have been able to see the glint of silver tables and chairs by the swimming pool. He could have smelt the spicy aromas hanging on the still, humid air where Debra lingered over her coffee and omelette. But she didn't shout out to him, 'come join me'. Normally she would be disappointed Sam had not waited for her but today she was more concerned by a note Mike had left at reception. Brief and to the point, he'd let her know he'd returned from the jungle but had gone out for the day. While she was relieved that he was safe, he didn't mention when he planned to return to the hotel or where he'd gone.

She picked up strands of the conversation between Kali and Sam as they relived their recent trip to the longhouse, expressing their enjoyment of the experience and acknowledging how impressed they were with the Iban people.

'I felt totally accepted,' Kali said, 'as if I'd known them all my life. Unlike a lot of people I know, they didn't judge me.'

'I love the way they share everything, even though they don't have much,' Sam said. 'They don't have hang-ups like us. I bet their mothers don't constantly nag them to quit smoking.'

'Or give up men and drinking,' Kali added. 'Perhaps your mum is hoping for a miracle by bringing you here, showing you where you lived as a kid.'

Debra listened more intently as Sam continued.

'I don't believe in miracles. I must admit though when I saw our old house the other day, I felt like a kid again. It also reminded me of Dad. I remembered the promises I made to him. I still feel guilty. He asked me to take care of Mum and to make something of my life.'

'Well, you tried your best, Sam. You got a job with that IT company.'

'But I stuffed up big time. At least that's what most people thought. When the company crashed, my boss lost everything, but I felt no remorse. My boss was ruthless, treated his staff like shit. I saw no reason to work hard. It convinced me money only corrupts people.'

'So, what do you do now?'

'Nowadays, I prefer the world of virtual reality. I have the power to destroy my dragons, defend cities, face battles. My wizards have control over their world and my avatars have extraordinary powers with everything they need. All Mum has is me and that's never been enough.'

'I don't think that's true, Sam.' Kali comforted him with softer soothing words. 'She cares about you, I'm sure. Has she told you she's disappointed?'

'She doesn't need to. I know when she stares at me, it's as if she's searching deep into my soul. I never meant to hurt her. She's been through enough already. But she makes me feel so guilty.'

'When my dad left us, I felt as if I'd also lost Mum.' Kali's voice faded. 'She was never the same again.'

Sam's voice lowered but Debra picked up pieces even though he whispered. *He heard voices at night? His dad? It really freaked him out?* Debra strained her ears to pick up more muffled words, aware that she was listening in on a conversation not meant to be shared. Now Sam's voice again. 'Something weird has been happening lately … I can hear strange noises … in the jungle.'

She felt goosebumps, and the hairs on her arms rose without warning. She was glad when Kali's voice became audible again.

'I think it's time we had some lunch. I'm starving.'

She imagined Sam stubbing out his cigarette, biting his nails and stretching his neck the way he did when he was anxious. Despite the humidity, a shiver ran down her spine. *No, please not the old demons, Sam. I don't think I can face them again.*

***

Such were Sam's past demons that Debra used to visit him in his rental property each day to reassure herself he was still alive. On many of these occasions, she couldn't wake him out of his drug-induced stupor. He would sometimes ring her at night when he was wandering around with his demons when all she wanted to do was sleep. After lying awake for the remainder of the night, too worried to sleep, she'd go round to check on him in the morning. It was no easy task entering his house and she gagged at the depressing sight always awaiting her.

She'd vowed not to go there again. It was his place and his problem. Let him sort it out. But the fear of finding him dead became overwhelming and her pulse quickened each time she tried to open the door. Duck in quickly, check on him and then leave.

But she found it difficult to ignore his towering pile of dishes in the sink, the dread of cockroaches and rats. Once, as she'd turned on the tap a long-legged spider clung to the web it had built across the neglected tower. It continued its precarious dance fighting against the rush of water and whatever else lay buried among the flotsam. A noxious-looking marinade had oozed its way onto the bench top, whatever had lain in its wake now stuck for eternity. Donning her rubber gloves, she'd dived into the bowels of the sink, pulling out mouldy, slippery mango slices in their rusty tin before gagging and running outside.

***

She gazed around at the blue sky, the vivid South China Sea with its waves crashing onto the sandy beach. She couldn't let these toxic memories pollute such picturesque surroundings. This was a holiday to help her heal and move on and was not for dwelling on the past. But the possibility of Sam's demons returning filled her with dread, and her stomach tightened at the thought. She was also disappointed in herself. Had she been misreading Sam's overt signs of contentment since they arrived in Brunei?

She thought Sam was enjoying himself, displaying a keen interest in everything they'd been doing. The other day when she left her camera in the car, he'd offered to fetch it for her. Parked outside the palace grounds, he was concerned it was too far for her to walk. Each day at the hotel, he cheerfully greeted the staff on a first name basis, happy to share a joke or chat with them about where he'd been and what he'd enjoyed throughout the day. She hoped she was wrong about his demons. Perhaps she'd misheard his conversation. But she had regurgitated too much of his teenage years for one day and her stomach churned, unable to finish her coffee.

She needed to swallow the past once and for all, to have faith that the future would be better. Whatever was going on in Sam's mind, she needed to believe he could handle it. He was now a capable adult no longer in his teens.

Pushing in her chair she took the crumbs of food from her plate and dropped them into the pond. As she fed the koi, she thought of Mike again. *What is he doing now and with whom?* Like Sam, Mike was also old enough to make his own decisions in life. She must step aside and let him do it.

A Perfect Union

Mike dodged the uneven slabs on the pavement as he rushed to meet his old muso mate, Roger, who once played lead guitar in The Banned. Roger now taught music at a prestigious college in Singapore. Mike should have known Roger would come to the reunion as his wife originated from this part of the world, across the river in Limbang, Sarawak, if his memory served him well. When Roger married Aisha, it caused a flurry of gossip among the ex-pat community.

After all, she was his amah and, with little education, she barely spoke English. His middle-class English family and friends were not complimentary when they described her, and they did not accept her as one of them. While he was ostracised from his English family, his friends in Brunei slowly accepted his new wife – not an uncommon occurrence in this part of the world – he was certainly not the first Englishman to have married a local girl.

But when Mike rang Roger earlier that morning, a niggling question prodded his mind. Had Roger's marriage that sparked so much controversy twenty years ago survived the test of time? It didn't take Roger long to confirm what Mike had been too reluctant to ask. Yes, he and Aisha were still happily married, with a string of kids and several grandkids on the way.

It just goes to show, Mike thought, *you can't rely on class and culture.* With little in common, Roger had managed to keep his wife happy all these years, whereas Mike and Jacquie with the same education, status, culture, and religion couldn't make it work. When he first began dating Jacquie, she'd commented on how well their stars aligned. 'Scorpio and Cancer,' she'd purred. 'What a perfect match.'

Some years later, when Charles and Diana married and subsequently divorced, he reminded Jacquie that people had made the same trite comments about their perfect union. It seemed that the royal couple had needed more than auspicious astrological charts to make their marriage work. With his limited interest in astrology, Mike had no idea what effect a sign like Scorpio could have on his marriage until he experienced the sting of Jacquie's tail. He could not have forecast how much pain she could inflict. Nor could he have predicted how much hurt he would feel as he shuffled back into the safety of his Cancerian shell.

Mike thought about what he'd endured since his divorce, including his experience in the jungle with Beth Worthington. It wasn't just about carrying a small dinghy on his head as he stumbled over large boulders. Nor was it tentatively wading through swamps with leeches clinging to his legs. Once the outboard engine stalled, they'd been eaten alive by mosquitoes, and deafened by the buzzing in their ears.

He glanced at his arm and rubbed at several bites which were still inflamed and aggravated by constant sweating. When the search party from the longhouse had finally rescued them, it was already dark. Beth had continued to recite her repertoire of inane jokes, which may have distracted her from darker thoughts, but did little to ease his angst. After arriving at the longhouse, she'd managed to find a hidden reserve of energy which she directed towards him in a display of rampant lust. Dick, who'd been out with the search party, returned exhausted, and had collapsed in a far corner of the longhouse.

In the opposite corner of the sleeping area, Beth had moved her mat closer to Mike, and covered his thigh with hers. Unaccustomed to such ardent displays of desire, he'd been blown away when her wandering hands traced a seductive trail down his body. While Beth was not unattractive and had many good qualities, she was the last person he felt like bedding that night.

Overly generous with Impi the boatman, Beth had insisted on paying for repairs to his outboard when it broke down. She had also arranged the helicopter trip and, in fact, the entire reunion was thanks to her adept organisational skills. But despite her many attributes, Mike didn't feel any attraction towards her. When she ran her fingers down his chest and along his groin, he rolled away, telling her the only thing he desperately needed was sleep.

'And here was me thinking you were a free agent, a recent divorcee? Could there be someone else who has captured your attention?'

'As a matter of fact, there is,' he'd murmured, conjuring an image of an appealing face he knew well, a shapely body he had seen often but never touched – a woman who, until now, he hadn't allowed himself to acknowledge, to admit how much she had crept under his skin and into his heart – someone who was considerate, witty, and intelligent, who also happened to have fabulous legs. *Now if those legs were wrapping around me now, I would not hesitate,* he thought. When he'd looked over at Beth, he could tell she was disappointed, but she had accepted his reluctance and moved her mat to the other side of the room.

After surviving his adventure in the jungle and his restless night on the longhouse floor, he was thrilled when the helicopter arrived early the next morning to take them home. Once he was dropped off at the Air Force base, he barely had time to drive to the hotel and grab a shower.

If he hurried, he'd still make his arranged meeting with Roger in town. They'd arranged to meet in a small café owned by Roger's Malaysian in-laws. With every step he took, his back and legs protested as he climbed a series of concrete steps to the café entrance. His muscles and joints creaked from sleeping on the uneven bamboo flooring and the scratchy woven mats strewn across the longhouse floor.

Roger and Aisha were waiting for him at a small table on the balcony. At the first sign of Mike arriving, several members of Aisha's extended family appeared from behind a kitchen screen. They covered the table with glasses of iced water, a pot of coffee and a plate of bright green pandan cake. Their happy smiling faces and waving hands beckoned him to have something to eat and drink. Mike thanked them before glancing at his friend sitting across from him at the table.

With his receding hairline and freckled skin, Roger appeared much older than his middle years, yet Aisha hadn't aged at all. Her smooth olive face and shining dark hair gave her the appearance of radiant youth. Confirming Roger's earlier assessment of their happy marriage, Aisha sat close to her husband, her hand resting on his forearm. She patted his hand when he needed reassuring, or lost the thread of the conversation. Keen to reminisce about the good old days and the songs they loved to play in the band, Roger excluded her from much of the conversation. Aisha's smile was wide and automatic, revealing crooked teeth, and every few minutes Roger glanced at his wife and returned her smile.

What would it be like to have a loyal, complacent wife, a woman you could trust wholeheartedly? Mike thought. *A wife who loved you unconditionally the way you were.*

'I was thinking about you the other day, Mike. I heard an old Billy Joel song on the radio, and it reminded me of the night you sang it to Jacquie.'

'Yeah. I remember. It was her thirtieth birthday. Not the type of song I would normally sing but she seemed to enjoy it at the time.'

'Which song did you sing?' Aisha asked, smiling now that she had found a link into the conversation. She regarded the men with renewed interest.

'Just the Way You Are,' Roger winked at his wife, before glancing at Mike with a strange smirk. 'So, Jacquie didn't come with you? What's she doing these days?'

'I could write a book about what she's been doing these days and who she's been doing it with,' he muttered under his breath. 'Not good I'm afraid. We've parted ways.'

'Bloody hell. I'm sorry to hear that, mate. I guess these things happen. It's as if everyone I talk to these days is going through a divorce.'

'Yeah? Not everyone it seems.' Mike nodded at Aisha with a mixture of envy and disbelief.

'Perhaps we're just lucky.' Roger nodded at his wife and several of his sisters-in-law who had emerged from the kitchen again, this time bearing plates of spring rolls and curry puffs.

***

Later in the day on the other side of town, Debra sat in another restaurant where the sign above the door bore the propitious name, *The Lucky Restaurant*. The fact that it was still thriving after twenty years was a testament to its auspicious name. While she waited for the others, she chose this serendipitous location to broach the subject of Sam's well-being. Without probing too deeply, she planned to draw him out.

'I've been worrying about you, Sam. Are you happy?'

'Yeah. I'm having fun. It's good spending time with Kali. Visiting our old house was great. It brought back lots of memories of Dad. I often hear him telling me what I should be doing. It was scary at first but I'm getting used to it now. It's sort of comforting.'

'I'm so pleased, Sam. More than anything, I want you to be happy. But I also want you to be at peace.' She listened as he described his emotions and insights but there was no mention of dreaded demons from the past.

'I probably feel happier than I've felt in years,' he said.

A knot slowly unravelled in her gut, and she sighed, releasing the last of her tension. As she waited for her friends to arrive for dinner, she scanned the menu packed with many popular Nyonya choices. For a small unobtrusive restaurant, it was always popular with locals and ex-pats alike. Offering a subtle blend of Chinese and Malay cuisine, it never failed to satisfy its patrons.

She found one of her favourite dishes, *laksa lemak* with noodles cooked in spicy coconut milk. *Yes, that will be my choice this evening.* Sam needed more time to choose as he was distracted by names he didn't know and some that sounded vaguely familiar. Colourful images accompanying each dish brightened the laminated menu, helping to jog his memory. He chose the vivid pink and green gelatinous cut squares for dessert – *agar agar* for old times' sake.

'This drink, *Chendol*. Is that the one with the green floating worms?

'Yes. Jelly-like shapes that take on a life of their own.' Supposedly made from green pea flour, they looked as though they were swimming amidst the shaved ice and thick coconut milk.

While he continued to scan the menu, Debra thought about Mike swimming in the river. She hadn't seen him or Jo since they'd been at the longhouse together. Sam told her Jo and Kali were resting after their exhausting day in the jungle, but she had no idea of Mike's whereabouts.

She ordered iced lemon tea and gazed around at the plastic tablecloths and rickety chairs that hadn't changed much over the years. Deep in thought, when someone crept up behind her and placed their hands over her eyes, she instantly thought it was Jo and grabbed hold of the hands – they were large hands, hands that belonged to a tall man who was now laughing as he plopped into a chair beside her. Jo and Kali followed behind him.

'Look who we found on the street. We've had an incredible day, haven't we?' Jo turned to Mike for confirmation, who grinned and nodded. 'He's back again safe and sound.'

'Good for you! Well, I'm glad you're safe.' Debra said, failing to disguise her disappointment. *Does Mike know how much I've worried about him, waiting all day for him to ring me? ... Of course, he doesn't.*

You could have rung him to find out sooner ... but she didn't want to appear too eager, especially if he'd been out enjoying himself with Jo.

'Sorry we're late. Mike crashed out on my bed, and I didn't want to wake him,' said Jo.

Lifting the glass to her lips, Debra gulped, and the glass slipped from her hand, drenching her shirt. Kali helped her by grabbing serviettes to mop up the liquid.

'Are you okay?' Mike stared at her, and she nodded as the waiter arrived to take their order.

Unaware of Debra's fluster, Jo, unusually animated and caught up in her own world, continued to rave about their recent trip to the longhouse.

'I'd forgotten how beautiful the jungle is. And the Iban people were so welcoming.'

'They sure were welcoming, but I would have preferred they had comfortable beds. I didn't get much sleep last night.'

'Well, it was your choice, Mike. You could have stayed with us. But you chose to go gallivanting up the river.'

'That's not very charitable, Debra. I could have been eaten by wild boar, ravaged by savages or worse. Did you not even miss me for a minute?'

A million and one questions whizzed around in Debra's head; she tried to tune them out, so all she heard was the end of Jo's question.

'… and can you imagine inviting strangers into your house?'

'No, I could not,' Debra replied automatically. Indeed, she'd guarded her privacy in recent years, not wanting the outside world to know about her dysfunctional family. Many times, she'd feigned illness or pretended she was busy when invited to other people's celebrations. Being among other people who led happy lives with perfect children was difficult for her to accept.

Her recent concern that Sam's past demons may have resurfaced reminded her of the many family occasions sabotaged by his anti-social behaviour. Sam, who was now tucking into his rice noodles, and smiling at those around him would probably not remember those past events or his actions at the time. It reminded her why they'd come on this holiday. It was time to forgive and move on.

Jo rambled on about the rural landscape and the river meandering through those lovely mangrove swamps. 'What a great opportunity for you to go upriver and see the orchids, Mike.'

'Except when Beth and I had to swim across the river. It was awfully muddy but was the only place to wash.' Mike lifted his arms pretending to sniff his armpits. 'Don't worry I've had a shower since.'

'You could have been bitten by a sea snake or monitor lizard, or worse still … by Beth.' Having let it out, Debra bit down hard on the end of her straw.

'You sound as if you have a little venom in your bite, Debra.' With a swift flick of his chopsticks, Mike stole a prawn from Jo's plate, and Debra felt a sting of jealousy as if he'd stabbed her with his chopstick. She picked at the paper serviette, separating each of the tissue layers with the concentration of an assembly line worker.

Jo flashed Mike her most encouraging look, keen for him to continue recounting his exciting night's adventure in the jungle. By the time the search party found them, they were desperately dehydrated. Impi, their boatman, had snagged the engine on rocks, and they'd had to help him carry the boat to where he said he could get it repaired. But the river was flooded in parts and blocked with debris.

'To think I'd previously complained about sleeping on woven mats, with cocks crowing from above and pigs grunting from below. It was such a relief to stretch out on the longhouse floor when we finally got back there. I'll never complain about a little discomfort again.'

'Fancy bumping into Roger this morning,' Jo interjected, keen to reminisce about her sailing days. 'Remember when the three of us slept on the island when our mainsail was damaged? It was a real surprise seeing you both in the café this morning.'

'It all sounds rather cosy,' Debra said, her smile resembling a grimace. When Mike detected her sarcasm, he didn't react but continued eating the last of his laksa.

Seated next to Debra, Kali had been observing her decimating the serviette, tearing it into shreds. She also noted her turned-down mouth and slumped shoulders and moved in closer, whispering.

'Mum enjoys talking about things that happened years ago, ' she said loudly for the whole group to hear. There's no way she could do it today. When Mike came around to our hotel room this afternoon, he was so exhausted he crashed out on my bed.

Within seconds, Mum was asleep in the chair, so I had to sit there listening to the two of them snoring. So much for reminiscing about the good old days.'

Glancing at the bottle of chilli sauce on the table, Debra imagined her face flushing to a similar shade of red. *Why should I be concerned about who Mike spent his night with, now or in the past?* She signalled to Sam that it was time to go.

'Can we stay a bit longer? Kali wants to show me some of her photos back at their hotel.'

'Yes, don't go yet. I'm just getting my second wind. Well, I should rephrase that. I'm celebrating life, after facing the thought of dying in the jungle last night. Let your hair down, Debra. The night, unlike us, is still young.'

Debra took a deep breath, thinking of her many options in life. She could choose to feel peeved or stay with her friends, especially those whose company she was starting to enjoy. *Isn't that why I came on this holiday?*

'Yes, let's go back to our hotel. It's not far from here and I still have a bottle of duty-free gin. If Kali hasn't already discovered it,' Jo laughed, winking at her daughter.

'Thanks, Mum.' Kali raised her eyebrows towards Sam, before shaking her head at her mother.

'Come on, let's walk there. Our mothers can get a lift with Mike.' Sam, playfully tapping her on the back, pushed her towards the exit.

Sam and Kali left their parents to pay the bill and find Mike's car, while they walked to Jo and Kali's hotel.

Kali produced her old photo album and Sam laughed as she pointed at amusing shots of them both as children. In one photo Kali was wearing her angel costume as she grinned at the camera. Sam, wearing nothing at all, laughed as he jumped into the swimming pool. When Kali saw a photo of her amah, her eyes moistened.

'Oh, how I loved Annie. She gave me endless cuddles whenever I needed them. She was never strict, and I was allowed to do whatever I wanted. I really missed her when I left, especially after I got married. I'd love to have her helping me now.'

'It was the same with our amah, Lena. I loved sitting on the floor eating rice with my hands. Life was so simple then.'

When Jo let Mike and Debra into her hotel room, Sam and Kali were propped on her bed, tears running down their faces. Kali pointed at the photo album smiling and Jo got the message – sad yet happy tears.

Once Jo had poured drinks for Mike and Debra, they again reminisced about happier times when they all lived in Brunei.

'It was the sense of community, the strength of friendships,' Jo said, and they all agreed. Without extended families to share special events like Christmas and birthdays, they'd developed stronger friendships to fill the gap.

By midnight, they'd weighed the merits of living overseas against staying in their country of birth. Mike's eyes were drooping, and his head nodded. Sam suggested life was complicated enough without having to survive on your own.

'I don't know how I would have done it without my family. Especially you, Mum. You were always there for me.' He looked at her with an expression much wiser than his years. She heard the sincerity in his voice and fought back awkward tears.

Sam fidgeted with the photo album, embarrassed by her display of emotion. He tried to lighten the mood.

'What about you, Kali? Any deeper insights into life?'

'I think life is about sifting through what is real and what is not. Dealing with stuff that I'm probably imagining.'

'Or hallucinating?' he suggested, elbowing her in the ribs.

'Maybe,' she said, returning his shove. 'But the sad thing is when you're having a good dream, it always comes to an end. You wake up and find your life is still full of crap.'

'Life can't be all that bad,' said Mike as he forced open his eyes. 'You're young, attractive with a great personality. There's still plenty of life to be lived.'

'Let's all drink to that,' said Jo. 'There's still plenty of time. To a life waiting to be lived.'

The Mad Hatter

Despite the alcohol he'd consumed the night before, when Mike woke the next morning, he felt like a new person. He started thinking about the type of person he used to be, which was rather confronting. The truth was he'd once had a quick fling with Beth Worthington, many years ago, a one-night stand. At the time it was convenient for them both. He'd invited her to crew for him after his own crew had taken ill at the last minute and couldn't sail.

Earlier in the day, he'd witnessed Dick criticising Beth for tangling the rigging, shouting at her until she stormed off in a huff. Desperately in need of a crew, Mike had also wanted the satisfaction of pissing off her husband.

'What's the matter with you, woman?' Dick had shouted at her in front of all the yachties trying to get their boats in the water. When Mike asked if Beth would like to crew for him, she'd gladly accepted – a timely salve to assuage her humiliation. She'd also been happy to spend time with him after the race had finished. His lips pursed, remembering that the sex had been good, but she wasn't really his type. Besides, he was flying back to the UK to see his wife and children. It was a convenient time to begin and end the relationship.

His most recent stay in the jungle confirmed his former instincts had been correct. He was still not interested in Beth. While she was good fun, most of the time, his thoughts were on another woman, a woman whose laugh echoed in his ears, and whose face was waiting for him whenever he closed his eyes. After Mike had rejected Beth at the longhouse, she'd still pressed him to come and stay with them at Labuan and, when he'd told her he was in a relationship, she'd said: 'Bring her along, it will be fun. There are a few other people coming.'

Thinking about Beth prompted him to reflect on some of his earlier decisions in life and former indiscretions. While he couldn't make excuses for his actions, he did have certain regrets.

As a child, his parents had encouraged him to always keep a smile on his face. They didn't want him moping around the house, looking miserable. This last directive was because they expected him to entertain his baby sister, Evie, who was born profoundly deaf. Hyperactive and often bored, she loved his amusing antics, which resulted in bursts of laughter from them both. Entertaining his sister, his parents assumed should be his number one priority.

'Will you come and mind her pet?' his mother would call out. 'I have to duck out to the shops.'

His father, not known for his patience, would shout, 'Eh, lad, will you come and amuse our Evie so I can watch the news on telly.'

Using exaggerated facial expressions and hand gestures, Mike had enjoyed reading Evie her favourite story, *Alice in Wonderland*. As they escaped via their own magical portal, the visual cues gave Evie a temporary distraction from her silent world. For Mike, the oddities beyond the rabbit hole often appeared strange and nightmarish.

But, for Evie, the brightly coloured talking cats and anthropomorphic playing cards held her focus for more than a few minutes. Enhanced by his encouraging grin, Mike's stories made her world more exciting. Trapped in this rehearsed state of perpetual happiness, Mike sometimes felt like the Mad Hatter. But who was he really? Where did he fit into this world of make-believe? As he questioned, Evie laughed, tapping her hand against her chest, 'More, more.'

His ability to entertain became his life's mission and proved useful when he decided to perform in a band. He would have chosen a career in theatre, but his old man had other ideas.

'You need to get yourself a proper job, lad. Something respectable that pays your bills.'

When he began teaching, he was once again the joker, entertaining his students with his well-modulated voice and regular supply of jokes.

When Mike left home to get married, Evie was devastated, and he felt guilty leaving her. After all, it had been his role to amuse and entertain her and ensure her happiness. At thirteen years of age, she couldn't understand his need to be with Jacquie or that she now had to compete for his affection. When he and Jacquie left on their honeymoon, Jacquie helped to take his mind off Evie and assuage his guilt.

'I love that you are always fun to be around,' she'd said.

And he loved to make Jacquie laugh. When he'd met her mother, he understood Jacquie's need for fun and laughter. Nothing could crack the mask on that old witch. Her face was permanently fixed with expressions of derision and disdain for those who failed to live up to her impossible standards.

'So, what happened, Jacquie?' he'd asked her as they were planning to divorce. 'If I was always fun to be around, where did I go wrong?'

'You were always living in the moment, enjoying every minute of each day. You didn't think about the future,' she said.

Unlike Dr Dan, he thought bitterly. *The good doctor had obviously been planning for some time, planning how he was going to steal my wife.*

When Mike married Jacquie, he'd thought he had no reason to worry about the future, believing his happy marital state would last forever. After the shock of his marriage ending, he now questioned the merits of setting long-term life goals. But were there any guarantees?

The reason behind his decision to settle in the UK was to give his family the stability they wouldn't have had if he'd remained working in Brunei. He'd hoped to create a tighter family circle where his girls wouldn't have to board at school, a place where he and Jacquie would spend more time together. While he hated to admit it, he'd never previously spent this much time in contemplation. He'd recently detected a more serious persona creeping into his psyche. *What's to become of this old joker and Mad Hatter? Have they completely disappeared down the rabbit hole?*

His thoughts momentarily returned to Beth. Previously, if he'd had the opportunity to spend a night with a willing woman, he wouldn't have hesitated. No doubt such a prospect would have led to pleasurable thoughts and gratifying outcomes. But spending his most recent night with Beth in the longhouse had shown him how much he'd changed.

Meeting with Debra after twenty years had also taught him the importance of long-term friendships. What was it she'd said the other day? *'A good friendship like ours can make sense of any amount of heartbreak, broken promises, or loveless marriage. It's worth far more as it gives us courage to believe in ourselves.'*

And he'd agreed with her when she'd said, *'I'm sure from here we can walk beside each other, whatever our journey.'*

A few days with her had been more fulfilling than a quick fling with someone he didn't really care about. He lifted himself out of the armchair and out of his reverie. What he needed was a swim, something to cool his body and ease his mind. He stripped off and lowered himself into the refreshing water of the swimming pool.

The Queen of Hearts

While Kali and Debra sat around the swimming pool waiting for Mike and Sam, Kali questioned Debra about Gareth. She had come over on her own, leaving Jo to have an afternoon nap. According to Kali, her mother needed time out, but Kali was also keen to know what Debra remembered about her elusive father.

'Most things I've heard over the years have been negative. Since I've been in Brunei, I've been having flashbacks where I remember childhood incidents and images of Dad.'

Debra reflected on when she first met Gareth and admitted they weren't great first impressions, even though the first time he introduced himself as their neighbour, he brought freshly made pancakes for their breakfast. It was a kind gesture … but she needed to delve deeper to find something that would please Kali.

'He did have some good qualities,' she started, but Kali interjected.

'From the many things I've heard about him, it sounds like he was a real prick.'

'I remember him teaching you to ride.'

Kali's bike had been second-hand and much loved by a neighbour's child, but Gareth liked to push her around the neighbourhood holding fast onto the tiny seat. Wobbling from side to side as she worked the peddles, Gareth ran along beside her ready to catch her should she fall. 'He continued to give you his support and encouragement, never letting go until you were ready to ride solo.'

'Really? I remember some of those times.' Kali had recently found some old childhood photos where her father was smiling at her with an expression of love or pride. 'It sounds as if he may have cared about me.'

'I'm sure he did. He was your dad. You used to race up the driveway on your little bike. One day you skidded and slid under the neighbour's car. Your dad was so upset he almost had a heart attack.'

'Oh, my God. I do remember that close shave. I was really frightened.'

'It was scary to watch.' Debra looked at Kali remembering the fragile child. Always highly imaginative, Kali had spent many hours on her own. But she often sought refuge in Debra's house and Debra had enjoyed her company. 'I'm sure he cared about you.'

'He hasn't bothered to keep in touch with me,' Kali said, twirling a strand of fringe around her finger, creating a fascinating rope of pink and black. 'Did Mum tell you about what he did with her plane?'

'Yes. Your mother loved her Cessna. It was her pride and joy. When your dad borrowed it to fly an illegal immigrant across the border, that was the final straw.'

'How could he do such a thing? Without her permission?'

'Everybody makes mistakes at times. I'm sure he felt ashamed of what he did. These things are not easy to face. Sometimes we need to forgive people and move on.' Debra thought of the times she had stuffed up in her life with bad choices and wrong decisions. As hard as it was, she had to let it go.

'I guess so. He's one of many men in my life who have let me down. But he was the first one.' Kali lifted her mobile phone and slammed it shut as if wiping those men from her life.

Debra remembered those small delicate hands and the affection she'd had for that little girl and now for the young woman she'd become.

'I remember another time we were at the beach when you almost drowned. A huge wave caught you and sucked you under. Your dad was the first to rush in and rescue you. He didn't hesitate for one minute. Perhaps you could focus on some of those positive memories.'

Kali stayed silent and gazed towards the ocean, deep in thought. Finally, she turned her wide-eyed gaze on Debra. 'If only Mum would focus on the positives in her life. For starters, she could do something about her hair. I've offered to colour and restyle it for her so many times. She says she has more important things to do.'

'I can understand you wanting to help her. But perhaps your mum's right. Her outside appearance is merely a facade. There are more important things in life.'

'What do you mean?' Kali stared childlike.

'Physical appearance is not as important as what's on the inside. Improving your mind and trying to understand yourself is more important than the way you look. Once you understand yourself, it's easier to understand other people. We don't always know why people act the way they do. Sometimes we need to accept them as they are.'

'I often feel ugly and worthless. That's why I like to change my appearance so often.'

'I'm sorry you feel that way. You're a beautiful young woman. Often our thoughts are not real, Kali. More like a Hollywood film. What might appear real is not always so.'

Kali stared into the distance. 'I keep thinking about my hairdressing salon and my lovely, lonely clients. Creating special styles to transform them lifts their spirits, and they feel empowered. My salon is like a haven for them, where we chat and connect. I pamper them, and they love me for it. And I really need that.

'By the time I am finished with them, they feel worthy of love instead of just being wives whose sole purpose is to please their husbands. Naomi Hoffman, one of my regulars, comes in every few days for a brush-up of her wig. She's recently widowed, and while she appears tall and strong, she's desperately lonely.' Kali brushed her hair behind her ears. 'I think she sees me as someone who listens and is willing to give her the nurturing she needs.'

She half smiled and went on. 'Another of my favourites is Hannah Levi. She's a small lady with a wizened face … she comes in every couple of weeks to have her roots touched up. We all had a laugh one day when she said, "I don't want Eli to find out I'm not really a redhead". Sometimes the gossip that gets spread around the salon is as important to them as the regular touch-ups. One day Hannah also brought in homemade cookies to share and a flask of my favourite, special black coffee.'

Debra nodded supportively.

'Would you believe,' Kali admitted, nodding, 'I once cut my own hair to please the latest man in my life. I took some horrendous liberties with the scissors and once I began cutting, I couldn't stop. My hair is only one of many things I changed over the years. There's also my weight which has become an obsession, to the point where I can't enjoy a meal without feeling guilty in case I stack on the kilos.

'My customers, though, are lovely women. They accept me the way I am – not like Miriam, my mother-in-law.'

Debra turned to Kali with keen interest, glad that she was opening up to her, so Kali kept on talking.

'Miriam had an endless supply of barbs she loved to spout at appropriate times. "Once on the lips twice on the hips" was one of her favourites. She'd used it the day before our wedding, and I bit my lip so hard not to say anything that I drew blood.

'The first time she said it to me, I just smiled meekly to keep the peace, to show Jacob I was fine with his mother. I wanted to be part of his incredible family and was willing to bend over backwards to be accepted by them.'

Kali stood and placed her hands on her hips. 'Look at me, Debra; no wonder I'm so skinny now.

'We'd been at the wedding caterers, Cuisine Élégante, in the middle of tasting a selection of hors d'oeuvres. Admittedly, I was working my way through each tiny delicacy, determined to sample each one. Miriam was tasting the healthier options on the opposite table but was keeping an eye on me at the same time.

'You might want to shed one or two kilos to fit nicely into your wedding gown,' she said, looking down her nose at me.'

Kali shook her head. 'I dropped the canapé I was about to eat, wiped the caviar from my mouth and sucked in my tummy so tight I struggled to breathe. I swore nothing was going to get in the way of our special day. His parents were footing the bill for the wedding, so I felt obliged to please them. I'd always dreamed of a fairy tale wedding and this was my big chance. To marry Jacob, I was willing to change everything … my religion … my appearance.

'Not long after our wedding, she started calling me Kelly. When writing it, she spelled it like the Irish name. 'It sounds more refined, less exotic,' said Kali, mimicking Miriam's condescending manner.

'Your mother-in-law sounds rather controlling,' Debra mused, watching Kali as she slowly chewed down another nail.

'Yes, she is. At the time I wanted to ask if she'd not heard of Ned Kelly, but instead I just gritted my teeth. Refined? I don't think so. But it was simply a matter of changing the spelling and pronunciation so, once again I agreed to the changes.'

'Oh, Kali. What a shame. You were named after a Hindu goddess. Your parents wanted you to have a special name. They saw you as a miracle.'

'I found out the reason she wanted me to change my name was because of her friend, Rani Patel, who often took her shopping in her chauffeur-driven Rolls. Apparently, dangling from the rear-view mirror was a picture of a dark woman holding various weapons and a severed head. I overheard Miriam once admit that she twitched and shuddered on hearing that Rani worshipped this goddess Kali whose darkness was believed to bring about transformation.

'Despite her frightening appearance, Rani assured Miriam, the goddess was regarded as some Great Mother Goddess. Miriam had told her friend outright that she wasn't interested in Tantra or alternative spiritual pathways.

'I heard her tell another friend that, while trying out a new beauty salon, she'd glanced at a magazine showing explicit images of people locked in erotic sexual poses. Tantra. The word had conjured up those images again. That was enough for Miriam. She couldn't have her daughter-in-law seen to be connected to such primeval beliefs and practices.' Kali's smile flickered.

'So, what did you do, Kali?'

'When I asked Mum about the origins of my name, she confirmed that Dad had indeed named me after the Hindu goddess. Apparently, Mum and Dad had enjoyed a brief interest in Tantric yoga, but Mum failed to mention any interest in erotic mystical states. She did admit to lighting joss sticks, sitting on the floor, and chanting. Dad had enjoyed it, though, and thought that naming me after a goddess might provide me with a blessed life.' She laughed. 'He sure as hell got that wrong.'

Kali bent her head. 'After seven years of marriage, I could see just how much of me I'd changed. I didn't know who I was anymore. I'd also made so many concessions regarding the children to meet Jacob's mother's approval.

'I desperately wanted to keep breastfeeding, but Miriam had other ideas. "Why don't you wean the baby, go on the pill, and get back to the gym. Then you can lose some of that baby fat" she told me.'

'Oh no, Kali. How awful for you. It's such a special time with your baby.' Debra reached out and patted Kali's hand.

'I cried that day and each time thereafter as I tried to wean him. The first time I tried to give Adam a bottle, he kept nuzzling into my breast, searching, ever hopeful. There was no way he was taking the rubber teat. You have no idea the guilt I went through denying him the comfort of breastfeeding. Life at home became more stressful, the prospect of returning to work more tempting. I longed for a world of my own, free from family pressures.'

Kali sighed deeply. 'I was often so tired and stressed Mum supported me where she could. Then Jacob insisted I quit drinking alcohol. I could play the proper hostess with a glass of champagne in my hand, but he didn't want me drinking alone. It all ended very badly when Jacob, courtesy of his mother, hired the best solicitor money could buy. To end the stress and financial burden, I settled for the crumbs I was thrown. Miriam's parting remark was to remind me of the privileged life I was leaving behind. I remember so clearly … she said, "Your problem, Kelly, is you are all hat, no cattle."

'I wanted to say, "You ought to know, you fuckin' old heifer. It's easy to see why you only had one child." But instead, I stormed out and bought myself a huge banana sundae covered in nuts, chocolate sauce and double dollops of cream. And the rest is history …'

Kali picked up the menu from the poolside table and scanned through the dessert options. 'I think it's time to reward myself again.' She waved to the attract a young Malay waiter hovering nearby.

'It sounds as though you've made many changes to please others. It's not easy when you're always trying to fix yourself.'

'No. It's very draining. I once tried to understand my father better by sleeping with a guy who was gay.'

'And did it help you understand?'

'No, he was more interested in the barman who was giving him the eye. I found myself with another guy who told me he was Michael Jordan. He was wearing a Chicago Bulls hoodie and I believed him. Later, when he began stripping, I saw he had a sailor's uniform on underneath. He was on shore leave.' Kali pulled at her pink and black fringe, stretching the longest strand towards her mouth.

'Isn't it a bit risky? Picking up sailors?'

'He was happy to use protection. Trouble was we were on Bondi Beach. Afterwards, I couldn't find my clothes in the dark. I still have the Chicago Bulls hoodie I had to wear home that night.' She stood again and stretched her arms above her head and took a few steps before staring at the beach in front of her. It had darker sand, a different ocean but was the same far-reaching sea.

'I hope the kids are enjoying their stay with Erin.' She looked around to Debra. 'I didn't dare ask Jacob to mind them just in case he tried to keep them. He'd love any opportunity to try and prove I'm negligent towards them.' She smiled, and Debra could see her reminiscing, a warmness spreading over her face.

'Sarah is three, and highly imaginative … like me. She loves to dress up in my colourful clothes. Adam, on the other hand, is more like Jacob. At five, he already has his father's air of entitlement.' She sat down again beside Debra.

'When I was young, I idolised my father,' she admitted as her mind drifted back. 'I was always eager to please him. When he left us, I was too young to understand what was happening. But I felt the hurt and rejection, the devastation of coping on my own. I knew Mum loved me, but she was stressed out trying to make a living to support us both. Not unlike how I feel now.

'It may have been easier to accept if Dad had left us for another woman, but I found it impossible to compete with another man.' She fiddled with her earrings, turning them in their holes, each semi-precious gem matching the sparkling stud in her nose.

'It takes time to make sense of family dramas, but you need to be kind to yourself, Kali. It can't have been easy for you or your mum. As parents, we all make mistakes. I'm sure you've discovered that by now.'

'I sure have. My kids must think I'm a terrible mother. I'm always tired and it's all so hard.' She opened her wallet and stared at the familiar photo – Adam and Sarah sitting on a seesaw, one high, one low, their faces radiating love and joy.

'Kids are resilient. I'm sure yours will be fine. But I still worry about you and Sam trying to find your way in this world. Thanks for being so supportive of him. I know he values your friendship.' She leaned in closer and lowered her voice.

'It's no trouble.' Kali let her endearing childish grin spread. 'I like being his friend and yours too.'

'Kali …' Debra hesitated, then decided to push on. '… I'm worried about your mum. She doesn't look well.'

'I know. She's not getting much sleep. She's always tired.'

'It's more than that. She looks gaunt, and her energy has been flagging. At the longhouse, she paused to rest every few minutes and fell asleep every chance she got. And she gets defensive whenever I ask about her health.'

Kali nodded. 'Yes, she overreacts to everything I say too. Always snapping at everyone.'

'I'm concerned about her. She was such a strong woman. She seems to be fighting constantly to regain control.'

'It's neurological. She told me not to tell anyone. She's scared people will view her differently if they know.'

'Oh no! I'm so sorry. It's not the sort of news anyone wants to hear. I can understand your mum not wanting people to know. She's never been one to ask for help. A couple of times on the phone I sensed she was trying to tell me something. She probably thought the timing wasn't right with Alex dying.'

'She's been through so much, like you, Debra, but I can't imagine you stuffing up big time.'

'Believe me, I have. Once it was over another man.'

'Really? Was it a love story?' She looked at Debra keenly.

Debra sighed, reluctant to reveal her mistake. 'Yes, it was a love story, and it transformed me – first by its presence and then through its absence. But it's a story for another time. I'll tell you one day soon.'

'Great. I can't wait to hear all about it. Speaking of other men … I reckon Mike has the hots for you, Debra. I've seen the way he looks at you.'

'Oh, go on. Don't be silly.' Debra laughed, but an unexpected flush spread to her face and neck.

The man in question had now arrived and was stripping off his shirt; he draped it over the back of a chair. As he walked towards the pool, they both stared after him, admiring his tight abs and muscled arms as he waved to them, beckoning.

'Are you girls coming in, or are you going to sit gossiping all day.'

Kali looked at Debra and they both giggled. Then Sam arrived and dropped his towel on the chair beside Kali.

'What's going on?' he asked.

'Nothing,' they replied in unison.

When Mike dived in, his tanned arms and shoulders rippled through the water with little effort, Debra watching him with interest. Kali's comments had surprised her, and while she had enjoyed the attention Mike had given her, she was not sure of his intentions. Perhaps he considered her purely a friend. Nor was she certain of her feelings for him. When she was Kali's age, she would have been thrilled if a man had the hots for her, but now she was ambivalent, unsure of how she felt or if she was ready to commit to another man.

During Alex's lengthy illness, she'd had many hours to reflect on her life, which at times had lacked the love and excitement she'd enjoyed while living in Brunei twenty years earlier. She still remembered how it felt receiving love, the touch of fingers exploring every part of her body … his evocative smell, full of promise and longing. But the love had not come from Alex, and she doubted she would find that intensity again or the way she'd willingly surrendered her heart to him.

She would tell Kali about Rahim one day, that like her, she too had longed for the fairy tale dream. She imagined clicking the heels of her ruby red slippers as she skipped along the Yellow Brick Road. Instead, what she'd discovered was something akin to a tale from Aladdin. Living in this faraway Shangri La was a sultan who sat on his jewel-encrusted throne in a gilded palace, not far from a majestic mosque that rose out of the clouds. On her arrival, she'd unwittingly rubbed the magic lamp and found a dark handsome stranger from another world. With his warm eyes and eloquent prose, this erudite lover of words had captivated her, until she was engrossed in his world of poetry and romance. Precariously balanced like a house built of books, their world had eventually come crashing down around them. But before it disappeared, his fascinating world had offered her insight and refuge in a way she could never have imagined.

While Kali might still be searching for the excitement of romance, Debra also remembered the pain of losing it all when the elusive dream she was chasing came to a sudden end. *But is there ever a happily ever after? Would any chapter that followed on from her former love story ever be enough?*

Before she could gather her thoughts, Mike returned dripping wet from the pool and stood behind her. He gently placed his hands on her shoulders.

'Come on in. The water's great. I've got something to show you.'

His face was so close she could smell the warmth of his breath. When she looked in his eyes, there was a promise of something more. She remembered a certain look, the gentlest touch, a shared thought, a moment in time. The hope and longing of what was to come. But was this the time or place?

Mike waited while she stripped off her shirt and trousers and left them hanging on the chair. As she followed him towards the pool, Kali gave her a last-minute wink that said:

'I told you so.'

He dived into the deeper end of the pool, and she dived in after him. He then guided her through the spray of water spurting out of the fountain in the middle of the pool. The deeper pool flowed into a larger infinity pool joined by a waterfall flowing from a fabricated mountain of rock. There was enough space to swim through the cascading water and she followed him in. She knew she was directly under the waterfall when the pitter-patter of drops became thunderous in her ears. It was like torrential rain pummelling her head and shoulders.

As she tried to lift her head, she shut her eyes from the onslaught of water and lost her balance. He caught her around the waist and drew her into his chest. His flesh felt slippery but firm and, as she opened her eyes, she felt the contact of his flesh against hers, felt the curves of his body and the smell of tanning lotion on his sun-kissed skin. As she turned her head slightly, she saw Sam swimming towards them, and Mike's misguided kiss brushed against her cheek.

'What do you think of this?' Sam yelled, waving his arms around to include the network of never-ending pools. 'It's awesome, isn't it?'

'I haven't seen anything better.' She laughed as Mike released her and she swam over to where Kali had now joined Sam.

'I'll race you back,' Mike challenged Sam and raced off for a head start.

'Look, there's Mum,' said Kali, pointing to where Jo stood at the edge of the pool. 'Are you coming in?' she yelled to her mother.

'No, I'll just rest for a minute. It must be happy hour. Time to sample another of those famous mocktails.'

Rising from the Ashes

Debra and Jo sat in the courtyard, sipping concoctions of coconut and lime juice, mint, and mango, as the others left to frolic in the ocean. A bevy of hotel staff fussed around them as they prepared the large fire pit for the special seafood barbecue to be held later that evening. The sous-chef placed a wide steel plate over the top of the fire where he would be sizzling locally caught fillets of fish, fresh prawns, and squid. He placed a large copper pot nearby to cook his traditional chilli mussels. As the kitchen hands brought in armfuls of firewood, Jo chuckled and quietly shook her head.

'Wow, that brings back memories. Dad chopping wood and preparing the fire at home. I remember the first time I lit a fire by myself; I was about seven and it was quite scary.'

'I'm sure it was. That's very young.' Debra nodded, wide-eyed.

'I arrived home from school one day to find there was no one at home. When I turned the door handle, it was locked. So, I lifted the terracotta plant pot beside the door to retrieve the key. It was one of those heavy old-fashioned solid keys, and I had to stand on an upturned pot to reach the keyhole.'

Debra listened, trying to imagine Jo as a small vulnerable girl instead of the fearless, capable woman she'd always seen. Jo continued with her story confirming there was nothing she couldn't handle.

'I can clearly remember the faded brown paint on the front door of the homestead and the way it squeaked when I pushed it open. When I went in, all was quiet, but there was a note on the kitchen table with my name on it. I could read enough to recognise the words 'Lad', 'Vet' and 'snake'.

'It was always Dad's job when he came in from tending the cattle to light the fire. He liked to think he was warming our home, filling it with love. That day, while I waited for hours in the cold room hugging my arms around my knees, I saw the matches. Dad had already laid out the fire and I thought he'd be pleased at how clever I was. It would make the room so much warmer. After about three attempts, I managed to get a match lit.'

'So was your dad impressed with what you'd done?'

'No. He said lighting fires was not a job for little girls. There are certain jobs which should be done by a man and lighting fires was one of them. It was dangerous to play with matches. He failed to comment on my achievement or how cosy the living room was as he walked in.'

'That's a shame. Lighting fires is quite a skill.'

'Most of the important things in life I learned from Dad. I kept a stash of useful items he'd given me in a battered old suitcase under my bed. A flashlight he said would help me see in the dark, and a mud map he'd drawn to show me the way home from school. A set of Dad's ancient aviator goggles took pride of place in that suitcase.' Jo circled her hands around her eyes. 'You know the old style. He taught me the importance of finding my way home as he had done after the war.'

'Sounds like you were close to your dad.'

'He said, if your vision should become cloudy, you could always rely on the stars regardless of where you were in the world, separated by space or time.'

'Yes, we're all gazing at the same stars,' Debra said, gazing up at the darkened sky. So close to the equator, the constellations looked clearer.

'As Dad and I sat on the old rickety porch, he on his rocking chair, me on the porch step, his words brought me comfort knowing we were all connected. When he pointed out the Venus star, first star of the evening, I knew I wasn't alone. When I rose early each morning, I saw the same Venus star waiting for me. I wanted him to be proud of me, to know that I'd listened to him and could find my own way in the world.'

'I think your dad would be proud of you, Jo.'

'I'm not so sure. My vision has become cloudy. I've lost my way, and I often feel alone. Perhaps I've wandered away from the guiding star.' Jo gazed into the sky above Brunei, with its firmament of stars, and Debra sensed she was searching for the brightest star of all, Venus. She pointed at it. It was still there.

'Maybe your dad is guiding you from a distance,' said Debra. 'Perhaps you just need to change your orientation, to trust in your guide. Your dad was right about the danger of playing with matches. My brother Trevor and I found out the hard way. When Mum saw his singed hair and eyebrows, she was furious.'

'Not long after this incident, my brother died tragically from an unrelated accident and the stars went dark that night. While I had nothing to do with his death, a sense of betrayal lodged in my gut as if I'd planted the identifying kiss to the waiting soldiers of death. I like to think he rose out of the ashes, like the phoenix as I often sense his presence around me.'

'You don't often talk of your brother, but you talk of the other deaths in your life.'

'His death was the first. Probably the hardest. I was only a child. Each subsequent loss is supposed to make you stronger, more resilient. But I think sadness starts to become the norm in your life. Loss is the price we pay for love.' She twisted her lower lip and rolled it over until the inner flesh was exposed, tender and raw.

Jo nodded with understanding. 'After my father died my life lost all meaning. He was my beacon, my rock. I expected all men to be the same as him, and of course, they weren't. While I appear strong and independent, Debra, the truth is, I think I still need a man in my life.' She pulled out a cigarette and lit it.

'At least you know what you need, Jo. I'm still not sure if I want to take that risk again.'

An awkward, bespectacled waiter approached but hesitated before slipping away. He left them pointing out the constellations, the Southern Cross, the belt of Orion, and the Hunter with the sword hanging from his belt. As children they'd viewed him as a saucepan, the sword as the pot handle. From a dark corner of the sky, a streak of light flashed across the sky and then faded as it fell. A tiny speck of space rock or dust moving so quickly it was hard to believe what they had just witnessed.

'Did you see that?'

'They say if you spot a shooting star while travelling, your voyage is supposed to be a success.'

'That's good. So far, this is shaping up to be a great holiday. In some cultures, falling stars are thought to represent the release of souls,' said Jo. 'I like to think that might be my dad.'

'New lives, new beginnings for us all. That sounds great to me.' Debra gazed around the garden now floodlit with tiny flashing lights.

'Is this a private discussion or can anyone join in?' Mike asked as he pulled out a chair. Sam and Kali followed closely behind.

'We were just stargazing. The stars are there for all to admire so come join in. How was the swim?'

'I love the beach, but I think this stretch in front of the hotel is mainly for show. No real waves.'

'The water was incredibly warm,' said Sam. 'Not exactly refreshing.'

'Too many sandflies. We stopped and bought Tiger Balm at the local Chinese store,' Kali added. 'I'm covered in bites.'

The same awkward waiter who'd been hovering earlier appeared at Mike's shoulder. 'You must come to the concert this evening, sir. Musicians from China. Famous bamboo music. They also play at the Sultan's palace.' The waiter's hands circled, including them all in his invitation. 'You will enjoy.'

'Bamboo? It sounds like your type of music, Debra. Very Zen.'

She thought of the bamboo wind chime hanging on her veranda at home. While the melodic sounds comforted her at night, she also welcomed them in the morning. They let her know if it was going to be a windy day. 'When the wind caresses the stems of bamboo it sounds like music. I'm happy to come along and listen.'

'I'm interested in anything that's soothing.' Jo read the promotional pamphlet the waiter gave her. 'This brochure says that the Buddha liked to meditate in a bamboo forest. No doubt he found it peaceful. I think we should go to this concert.'

'If Rahim were here, he'd say bamboo was an important Sufi element because of its connection to the reed flute.' The words escaped her before she could stop them.

'But he's not here, is he?' Mike's expression darkened, his eyes questioning.

'No, he's not here,' she replied sadly. She too had a sudden need for soothing. The idea of bamboo music sounded quite inviting. 'Let's go.'

***

The musicians had set out their unique array of instruments in a large room off the dining area. Several of them looked like harps or xylophones, while others were more easily recognised as flutes or pan pipes. Bamboo flame torches erected outside the room filled the entrance with the smell of burning fragrant oil and minimal flickering light. As Debra entered the sacred space, aromatic incense filled her nostrils, transporting her to another time and place. In an instant, she was strolling through Chinatown breathing in the smells on a sultry Singaporean evening.

The staff arranged seats in a semi-circle and dimmed the lights, except for the spotlight on the musicians. With a subtle flick of his wrist, a bow-legged conductor provided the cue for the orchestra to begin. With precise timing, each of the musicians followed his lead, each haunting, mournful note evoking images of Chinese mountains, towering temples and cypress trees covered in snow.

The musicians embraced their instruments, tapping into their inner source, gently emitting sad melodies of hope and longing. The final harmony lingered, bouncing off the walls, and Mike reached across to take her hand. He stroked her fingers as the musicians reached their natural crescendo, the final melodic chimes barely audible. It was time to be still and listen to the healing vibrational energy emanating across the room.

Mike was the first the break the silence. 'Well, I must admit, they brought that old bamboo to life. It just goes to show that even the most ancient instruments still have something to offer.'

'I guess there's hope for you, Mike,' Sam laughed, and Mike pretended to look hurt. 'But the acoustics were pretty amazing.' He looked at Kali, who nodded.

'Who would have thought there was so much magic in bamboo,' Jo mused.

'I guess there's magic in many things. But we don't always choose to see it,' said Debra.

As she stared into the burning torch flames, Mike watched her and there was something serene about his expression. Long after the music faded, he continued to hold her hand, circling his fingers around her wrist. Something that burned brighter than the candle flames spread through her chest. While the others stood to leave, Mike and Debra remained seated, enjoying the moment. She looked at him quizzically. There was a definite look of promise in his eyes, and she breathed more deeply to regain her focus. As they finally stood to leave, he moved his arm around her waist, directing her towards the door.

The Reunion

The long-awaited evening finally arrived. The casuarinas bordering the yacht club driveway twinkled like Christmas trees and a strong fragrance of citronella drifted in the still night air from the flaming torches lighting the path. A transformation had taken place since they were there a few days ago and a buzz of excitement now filled the air. Sweatshirts and work boots were now replaced with white dinner jackets and black silk shirts.

'Formal dress,' said Mike. 'Red Sea Rig, like the good old days.' Earlier, he'd threatened to wear only his crimson bowtie and waistband with nothing else underneath. But when he arrived at Debra's door to collect her, he was handsomely decked out in a dark dinner suit and formal white shirt. She inhaled his spicy hint of musk as she kissed him on the cheek.

She couldn't remember the last time she'd attended such a fancy function. Most special events in her life she'd recorded in her memory as occurring either before Alex's illness or after his death. Functions similar to this she had experienced only before his illness.

As she'd slipped on her midnight blue dress, she felt like a teenager trying to balance on her stiletto heels. As they arrived at the clubroom entrance, Jim Lyons put up his hand to stop them from entering as he reattached the "Welcome Back" banner that had slid from above the door. Then he welcomed them before moving the ladder out of the way.

A large photo board stood to one side of the entrance, a testament to the thousands of members who had sailed in these waters and socialised at this bar. Debra laughed at a sailing photo of Mike, his hair plastered flat on his head as he leaned against the bow of his Laser. He immediately looked for an equally amusing shot of her and found one of her on the dance floor with her arms thrust above her head, her mouth wide open as if caught mid-song and her purple hot pants revealing most of her thighs.

'Nice legs, Debra,' he said, scanning the length of her body. 'In fact, they're still pretty good.'

'And you're still a smooth talker.' She ruffled his gelled hair, and he wrapped his arm around her waist as they headed for the bar, greeting everyone along the way.

Rosa Lyons busily sprinkled a handful of sparkly confetti over each tablecloth. As the shiny words slipped through her fingers, glittering piles of "Congratulations", "Happy", and "Reunion" spelled out the message she was trying to create. She waved to them, sprinkles still attached to her palm.

Beth Worthington had cut hibiscus from her garden. She now arranged them as the centrepiece on each table, hoping when they warmed after being placed in the fridge overnight that their blooming would coincide with the unfolding of the guests in this tropical night air.

Dick stood admiring his reflection in the trophy cabinet where the barman had recently polished the spoils of their sport. A testament to battles fought on the water and on the cricket pitch, each trophy basked in its new shining image. The waiters hovered, readjusting the balance of champagne glasses on silver trays. The room soon buzzed with people smiling, hugging, and laughing their way across the dance floor. As they spied a familiar face or voice, they carried on from where they had left off twenty years earlier.

Mike made a beeline for Roger and Ayesha to continue his conversation from two days ago. Rosa finished her decorating tasks and bustled over to join Debra at the bar. She chatted non-stop, like a wound-up gramophone pushing the needle towards the topic of her former gardener. Debra tried to change the subject as she looked to see if Jo had arrived. She wouldn't want to be reminded of her ex-husband's former liaison with Rosa's Malay gardener. But Rosa was not easily distracted and continued to crank up the volume of her well-worn opinions.

'Imagine Jo tolerating him for all those years. I'm surprised she didn't leave him sooner.'

Before anyone could comment, Beth wrapped her arms around Mike and threw her head back, laughing. Debra followed the sound of Beth's horsy snorts and moved closer to Mike.

'She means well,' he whispered as Beth tried to fix his bowtie. He rested his hand on Debra's thigh and moved his head in closer towards her, but Beth was unperturbed. She continued to turn his collar and smooth out his shirt front.

'Dick always gets me to loosen his bits. He can't get his fingers around to fix them properly himself.' She looked at Mike, but he just winked and turned to Debra.

'I think she belongs on the stage,' he whispered.

'Yeah. Burlesque, I'm thinking,' Debra forced a laugh.

One time commodore of the yacht club, Dick, with his ruddy cheeks, looked quite at home leaning on the bar, but he leant in closer to Debra.

'You're right there,' he said. 'My wife's a real performer.'

Rosa had gathered a group of people around her, including her husband, and reminisced loudly. When Debra heard Jim mention Alex's name, her pulse quickened as she tuned in. So, too, did Beth, keen to hear everything Jim recounted about his fateful business trip to Manila with Alex.

'What a shocking accident. It must have been awful for you, Debra.' Throwing her hands to her face, Beth looked like an aging thespian.

'It was no accident. Somebody drugged Alex.' Jim looked at Debra and she turned back to the bar. When Beth pressed him for further details, he said, 'The toxicology report found drugs of a dose designed to kill him.'

At the time of the accident, the doctors had given Debra these details, but it hurt to hear them repeated now. She grasped her glass tighter, her thumb rubbing hard across the smooth surface. Jim had previously told her how the cab driver had offered them orange juice, which he had refused, but Alex had accepted. She'd always wondered if it had been a random attack or had someone been behind the cold, calculated plan.

Sensing Debra's discomfort, Mike pointed to the framed sporting photos around the walls. He showed her a photo of the last time the yacht club had beaten the college cricket team. Before too long, they were all reminiscing about the yacht club team's past cricket victories and the challenges they'd faced.

'Who was that Malay chap who used to play for your college team? An incredible batsman. What was his name?' Dick asked.

'Rahim,' said Mike. 'Or Harry as he liked to be known. He was our best batsman … used to play for Worcester County.'

'Yes, I remember him,' chirped Beth. 'He always looked mighty fine in his whites … had his creases in all the right places.'

Debra's cheeks flushed at the memory. While some of her memories had faded, she had no trouble conjuring images of him the way he looked when she last saw him. She looked around the room as if he might miraculously appear through a side door. There were times when she'd come here to socialise with the crowd, to enjoy their company, but there was only one person she sought out. Sadly, he wasn't there tonight, and the reality was he never would be.

Mike interrupted her thoughts. 'Beth has invited us to stay overnight with them in Labuan. There are a few other couples going but I won't go unless you come with me.'

'Oh …' Debra considered the possibilities. '… okay. That might be fun.' She blushed at the thought of spending time on her own with Mike. 'But I'm not sure what Sam wants to do. I'll check with him first.'

She looked out over the railings to the staircase below and heard Sam's and Kali's voices as they walked up the stairs together. Dressed in formal attire, Debra barely recognised Sam. True to her promise, Kali had completely transformed him from his leather shoes to his spiky hair. She herself looked stunning in a strappy pink dress that matched the streaks in her hair. With a substantial split on one side, it also showed off her shapely legs.

Kali spied the photo booth sitting in one corner of the room and dragged Sam with her. After rummaging through the box of props, Sam chose a fake moustache with John Lennon glasses while Kali propped a black top hat on her pink curls. She threw a red feather boa around her shoulders, deliberately flicking Sam in the face with the tail. He pretended to flinch, and they both laughed as the camera clicked into life, capturing an image of a happy, carefree, young couple.

Debra waited as Jo puffed her way up the stairs, pausing every few steps. When she finally reached the top, Jo, too, was barely recognisable. Resplendent in an emerald-green gown that highlighted her hair, now a bright shade of copper, it appeared Kali had finally performed her magic.

As Debra continued to stare at the entrance, her pulse quickened. She threw her hand to her open mouth aware she was gawping. Out of the dark shadows, a man climbed the stairs behind Jo. *No, it can't be!* The years had not been kind to him, but it was the same man she knew twenty years ago. She would recognise him anywhere.

Seeing the look of shock on her face Mike turned to see what had caught her attention. His eyes also widened in surprise. 'Oh, my God! Who would have thought?' Mike's words mimicked her own, but she couldn't get the words out of her mouth. 'I never thought we would ever see him again, certainly not here.'

At their surprise, Beth also spun on her barstool. Not afraid of voicing her thoughts, she gushed, 'Is it who I think it is?'

'Well, it sure as hell isn't Lazarus,' Dick said, following her gaze.

Now, everyone at the bar had turned and were staring, but Rosa was the first to confirm their disbelief. 'It certainly is him. I'd recognise him anywhere.'

By the time Jo joined them at the bar, it was obvious she had not come alone. She registered the shock etched on Debra's face, and mouthed the words, 'I tried to tell you.'

While they had recently discussed Jo's former husband on several occasions, Debra couldn't recall Jo telling her that Gareth was coming to the reunion. She would have remembered. Instead, Debra had commiserated with Jo at how lucky she was to be free of him, telling Jo she hadn't deserved him. On none of these occasions had Jo defended Gareth. Yet here he was now standing with one arm around Jo's waist, asking her what she wanted to drink. In the way she smiled as she gave him her drink order, Jo didn't look as though she was objecting. Unbelievably, Gareth appeared totally at ease, unaware people were gawking at him. He grabbed Debra in a hug before she could object.

'Debra, it's so good to see you again.'

Lost for words, Debra stammered something incoherent into his shoulder. Looking at the aging man in front of her, she tried to recall the man she once knew. She remembered meeting him for the first time when he waltzed into their house as if he owned the place. Debra had been surprised then at his brashness, his disdain for formalities or protocol. What made him think he could waltz in here now after leaving under such a dark cloud?

When they were later seated at their tables, Debra grimaced at finding herself seated next to Gareth. Her irritation was like an itch she couldn't scratch. She watched Kali trying to gauge her reaction to her father's surprise visit. But Kali appeared to be engrossed in her conversation with Sam, although slurring her speech and prattling at a higher pitch. Since Gareth had walked out on Kali and Jo after sabotaging Jo's career, Debra found it difficult to forgive him. *Am I being unfair? My own behaviour before leaving Brunei was not above reproach. Perhaps Jo is more forgiving.*

Now that she was aware of Jo's health issues, she could better understand her need for support. It wasn't only what Gareth did to Jo; it was the niggling doubt concerning Alex that still festered and the lack of answers regarding his drugging. *Did Gareth have some involvement in Alex's accident?* Before she could stop herself, the resentment she'd kept bottled up all this time spurted out.

'There is something I have been meaning to ask you about Alex.' Her voice sounded louder than she intended.

Gareth scowled and Jo spilled her drink, quickly mopping it with her serviette. Everyone in the room stopped talking. But a lot happened in the silence that followed. It was as if the fans stopped whirring, the glasses no longer clinked. Everyone stared at her, waiting for her to continue. Her pulse thumped in her ears, but she paused to take a deep breath. She looked around the room, at the eyes watching her every move.

'Never mind. This is probably not the right place or time.'

The hibiscus flowers in the centre of the table chose this auspicious moment to unfurl as they spread their glorious colour from white to brightest pink. Like the intoxicating fragrance they released, the conversation was left lingering in the sultry night air.

As the moon silvered the balcony railings, *Dancing on the Ceiling* bounced across the water and the Filipino band played as if they would lift the clubroom ceiling. Their voices, like their guitars, were well-tuned. Mike pulled Debra onto the dance floor, and they slipped into a lively jive routine. She kicked off her shoes and twirled in bare feet as Mike spun her around and under his arm. The dance floor soon filled with people grooving as they sang the lyrics of every Lionel Ritchie song they knew. Sweaty, writhing bodies danced to their own secret rhythm, letting the magic of the music lift them to another place and time.

Roger appeared at Mike's side, tapping him on the shoulder. 'Sorry, mate. You told me to let you know when we're on. I've already spoken to the band.' He directed Mike to where he'd stashed some gear behind the stage and, opening a case, pulled out his guitar. Mike grabbed the guitar propped next to it and before the crowd knew it, Mike and Roger had taken over the microphone. As they tuned their guitars, a drunken man in a white dinner jacket and vivid pink shirt shouted from the back of the room.

'Get off the stage, you old buggers.'

'Give them a chance. They're just warming up,' Beth yelled back, glaring at the man.

Without any introduction, the two old buggers launched into their theme song from days gone by, their version of

Sultans of Swing. Some of the women waved their arms from side to side, while others began to dance. Those who remembered the Dire Straits lyrics, sang along, saluting a small-time band who once played in empty dingy pubs south of London town.

While Sam grabbed his mother, Kali took Jo by the hand and led her onto the dance floor. 'Here's your big chance, Mum. Let's see if you've still got what it takes.'

They followed Kali, who choreographed the moves, swaying her body, shaking her head, tapping her feet to the rhythm. Before long, Gareth joined them, as did Dick and Beth, their circle growing larger, moving faster, throbbing with music, and sweaty flesh. When the song ended, the crowd called out for more, but the Filipino band was warming up for their final set. Debra sidled towards her chair, the promise of a cold drink and a breath of fresh air when Mike pulled her by the hand.

'They are going to play a slow number. Stay for one more.'

He removed his jacket and she folded into his slippery arms. When the Filipino lead singer caressed the words of *Endless Love,* the second vocalist joined in. As he sang the poignant melody, he embraced the lyrics that were written for two voices, two people in love.

As Mike waltzed her across the room and out to the balcony, she could have floated away. As the song reached its natural climax, Mike joined in, softly serenading her with the same words of love. When they kissed, it sealed a perfect evening.

Labuan

When Debra woke in her hotel room the next morning, she felt lighter and brighter. It wasn't just the sunshine filtering through the shutters that added to this feeling of contentment – when she looked in the mirror, her face had a new glow. She skipped to the bathroom and turned on the shower to let the warm water wash over her. She wanted to spend longer pampering herself, but after last night she couldn't wait to see Mike again.

As she hurried into the lift, she bumped into Gareth who was staying at the same resort. She had always believed that Gareth was somehow involved in Alex's death, and every time she saw him, she felt an urge to glare or lash out at him. It was part of her own inner struggle, a feeling of resentment that he was alive, and Alex wasn't.

Her eyes widened when she saw Jo and Kali joining him for breakfast, but Gareth happily explained. 'I've invited them to stay here with me at the resort. I've got an enormous suite. They'll be more comfortable here. Better facilities than the smaller hotel in town where they were staying.'

'Oh! That's a surprise. I'm sure Sam will be pleased.'

'We can keep an eye on Sam if you want to go to Labuan,' Jo offered.

'Thanks. I'm not comfortable about leaving him but he says he'd rather stay with Kali. I think he wants to show her the bowling alley and video game arcade.' Sam had also reminded her that he was old enough to survive for one night on his own.

'Yes, please let him stay,' Kali pleaded as she walked to the buffet with Debra. 'It's awkward, you know, with Dad,' she whispered. 'It would be good having Sam here with me.'

'Okay. It is just for one night.' She understood this relationship with her father couldn't be easy for Kali. She would need some time to adjust to the new arrangements of having him in her life again.

As she reached for the fruit platter, she sensed the gentlest touch on her shoulder, his hand brushing across the back of her neck. A shiver rushed up her spine and she didn't need to turn to know who caused it. He was wearing a blue polo shirt she'd seen before, but today there was a new vibrancy, an added sparkle to his eyes. When she turned around, he didn't step back so she was forced to move within his space, and his body pressed against hers. He moved his hands to her waist, then quickly to her plate as her fruit started to topple.

'Let me take that for you.'

'Thanks. I've decided to go to Labuan with you,' she stammered before she could change her mind.

'That's great news,' he beamed.

Later that day, when they climbed into the cab, she told herself Sam would be fine. *I'll be back in no time at all.*

The cab driver dropped them at the ferry terminal in town, which had changed since her first trip to Labuan. It was much larger with an added second storey. Her mind flooded with memories of the day, not long after arriving in Brunei, when she had taken her amah to Labuan to get her visa renewed. She'd bumped into Rahim, who'd offered to accompany them, to assist in getting the visa. Only a two-hour trip to this island off East Malaysia, it had been an unforgettable crossing into another world. Equally memorable, the beginning of their relationship with Rahim, which, once started, was difficult to end.

The ferry ride on this occasion proved less eventful. As the heavens opened with a familiar monsoonal downpour, she remembered a similar darkening sky and angry clouds that had threatened their idyllic world. She looked at Mike, who felt squeamish from the choppy swell, his face turned a ghoulish green.

'And I thought you were a weathered seafarer.'

'I can't blame the waves. I confess it's more about the alcohol I consumed last night.' He looked out at the horizon while she gazed around the ferry, noting the air-conditioning, comfortable seating, and pleasant interior, all recent additions since her first ferry crossing.

'It's a real improvement on the old ferry. This is so much smoother. No more people throwing up all over the deck.'

'I think we should change the topic. With my stomach about to turn cartwheels, it's the last thing I want to hear.'

They moved to the outside deck, where the sheets of rain stopped as if on cue and the clouds no longer looked angry. Even though the humidity still clung to the air, a slight hint of breeze flapped the small flag on the stern. Leaning against the railings with the cooling spray blowing on his face, Mike stared out at the spuming waves crashing over the gunwales.

'Nothing like the white cliffs of Dover but at least it's not freezing cold.'

'Does your mother still live in Dover?'

'Sadly, no. She has dementia. She's now in a nursing home in Ramsgate.'

'Sorry to hear that. It's never easy watching the decline of loved ones.'

'Yeah. It's been hard on the family.' Mike gazed out to sea keeping his eyes fixed on the horizon. 'Did I tell you I met Rahim's mother there?' Mike didn't see Debra's eyes widen nor did he notice as she strained her neck, leaning in closer to hear his words.

'No! You didn't tell me. Rahim's mother?' She had to shout to compete with the noise of the engine. Her pulse now thumped in time with the lapping waves.

'The nurses told me about a woman who didn't get many visitors. As Mum is often silent, I popped over to say hello to this other woman. Fiona Walker. I never dreamed it would be his mum.'

'So how did you know?' Her words tumbled out in quick succession.

'She had a photo of him by her bedside. Playing cricket at Leys College. She talked about him as if he was a little boy. Of course, she always called him Harry.'

'So, you don't know if she ever saw him again?'

'No. I visited a few more times. Some days were better than others. The nurses told me she had a daughter who sometimes visited her.'

'Her daughter's name was Sophie,' Debra reflected on what Rahim had told her about his sister. He'd been estranged from his sister and mother since he was a child when his father took him to live in Malaysia. 'So, we don't know if he ever got to see his mother again.'

'Once when I visited, Rahim's mother mentioned her parents' house in East Grinstead, not far from where we used to live. I had a rough idea where it was.'

'You went to his grandmother's house?'

'Yes, I found their house and their Pakistani neighbour who made me tea and wanted to chat all day. She was a wealth of information. She reckoned Rahim's grandmother died of a broken heart, never having known her grandson. A nice woman, she said but the grandfather was rather hostile. Apparently, he used to cross the road instead of walking past the neighbour's house. She said he was probably scared of catching something.'

'When Rahim's mother took her Malaysian husband to meet her parents, she was barely nineteen, still at Cambridge. Her father would not accept him.'

'I'm not surprised. I guess a Malaysian was considered quite foreign during the fifties. They would have expected their daughter to marry an Englishman.'

'By the time Rahim was born, Fiona had cut all ties with her parents.'

'So, Rahim never met his grandparents. Once her husband left her, Fiona was probably too proud to go home. It would mean her father had been right.'

'From what I heard from Rahim, his own father in Malaysia was not a pleasant man.'

'Yes. I think Rahim came to Brunei to get away from him. But you said he returned to KL after his daughter's car accident.' *How can someone disappear so easily without a trace? Did he ever think about me as I'm thinking about him now?*

As she stared out through the foaming spray, a smattering of tiny Lego-looking houses and buildings appeared as they drew closer to the port of Labuan. Crowds of people stood beside piles of baggage, wooden crates, and woven baskets of fruit lying on the wharf. They looked like people who belonged and knew where they wanted to be. *Did Rahim ever find the place where he truly belonged? Or, like me, is he still searching?*

Passengers and crew busied themselves on deck as the captain slowed the engines, the boat chugging and spluttering as it slipped in beside the wharf. A modern ferry terminal of chrome and glass loomed in front of them where once a collection of older wooden sheds had stood. A deck hand threw ropes around bollards while another pulled out ramps to bridge the gap for passengers to disembark.

Walking inside the terminal, she caught sight of their reflection in the glass — a tall man who still looked good for his age and a mature woman with a trace of the younger woman within. They collected their bags and stretched their legs as they walked towards the taxi rank. After giving the address to the driver, they arrived at Dick and Beth's house a few minutes later.

The Worthington's house was architecturally designed to suit the eclectic needs of its eccentric owners. Facing the ocean, most of the rooms had access to glorious views. Beth guided them into a study upstairs which had been converted into a guest bedroom with its own ensuite. As she pointed out the fresh towels lying on the bed, there was only one blow-up bed, and it was a double. While Debra's cheeks flushed, the expression froze on her face.

'I'm sorry it's only an inflatable mattress, but I thought you might like some privacy,' she said with a wink. 'Jim and Rosa will be sleeping downstairs off the living room. Drop your bags and join us for sundowners. Our amah, Nina, has made a lovely fish curry so we can eat as soon as the others arrive.'

'Does Beth think we are an item?' Debra whispered to Mike as they placed their bags on the floor and picked up the duty-free alcohol they'd just purchased.

'Yes,' he grinned, 'I'm sure she does. I told her I was committed to someone else to stop her jumping on me in the jungle. After fighting her off all night in the longhouse, there was no way I was coming here alone.'

Dick insisted Mike take his drink outside so he could show him the garden before it got dark. With his swimming pool business now well established in Labuan, he was keen to show off the perks of his thriving empire. More concerned about the mosquitos, Beth steered Debra towards a comfortable sofa and lit a mosquito coil in a ceramic pot. She brought them both a large gin and tonic with plenty of ice and slices of lemon.

As they stared out at the sun fading into the distance, Beth moved a little closer to Debra's side of the sofa, nonchalantly readjusting the cushions. *She's going to ask me about Mike*, Debra sensed and reeled when she said: 'Tell me more about your dark handsome lover.'

Beth had a definite glint in her eye and grinned widely. 'Oh yes, there are some things I never forget,' she added

'What on earth has Mike been telling you?' Debra demanded but it was hard to stay serious at Beth's obvious mirth.

'Debra, I'm deprived of gossip these days. A tale of forbidden love will make my day.' Her laugh sounded more like a whinny, and she flicked away a strand of her enhanced chestnut mane.

'It was a long time ago. Not something I'd planned.' Debra gulped a mouthful of gin, reluctant to disclose a love story she'd always kept close to her heart.

'I understand.' Beth immediately launched into the details of a casual fling she'd had while living in the West Indies. 'There's so much mystery and fascination surrounding dark men and the myths about size. It's as if we need to break the spell to discover the truth for ourselves.

'No. No. It was nothing like that. It was a blending of hearts and minds.'

'Your minds?' Beth looked incredulous, spluttering in her drink. 'You've got to be joking.'

'It began with our shared love of poetry, especially the poems of Rumi.'

'Rumi? Good god. It doesn't sound like much fun.'

'I'd recently lost my daughter. He was estranged from his mother. We were both in need of love and nurture.' There'd been a time when she used to imagine the sadness in the cells of her body mingling with the sadness in his, but she didn't dare tell Beth that. *She wouldn't understand.* While it didn't justify their adultery, it had been a distraction from their personal pain. 'When he had to leave his mother in England, he was devastated. His father took him to KL and arranged his marriage to a distant cousin.'

'How awful. And he wanted to stay in England?'

'It was a lonely life for him when he first arrived in Malaysia. He couldn't speak Malay and the other kids teased him. His father took a second wife, and she had five children in five years.'

'Five children? My God. And what about your lover's wife?' Beth spluttered into her drink, her eyes widening with disbelief.

'She was young and innocent. There was an accident where she grazed her knees. Rahim was bathing her wounds when his stepmother walked in and found Mahani lifting her sarong. He was kneeling on the floor beside her. They were forced to marry immediately.'

'No! Oh, my God! How awful.' Beth threw her well-manicured hands to her face.

'Yes, so he married young and his dreams of going to Cambridge came to a sudden end. Coming to Brunei was as far as his wife wanted to travel. She wanted to be close to her family in KL.'

Beth moved in closer until their knees were touching on the sofa. Her eyes wide as she slowly shook her head. She patted Debra's arm comforting, commiserating.

'What is Beth telling you, Debra?' Mike crept in behind them while Dick replenished their drinks from his bar.

'I'm telling her you're a great guy, Mike. She shouldn't pass you up.' Beth lifted her hand to grasp the fresh drink Dick was passing to her.

Debra blushed at the thought of the small inflatable bed awaiting them in the guest room. Mike sat beside her on the sofa.

'Dick has been telling me all about your business, Beth. Sounds like a thriving enterprise you have here. Who would have thought selling pools would be so lucrative in this part of the world.'

'Yes, it pays for our creature comforts. We like to travel to Europe each year. It helps to remind us that we're British.'

Gazing around the room, Debra admired the spoils from such trips abroad. Venetian glass and fine bone porcelain adorned the shelves. As they sipped from their Waterford crystal, she appraised the Persian rugs strewn across the floor. Everywhere she looked were brightly coloured furnishings both modern and luxurious. She adjusted a cushion behind her back, noting its French provincial design as Beth flicked a switch on a standard lamp. An arc of Turkish mosaic globes burst into light, reflecting ceramic colours of every hue.

A taxi pulled into the driveway and Jim and Rosa climbed out, depositing their small bags around them. Beth showed Jim and Rosa to their room, while Dick fetched more drinks. Rosa enthused over Beth's house and furnishings, examining every item of *design d'intérieur* by scanning each label.

'I've got a lamp just like that one,' she said, pointing to the Turkish standard lamp.

Each piece of art or decoration reminded Rosa of something she had in her own home or somewhere she'd been. Jim didn't comment but reserved his enthusiasm for the dinner that was being served. He expressed how much he missed the curries from this part of the world.

'Being able to buy fresh fish from the local markets … what a bonus! And it's so cheap. At home in the Whitsundays, I catch my own as it's too expensive to buy.' He tried to engage

Dick in fishing stories and wanted to know whether Dick was catching anything. Dick said he had no need to fish as Nina bought it fresh at the markets each day.

After dinner, Beth insisted they play games. While she loved games of all kinds, the one she enjoyed most was Twister enabling her to entwine her body around the other players. She was in her element as she rubbed herself against Mike whenever she got the chance. Dick did not appear to be complaining as he groped Debra's breasts while ostensibly losing his footing. An opportunity for a bit of smooching, with everyone laughing and enjoying harmless fun.

It had been some time since Debra was able to relax so completely, let alone enjoy a night of fun. And she realised that she hadn't thought about Sam since she'd arrived in Labuan, and it felt strange not to be worrying about him. Mike paid particular attention to her throughout the evening, keeping her to himself whenever he could. He placed his arm around the back of her chair, touched her arm, held her hand, and she felt flattered by this show of affection and his need for proximity. He also checked in with her to make sure she was okay and whether she needed another drink. Living in a duty-free port, there was little chance of running out of alcohol, but their night of reckless fun and frivolity finally came to an end in the early hours of the morning.

Mike and Debra transitioned from the foreplay of Twister to the inflatable bed that awaited them upstairs. As they tried to get comfortable on the wobbling rubber mattress, they expressed their emotional unease and reservations.

'I feel nervous. I'm scared my inner workings have permanently rusted over.'

'Don't worry, Debra. I'm sure Dick has some WD40 in his garage.'

Debra laughed and relaxed, tuning into the surroundings. There was a softness about Mike as she gazed into his large playful eyes. She was also aware of the sympathetic croaking of frogs calling to their lovers on the other side of the fence. She heard the gentle rise and fall of the waves as they crashed against the seawall, then lost herself in the moment, the urgency and surging rhythm of their bodies until they finally reached their natural climax.

'My god! Oh, my god!'

They lay there panting as the air rushed in and out, aware of the synchronous cries of release as they both muffled their sounds of joy. But the gentle sighing sound continued, of air rushing out and, with it, the sensation of sinking deeper, deeper, closer to the floor.

'Holy shit. The mattress. It's deflating,' Mike laughed, while she giggled uncontrollably. 'We should see if they've got a pump,' he chuckled.

'No, let's not disturb them. It will soon be morning. Just pretend you're lying on a yoga mat. It's great for your back.' She giggled into the sheets, pulling them over her head.

'It's easier to pretend I'm still lying on the longhouse floor, waiting for the cock to crow.'

'I think he already has,' she whispered in his ear and, when he bellowed loudly, she placed her hand over his mouth, smothering his mirth, aware of Beth and Dick in the adjoining room. But they couldn't stop laughing, one setting off the other until their laughter bounced off the walls, which, though architecturally designed, were only made of plywood.

'Well, everything appears to be in good working order. No rust at all.' He brushed a strand of hair from her eyes before kissing her again and wrapping her in his arms.

'It was incredible,' she whispered, 'Not bad for a couple of has-beens.' She chuckled and nuzzled her face into his shoulder.

Despite their discomfort, their bodies were spent, and they soon fell asleep. But it was a restless night, a fitful sleep where neither head nor body relaxed comfortably on the flattened bed or the squashed pillow. Debra dreamt she was sinking into the earth, like a waterfall tumbling over rocks. She awoke in the morning with an aching back and twisted neck. Mike also groaned.

'Bloody hell. I can't get the crick out of my neck.'

'I need to do some spinal rolls to massage my poor back.'

'I dreamt I was lying on the longhouse floor. What a sucker I am for punishment.'

'And I thought it was the earth moving. What an amazing night.'

As they staggered out into the living room, Jim and Rosa were already up, sitting on the sofa, Beth supervising Nina to lay a table piled high with breakfast foods, including what looked like a pot of soup.

'Scotch broth,' she said. 'Great for hangovers.'

'We could have done with some of that in the longhouse,' said Mike. 'That rice wine was a potent brew. I've never had such a terrible hangover.'

'Luckily, I had some Valium with me,' Beth chortled. 'I couldn't have got through the night without it. There was no way you could sleep in though. If you weren't woken by the squealing pigs rooting under the longhouse, the noisy rooster started crowing before dawn. It was so loud I'm sure he was sticking his head through the window.'

'I'm disappointed we didn't get to go. It sounds like an interesting experience,' said Rosa.

'Oh, it certainly was an adventure. I broke my nails hauling a canoe over rocks up the river. Covered in mozzie bites and spent all night fighting off other creatures crawling all over me.'

'It was probably Mike crawling over you,' said Dick as he entered, carrying a jug of orange juice and a bottle of champagne.

'I couldn't move,' said Mike. 'My sweaty back was stuck to the woven mat on the floor. Speaking of backs, we've just spent another night on the floor. That bloody inflatable mattress deflated during the night.'

'You need to be less rigorous with your lovemaking, Mike. That poor mattress hasn't seen so much action.'

'Yes, it takes post-coital depression to a new level. Absolute deflation.'

As the heat crept up Debra's neck and face, Mike put his arm around her and drew her in closer.

'It was worth it, though.'

'I think I need a drink,' Debra said, moving towards the breakfast table and pouring a glass of orange juice.

'It's a good thing you're not an atheist, Mike.' Beth ladled the Scotch broth into bowls and handed one to Mike.

'Why's that?'

'Because you'd have no one to talk to during orgasm.'

'Oh, my god!' Mike dropped the soup spoon, slopping the soup on his shirt.

'I told you the walls were thin,' Debra whispered as she slid past him.

'Well, it's been a wonderful night.' He gave his sheepish grin.

'So, do you believe in anything, Mike?' Rosa questioned him.

'I believe in many things, but I am no God botherer. I had a similar conversation with a devout young woman recently.

Other people appear to be more concerned about my beliefs than I am.'

'Let's hear it then, Mike. Who did you upset with your blasphemy?' Beth called from the kitchen, where she was making more coffee.

'It wasn't my blasphemy which upset her. I was in a café waiting for my coffee. A young woman was reading what looked like a dictionary. The teacher in me reacted before I could stop myself. In hindsight, I should have worn my glasses.'

'What did you say to her?' Debra asked, her eyes widening.

'I said I was impressed she was reading a dictionary, which is not something many people do these days, especially in a café. She gave me the dirtiest glare and said, "It's a Bible."'

'So, she didn't try to convert you?' A grin spread across Debra's face.

'No! The look she gave me said, "You are the lowest of all God's little creatures."'

'She doesn't sound like a real Christian,' Beth said, but the telephone ringing in the hall drowned out her words.

Dick answered the phone and the look of concern on his face registered with them all. He signalled Debra who raced to grab the phone.

'Oh, my god. I'm leaving now.' She dropped the phone and turned to Mike. 'It's Sam. He's had an accident in the hotel pool. That was Gareth.' As she broke into a sweat, the old fears from long ago whizzed around in her head. Her stomach tightened, twisting into a knot of shattered hopes and broken promises. 'Gareth says Sam and Kali drank his bottle of vodka and were running amok in the fountain.'

'Holy shit! There's a ferry leaving in about half an hour. Grab your things. We'll go now.'

Mike threw his few clothes into a bag and tidied their room while Debra moved like an automaton, acting without thinking. Her brain said it was too difficult, too painful to experience another of Sam's episodes. She didn't want to think about the many possible scenarios. *What might have pushed Sam over the edge? He's been so good for so long.*

Dick grabbed his car keys and Beth thrust plastic containers into Debra's arms. 'You might need some food later,' she said. With a frenzy of frantic thanking and hugging, they were bundled onto the ferry.

'He was doing so well. I thought he was over all that stuff.' She choked back tears as Mike reached out to pat her hand.

'It may not be as bad as you think.'

From past experiences, it usually turned out worse than she had expected. It was often hard to imagine, let alone experience. A challenge for any parent was to love their child, whether they were an addict, unemployed, trashing the house or in this case, drunk and throwing himself in a fountain.

Mike offered to get them coffee once they were on board, leaving her on deck with her darkest thoughts. Matching her mood, the dark menacing sky hovered above angry waves crying out, thrashing, and smashing against the gunwales. Inside the ferry, recorded music played through the speakers but the wind snatched away most of the tune. Along with her fading memories of hope, the odd syncopated notes were lost in the sea spray.

Her aspirations for Sam had changed dramatically during his teen years, from hoping he would get a successful career to praying he would just get a job, any job at all. Then it hadn't mattered whether he had a job, but she'd prayed he'd get out of bed each day, and just eat a normal meal.

Mike arrived with coffee and opened Beth's container of samosas. Normally, the smell would tempt her to bite into the greasy pastry to savour the curry-flavoured centre. But today her stomach churned, wound tightly with fear and concern for her boy. Before they'd left on this holiday, he'd just started eating regular meals again. It was a joy she couldn't describe. To see him taking an interest in cooking a meal and shopping for the necessary ingredients was an added blessing. She looked at the samosas and shook her head. 'No thanks. I'm too hurt and angry.

The Dragonfly

While Jo and Gareth were out shopping Kali had invited Sam into Gareth's suite, tempting him with Gareth's duty-free vodka.

'I'm so fucking angry,' she said, emptying her glass. A small drop of liquid dribbled down her chin, which she tried to lick with her tongue but then wiped it away with the back of her hand.

'Why? What's the matter?' Sam moved to the coffee table where she poured herself another glass, telling him to drink up quickly so she could pour him another. From the way she struggled with the lid on the bottle, he doubted this was her first or even second drink.

Sam looked at the glass in his hand. He was not supposed to be drinking but he didn't want to disappoint her. He sipped the neat vodka, reeling as the first mouthful burned his throat. He hesitated before taking his second sip, gagging as it went down.

'How's it going with your dad?' he asked, waiting while she sculled the vodka as if it were water.

'All those years when he could have helped me. He didn't care at all. My life has been so screwed up. It's been a fuckin' struggle.'

'At least he came back. He's here now. He must have cared enough to come. I wish my dad would suddenly reappear.' He thought of his many regrets. The things he'd like to say to his dad that he should have said years before.

'I want to hurt him the way he hurt me.'

A furnace burned within him as the vodka warmed his insides. His head felt on fire and, in the mirror above the dresser, he could see a red bloom rising in his face and neck. Kali was now balanced precariously on the balcony railing, staring at him from her perch. As she slid from the railing, her breasts bounced up and down in her leopard print bikini top. She adjusted the matching bikini briefs which had slipped while she was sliding down. He stepped forward, taking her arm.

'Let's go for a swim. I need to cool off.' He took her hand and led her to the door.

But she flopped herself on the bed before leaping up and wandering around the room, kicking the leg of a chair. Finally, she agreed to a swim, and he led her to the first of the larger hotel pools. He dived in but Kali stretched out lazily, sunning herself on the edge. When he emerged from the pool, his head felt cooler but slightly dizzier and he tried to ignore a bout of nausea in his chest. When he looked up, Kali stood by the fountain at the edge of the pool.

'There's a dragonfly trapped in a spider web. Can you climb into the fountain and get it out?'

'And what's wrong with your legs?'

'I've sprayed them with instant tan. I don't want to get them wet.'

Since arriving in Brunei, Kali had been fascinated with the brightly coloured dragonflies hovering around the water; fascinated by the transformation they underwent from nymph to adult.

'When they're mating, they connect tail to head and form a heart shape. How cool is that? It's not just about change, is it? It's learning to love yourself.' Her speech slurred as she struggled to pronounce the words.

'I don't think the dragonflies would view it that way. It's about survival. Do you know how long it takes the nymphs to crawl out of their exoskeleton and free their wings?' He tried to keep her alert, to distract her with scientific data. 'It must be an exhausting task. You know they're the oldest insect, even predating the dinosaurs.' He looked at Kali, who, although several years older than him, wasn't interested in science. She was on a spiritual quest, looking for existential answers to her never-ending questions.

'The trapped dragonfly. Do you think it might be an angel or messenger?' As her head dropped to her chest, she struggled to move her tongue around the last word. The rest of her body wobbled as she slid off the edge of the fountain.

Sam tried to keep her awake by telling her everything he knew about dragonflies.

'Right now, that dragonfly is part of the natural food chain. We're depriving a spider of its food.'

He thought of the dragonfly living most of its life as a nymph or an immature adult, much like himself. The opportunity to fly lasted only a mere fraction of its precious life. He would certainly make the most of his short time ahead when he finally got his wings.

Climbing into the fountain, Sam waded out to where the iridescent blue dragonfly was solidly stuck in the sticky threads of the spider's web. As he tried to free it, one of its legs not totally entangled, wiggled and wrapped itself around his forefinger. At least it was alive. In the meantime, Kali, ignoring her recent leg tan, had joined him in the fountain. The dragonfly flapped its wings to escape, but the threads held firm. Sam pulled a little more and one of the wings was freed from the web. As he placed his fingers behind its wings, he saw a tiny piece of silk holding the right fore and hind wings together.

'Give me your hair clip.' He took the clip Kali pulled from her hair and cleared the remaining piece of silk. Slowly, the dragonfly came free; it landed on Kali's finger, where it rested for a few moments, which set her to sobbing. In between the sobs, she whispered, 'Do you think this is a sign of good luck?' She sighed as the dragonfly rose into the air, hovered for a few seconds, and then was gone.

By now, two waiters had run towards them, yelling and waving their arms. Sam and Kali waded across the fountain to the far side of the pool away from the hotel staff. Focused on keeping her arms and mobile phone out of the water, Kali stumbled, and Sam reached out to grab her. His feet slipped from under him, and he heard the crack as his head hit the concrete edge. Clambering onto his knees, he touched the back of his throbbing head and felt the blood as it ran down his fingers.

Kali screamed. Ripping off her white T-shirt, she held it to Sam's head, leaving the two waiters standing, staring at her breasts which had spilled out of her leopard-print bra. The white T-shirt was soon soaked blood red, her bikini briefs, slime-coloured green, and her legs splotched with patches of instant tan.

As they climbed out of the pool, a hotel waiter tried to wrap a towel around Kali, but she shoved him away. Another waiter used a towel to stem the flow of blood dripping from Sam's head. Hearing the commotion, Jo and Gareth appeared as the manager gave instructions to wipe the blood from the tiles around the pool.

'What the fuck are they staring at?' Kali pointed at a gathering of Malay men looking in her direction.

'You are half naked, Kali. I've told you to cover yourself up. That's why they stare.' Jo grabbed a third towel which the manager handed her. Looking at Sam's head, she said, 'You might need stitches, Sam. I'll take you to the hospital.'

Turning to Kali, she added, 'Get some dry clothes for yourself and Sam.'

When Kali returned with the clothes, Sam looked at what she'd chosen for him: Her mother's baggiest shorts and a large pink T-shirt printed with the words, Party Princess. 'Did you have to choose a pink one?'

'I thought it might cheer you up. You know we all shimmer in our own way. We just need to unmask ourselves.'

Kali showed Sam a photo she'd taken of the dragonfly. While the insect clung to her finger with its tiny front legs, she'd clicked the camera button with her other hand. The screen image, though blurred, displayed a brilliance of vivid blue and silvery gold.

'It's beautiful,' she said. 'Shame it didn't bring us good luck.'

'But it brought you joy.' Sam watched her pout, childlike.

'What on earth were you doing in the fountain? Why the crazy antics?' Jo asked.

'Perhaps it was all the weed on the bottom,' Kali laughed. 'I didn't eat breakfast.'

'And you shouldn't have drunk your father's vodka. He's furious.'

'I need to have a shower and put on some proper clothes.'

While Gareth tried to placate the hotel manager, Jo helped Sam back to their room so he could shower.

To Paradise and Back

By the time they arrived back at their hotel, Debra and Mike were saturated from the sea spray on the ferry and the light showers that fell, followed by heavy soaking rain, which had drenched their clothes. Mike suggested a hot shower, but Debra was desperate to see Sam.

Gareth greeted them at the door but failed to make eye contact. He whisked them inside where he paced the floor. 'We're in so much strife over this. The hotel manager has threatened to kick us out.'

'How did he get the drink, Gareth? Wasn't someone keeping an eye on him?' Debra's anger moved its way up her chest.

'I'm so sorry, Debra. We ducked out to do some shopping.' Jo folded her arms, trying to control her trembling hands.

'The kids were cursing and swearing at the hotel staff. It was so embarrassing,' Gareth sighed.

Yeah, I've had years of embarrassing moments, Debra wanted to shout. She looked at Gareth with his hand on his hip, a blue vein pulsing in his temple. 'I'm terribly sorry for your embarrassment, Gareth,' she said, enunciating each word. 'But what about Sam?'

'He has a nasty cut on his head,' Kali took her arm and led her into the bedroom. 'I've put a bandage on it, but Sam was adamant he didn't want to go to the hospital. Mum thinks he needs stitches.' Kali left Sam lying on the bed.

Debra noticed the blood-soaked white towel lying discarded on the floor. 'Oh, Sam! I thought you were over all this stuff. I thought you were clean. On the mend. You promised me.'

'It's not what you think, Mum. I only had one glass. It was Kali who'd been drinking.'

'But why such weird behaviour? Why were you in the fountain?'

'It was the dragonfly. She wanted me to rescue the dragonfly. It was caught in a web. She didn't want it to suffer.'

'Gareth says you were drunk and abusing the hotel staff.'

'That's not true, Mum. You must learn to trust me. Listen to what I'm saying.'

She looked at his face. He seemed to have matured; his voice, too, had deepened, but was it enough to convince her? *Can I ever trust you again?*

'It's not that I don't trust you, Sam. I want to believe you. It's just that sometimes when I listen to my intuition, it lets me down. But I do it anyway because I love you.'

Regardless of people's warnings, she'd always listened to her heart. She wanted to trust him and believe the best in him. But often what she saw was the worst.

'I think Debra could do with a strong cup of tea.' Jo hovered near the doorway before entering the bedroom and gently touched her on the shoulder. 'I think we should get him to the hospital.'

A loud knock interrupted Jo and, when Gareth opened the door, an angry hotel manager and uniformed security guard filled the doorway.

'Some of our guests have complained about the young people staying here. Guests are not allowed to consume alcohol on the premises,' the manager said sternly, his words sharp and clipped.

'I'm terribly sorry. We have spoken with them, and it won't happen again.' Debra joined Gareth at the door.

'We cannot have them upsetting our other guests. You understand?'

'We understand and we do apologise. We'll pay for any damages they may have caused,' Gareth added. The manager didn't look convinced and before he left, he issued a reprimand.

'Please take this as a final warning. If there are any more complaints, you will have to leave the hotel.'

After the manager left, Gareth continued to rant about what he had to endure. 'Everyone kept staring at us as if we were the guilty ones.'

Debra glared at Gareth, his arms flailing as he spoke. The anger in her chest now moved into her throat and she heard herself scream.

'I've heard enough about you, Gareth. What I want to know is why didn't you look out for Sam?'

'I didn't know what to do,' he muttered, wringing out his hands.

'Like you didn't know how to help Alex?' Her face now felt hot enough to explode. 'Why weren't you there with Alex?' She choked back tears. 'Did you know Alex was in danger? Should it have been you in the taxi? Were you the target but Alex got in the way?'

'Debra, this is not the place.' Mike bustled Sam towards the door, Kali on Sam's other arm while Gareth hovered in the background.

'I didn't know what they were planning. I didn't know,' he said.

'Gareth, let it rest, mate. Thanks for your help.' Mike ushered Debra through the door and into the lift, and Jo hurried after them, insisting on going with them to the hospital. As the lift doors closed, Debra turned to Mike.

'Thanks for his help? He was the bloody cause!' When Debra thought of Gareth, mean little subtitles appeared in her mind. The engine inside her head screeched as she remembered the menacing details of Alex's last trip to Manila. Gareth was meant to fly with him but cancelled at the last minute. And today he was supposed to be taking care of Sam.

'I would have brought him to the hospital straight away, but Sam was adamant he didn't want to go.' Jo hunched her shoulders as if she couldn't bear any additional stress.

'I can understand that. He's had so many visits over the years.'

As a youngster, Sam had loved to explore everything which had resulted in many accidents and visits to outpatients. It had begun with him drinking kerosene and having his stomach pumped. By the time he was due for his follow-up appointment, he'd fallen off a garden wall, splitting open his head. And then, of course, there'd been his more recent visits.

As she clambered into the front seat of Mike's car, she still fumed. Mike patted her knee.

'You can't blame Gareth. Sam is an adult.'

'But he was doing so well,' she whispered. 'Someone should have been keeping an eye on him.' She suddenly gulped. 'I guess it should have been me. I should have been there with him.'

Debra, you need to stop blaming yourself. Shit happens. You need to let go of the past. Move on with your life,' said Mike as he pulled out, manoeuvring into a busy lane of traffic.

She wanted to snuggle her face into his chest to cry a history of tears. She wanted him to stroke her hair, kiss her wet cheeks with soothing sounds of love, but as always, there were others whose needs were more urgent than hers.

As Mike drove to the modern multi-storeyed hospital outside of town, Debra pointed out the site where the old hospital used to stand. Demolished to make way for a new shopping centre, it had once stood adjacent to the mosque.

Jo also remembered the old low-lying wooden hospital surrounded by verandas and rats running around the wards. 'Once when you were a child, Sam, I drove you to the hospital. You'd burnt your back throwing leaves onto a fire. Do you remember?' Jo asked.

'I remember being burnt but I don't remember the pain or the hospital.'

'Well, it's probably good you don't remember,' said Debra.

They'd spent hours in the hospital waiting for doctors to examine him. Arriving as the muezzin called Muslims to noon prayer, they were still at the hospital when the next call for afternoon prayer reverberated around the room.

'What a childhood I had. Are there any other traumas I can attribute to my screwed-up life?'

***

Sam was not alone, Jo thought. Kali had displayed more weird behaviour than Jo cared to remember. She wanted to tell Sam how he should come and live with them for a while. Then he would feel quite normal. Instead, she said, 'Your poor mother was a mess. She kept blaming herself for your accident.'

Sam thought about the many times he'd screwed up in life and how often his mother had been there to rescue him. He'd had no way of knowing hospitals would come to feature significantly in his life. Fortunately, time had erased the pain and healed past wounds. Now when he tried to recall a past traumatic event, it was often diluted, the images blurred.

***

Debra recalled her first visit to the old hospital the day after she arrived in Brunei. Her contact lens had scratched her eye, and as she stumbled along the unfamiliar streets she'd crashed into Rahim. Despite her lack of vision and orientation, fate had brought them together.

When they arrived at the hospital, Mike dropped them at the entrance and drove off to find a parking space. While they waited for a doctor, Jo tried to distract Debra, entertaining her with some of Mike's amusing antics.

'Mike says he's compiling songs from the sixties and seventies to play at a gig he's doing in London. He's giving everyone a chance to name a favourite song from their past. You know how Mike has a way of connecting everything in life to music.'

Mike walked in picking up the thread of their conversation. 'So which song encapsulates an important part of your life, Debra?'

She closed her eyes trying to recall songs that made her happy, lyrics that made her sad, and tunes that could transport her to another place and time.

'Why is it when we hear a certain song, we experience the same emotion we felt when we first heard it? As if we want to relive those experiences, even the ones that make us sad.'

She knew the lyrics she would like to hear again, and the tunes she continued to play in her head. She'd held onto those memories for even the saddest ones brought her the greatest joy. She remembered one song, a haunting tune she listened to over and over hoping to recapture the mood. *"Love Letters Straight from your Heart,"* she said.

'Ah! The old love letters. So, he still has a hold on you?'

Moisture gathered in her eyes, but she was not yet ready to disclose how she felt. She turned to Jo, who, like Mike, was waiting for an answer.

'What about you, Jo? What song would you choose?'

'Well, I've been reflecting on my life a lot lately. Despite all the challenges I've had, I've also travelled and seen the best life has to offer. Yet while I've been to paradise and back, *I've Never Been to Me*.'

'Bloody hell! Why all these tearjerkers? Don't you remember any happy songs from that era?'

'As Jo says, we've been reflecting on the past. Memories often evoke emotion, especially sad stuff. What about you? What would be your song, Mike?'

'There are many that would fit the bill, but I think my favourite would have to be *Don't Stop Me Now*. I just love those crazy Queen lyrics.'

'And they are so like you.' Debra laughed as Mike walked off to join Sam and Kali by the vending machine. Debra turned to Jo, gently brushing her fingers over Jo's hand.

'I hope you finally find yourself, Jo, and whatever it is you're looking for. I also hope Gareth does the right thing by you. I'd like to think someone is taking care of you when you need it most.'

'I used to think if I loved Gareth, I owned that love. It was mine. No one could take it away from me. I thought I was defined by the love I felt for others, not by the love they had for me. I know I'm still capable of giving love.'

'I hope you're also capable of accepting love when it's offered. I've discovered it's not always that easy.'

'I'm learning that I don't always have to be the rock. I can be the sand that moulds into whatever shape is needed.'

'I'm glad you have a sense of what you want and where you're heading. I'm still not sure.'

When Mike signalled that the doctor was ready to see Sam, they rushed to join him. The doctor instructed a nurse to suture Sam's head while he prescribed antibiotics. After waiting an hour to see him, the consultation was comparatively brief.

When they arrived back at the hotel, Gareth was waiting for them.

'Can I have a word, Debra. Just you and me. Let's go downstairs to the café.'

They ordered coffee and Gareth took a seat opposite her at a small poolside table.

'I know you still blame me for Alex, Debra, but it wasn't my fault.'

'But you should have been on that early flight, in the taxi with him. It should have been you that was drugged.'

'I know but they blackmailed me. If I didn't help them, they threatened to tell management about Azri and me. I was only trying to help Azri.'

'But you knew Azri was involved with illegal immigrants … helping them escape across the border.'

'I knew it was dangerous, but I never meant to hurt Alex or Jo. I never expected to fall in love. But Azri, with his large soft eyes, pleaded with me.'

'And he betrayed you.'

'The last time I saw him at the airport, I reached out to touch him, but he turned away, shunned me. It felt as if he'd thrust a hot poker into my gut and twisted my insides. When I first met Azri I wasn't looking for love. But he sensed the passion within me that I'd been denying most of my life.'

As Gareth writhed with anguish, she saw a vulnerable side he'd previously kept hidden. She recalled how Azri with his childlike appearance and gentle spirit, had managed to unfurl Gareth's affections like a ship in full sail. Whenever she saw the pair together, Gareth purred with contentment.

'He was using you, Gareth.'

'Love falls where it may. I thought you, of all people, would understand. I always kept your secret, Debra. I never told anyone.'

'Love's not easy to understand. It's the circumstances surrounding it that often make it difficult. But I understand the pain of finding someone special and then having them wrenched away from you.'

'Thanks for trying to understand.'

'Take care of Jo. She's going to need you, Gareth.'

She thought about the complexities of love in her own life. *Am I willing to take the ultimate risk to commit to something so precarious? Those who've known a fairy tale ending, tend to believe in love. But those who've never finished the final pages are unsure how the story will end.*

Love in Confined Spaces

When Debra arrived for breakfast, Mike sat at their favourite table by the pond, engrossed in reading a small book. He looked up when he saw her.

'Ah. There's nothing quite like the feel of a good book in your hands.'

'Yes. They seem to turn up in your life just when you need them.'

'Have a seat and I'll show you a book to warm your heart.' He pulled out a chair before handing her the book. 'It's for you. I found it in a small bookshop. I believe you know the author?'

Stroking the red leather binding, she stared at the author's name on the hardback cover. Small and compact, it met the criteria they'd agreed upon when they first began sharing poetry twenty years earlier. It was the need to fit into one's pocket – to take it with you and enable the reader to pull it out at opportune moments – to be able to read again and again the comforting words of another, words that spoke to lovers searching for love.

As her eyes lingered on the gold leaf imprint of the author's name, a familiar tingling sensation crept through her body. She lifted the book to her nose, inhaling the earthy smell of the leather. Flicking through the pages, she heard Rahim's words in her head and sensed him on every page.

'You will enjoy the last poem. It seems he had a muse. Someone who influenced his life perhaps more than she knew.'

'That's amazing. He finally published.' When she reached the last page, she read the words of a poem she knew well. He wrote it for her just before she left Brunei. She knew he'd been writing poetry most of his life and intended to have it published one day. And his dream had come to fruition. He had managed to create magic from his words, caressing the lyrics as he breathed new life into them. There were poems that expressed his despair, displacement and disappointment, his sense of loss at his daughters leaving home, his deepest fears at the challenges they faced. There were also poems that expressed a lighter side to his life with outpourings of joy and desire, but the best poem was the one he wrote for her.

She brushed her fingers over the pages once more before turning to the dedication page. The book was dedicated to his old tutor Haji Hassan who taught him to expand his awareness of divine love which was expressed so intensely by poets such as Rumi, in the hope he too would find the elixir to soothe his restless soul. When she'd first met Rahim, he'd told her two factors had helped him survive his early years in Malaysia. The first was his love of poetry and the second was the guidance of his Malay tutor. Even then, poetry had helped Rahim to find meaning in a mosaic of otherwise inexplicable emotions and events in his life.

'When he stopped writing to his old friends, we thought he'd lost contact with the outside world? But it sounds like he's reaching out in his poetry.'

'I don't think he ever lost contact with England. Each time I'd fly back to the UK he'd say, "Give my regards to Leys College." And when I returned, he was keen for cricket scores from his precious Worcester County.'

As Debra turned the pages of his evocative poetry, she hoped Rahim found the comfort he once desperately sought in Rumi's devotional words. Rahim had felt a comfortable connection with what Rumi wrote on states of longing, emptiness, and grief. He believed that the deeper the grief, the more radiant the love. In Rumi, they had both discovered a secret world into which they could immerse themselves. Perhaps it was time to deal with her own grief by finding comfort in the words of another. She looked up to see Mike waiting for her to respond.

'Sorry, what were you saying?'

'Did I mention Roger bumped into him in Singapore recently? Roger knew him from his days at Leys College.'

'Rahim?'

'Yes. Rahim told Roger when he first left England, he was keen to keep in touch with his school friends. However, his life changed dramatically and the young lad who left England lived a very different life in KL than the one he thought he was destined to live.'

'Roger saw him recently?' Debra closed the book, giving him her full attention.

'Yeah. According to Roger, those former classmates spent their gap year skiing in Switzerland, recklessly partying and bragging about their conquests. But Rahim's life was dictated by his father. By the time he was twenty, he was married with children.'

'He always thought he was English. It was only other people who viewed him differently. So … Roger spoke to him … recently?' She rolled the last word over her tongue, allowing it to sink in.

'That's right. Those who knew him well understood the words of Byron and Keats still burned deep within him. He was more British than the British.'

Rahim once told her how Keats had resonated with him, consoled him at a desolate time in his life. Right now, all she could focus on was *Roger has seen Rahim recently*. She thought of his connections to England, the mother and sister he'd left behind.

'So, where is he now?'

'I don't know.'

Debra inhaled, feeling her shoulders slouch. She let those last words slip through the part of her mind where she stored a myriad of unanswered questions. There was another she needed to ask, dreading the answer.

'Speaking of England … when do you fly home?

'I have one more day. How would you like to spend it?'

'We've been so busy. It might be nice to have a quiet day just chilling out.'

'I agree. Let's spend the day around the pool.'

And so, they began the last day by sleeping in before slowly making their way to a late poolside breakfast next to the fishpond. They took their time, eating in silence, content to absorb the energy of the other. Time was running out and there were many things she wanted to say.

She looked at Mike, who was still larger than life itself and whose affection she had come to rely on these last few weeks. She came on this trip searching for answers but had found something far more meaningful than she had thought possible. As she bit on a mouthful of marmalade toast, she poured them both another cup of tea.

'I want to thank you, Mike. This holiday. It's been fabulous.'

'Yes, it's certainly exceeded all my expectations.' He beamed from ear to ear.

This encounter had been good for them both. The experience had given them the confidence to reconnect, to be accepted and loved, to know there was a life in them waiting to be lived. But she waited, wanting to hear how he really felt about her.

But instead, he said, 'And now you have all your answers, thanks to Gareth.'

'Most of them. There is one I will probably never know.'

'And until you do, you will never be ready to start again.'

'It's not that. I think it's just the timing is wrong. After Alex, I'm not sure if I'm ready for anything yet.' The thought of uprooting to another country, to live a different way of life, with another man. There were so many decisions she needed to make. It would take time.

'Whatever we have together, it's worth keeping. We'll stay in touch, visit each other, and maintain our incredible friendship.'

'We sure will. Your friendship means so much to me.'

Like looking in a mirror they had seen themselves through another's eyes. As friends, they knew the difficulties and understood each other's vulnerabilities, as well as their triumphs.

'Unlike Jacquie and me. We were like Baroque double violins, sometimes in harmony, but most of the time in discord. It was unpleasant to the ears but even harsher on the heartstrings. Perhaps we'd just reached our natural coda.'

'I don't think it's always about the person you are with, but how you are when you're with them. We all play our roles within the relationship but sometimes we're just heading in different directions.'

'Well, I kept waiting for that sharper note to uplift an otherwise series of flats in our marriage. But it never came.'

'Sometimes it's the sounds that are missing from a relationship. Silence has a power of its own.' When she looked back at her own marriage, she remembered lovemaking with the lights out and none of the shared looks, gestures, or whispered words of intimacy. Just the silence. 'There were times when I longed to fall asleep with his arms encircling me, but he told me I was far too needy. He didn't appear to need anyone.'

'It sounds as though you weren't dancing to the same tune. You think you know the music, but then your partner changes the tempo. The rhythm is never the same again.'

She heard the passion for music in his voice but also his hurt. 'If you observe any two partners you can see the alchemy taking place between them. If one of them feels hurt, you see the space between them widen.' She thought of the connection she had with Mike. So much that was unexpected had brought them together. He had strengthened her with his vitality when she'd felt vulnerable and drained by grief. His gaiety and humour had showed her how to laugh again. His affection had reminded her how to receive love. *But am I ready to freely give it in return?*

'I've been reading about a scandalous love affair that allegedly occurred here in 1452 around the time of Sultan Sulaiman.' Mike pulled out a folded page from the local newspaper. 'In fact, we've probably walked past this site where they're buried.' He described a small, roofed structure opposite the post office. 'Not just any gravesite but one surrounded by mystery and intrigue. Originally, the site was a much larger mound, but it was bombed during the war. At that time, the grave appeared to be empty even though, according to the legend, two people had been buried inside.'

'Wow. That was a long time ago. Who were these infamous lovers?'

'The grave was said to belong to a lady of royal blood. Those familiar with the grave called it *Kubur Raja Ayang*. She was buried with her lover as punishment for her crime.'

'Oh, my God. What was her crime?'

'The worst sin of all. Brother and sister. According to local law, they should have been stoned to death. It appears the authorities took pity on them.'

'What? So, instead, they buried them alive in a grave!'

'It was more like a sealed cave. I don't know how long they were there, but people brought them food. The cavern was fitted with ventilation. Any smoke seen coming out of the chimney indicated they were still alive. Then, one day, there was no more smoke.'

'Gosh. Forbidden love. What a tragic way to live and die.' She remembered the significant danger for any illicit lovers in Brunei, not only back then, but even now. 'So, did the authorities think forcing them together would be punishment? I wonder if they grew tired of each other under such extreme conditions. Or did they embrace their confined space knowing at least they were together?' Debra would never know. But she knew the pain of being forced apart, how it only served to increase the heartache.

'It would have been a punishment for Jacquie and me. We would probably have murdered each other on the first night. She was not good being denied her creature comforts, which would have included a lover on the outside.' He shrugged. 'But now is not the time for revisiting old grudges.'

'Maybe it would have transformed you, Mike.' Debra half-smiled. 'Are there any records of the young woman? I could do some research when I go to the museum. An unmarked grave is a rather sad testimony to a young couple whose sin was falling in love.'

'According to this article, although she wasn't named, there were remnants of a broken tombstone and a description in Arabic.' He peered at the text in the newspaper article with the English translation provided: *It is hoped the punishment complied with religious laws, sufficient compensation for the sin committed. Pray the lovers are in peace and the Al-Mighty will forgive them.'*

She thought of the legendary lovers and what they'd endured. *Could anyone ever re-imagine living their past with a different outcome?* With its evocative forces, nostalgia lived with them all. The past was something already lived but often not lived fully enough. *There's always an element wanting to be lived again, yet would it ever be as good the second time around?*

A Circle of Light

'So, you never found your pangolin, Sam?'

'No, despite my long nose and curious nature, I didn't manage to find one. But I will keep searching. Like the pangolin, I'll keep digging.'

Time had run out for Sam and Kali as their holiday came to an end. They reminisced about their childhoods, the good times and bad; they reflected on how life had robbed them of some of the joy, but that tiny miracles in nature were still waiting to be found.

'I've been reading up on the pangolin. Like you, Sam, it is shy and nocturnal.'

'Did you also know they roamed the earth alongside dinosaurs eighty million years ago?'

'No, I didn't. But I know they have a long prehensile tail. They carry their babies around on it for the first few months. Can you imagine? How cute is that?'

'As cute as you.'

Kali heard the affection in Sam's voice, but also his sincerity. She knew he saw her for who she was. He wasn't interested in her body or how she looked. When she thought of her past relationships, she was reminded of the times she gave her body willingly to men and the times they took it without asking. She wanted them to love her, and her body was the only power she had.

But now she knew that giving away her physical power had robbed her of what little inner strength she had. Like an empty shell, vulnerable, skeletal, with no connection to her inner beauty, she felt her essence had seeped out of her. Now she needed to grasp it before it disappeared. She looked at Sam who, as a child, had never feared anything. Spiders, scorpions, he wanted to defend them all. She could do with some of his fearless passion right now.

'Wildlife Warrior. It might be a good career choice for you, Sam. You could follow your dreams, pursue your pangolins.'

'I've been thinking the same thing. It would be nice to live in this part of the world. I also think it's time I stopped riding on my mother's tail. I need to make my own way in the world.'

Kali thought of her mother and knew she must also stand on her own two feet. But before she left Brunei, there was one more thing she needed to do.

'There's somewhere I need to go. I'll take the car.'

Dressing in trousers and a long-sleeved shirt, Kali drove to the mosque in town. It was closing time for tourists and the holy man no longer stood at the entrance. As she moved towards the front door, she could see him inside getting ready to leave.

'I'm sorry I was rude the first time I came here,' she spluttered. 'I refused to wear the black robe. I know I embarrassed my mother. I didn't mean to offend you.'

He stared at her, listening, but took his time in answering. 'Before we choose our actions,' he said, nodding slowly, 'we should make sure they align with our thoughts and beliefs. None of us is perfect. But if we are acting in line with our highest self; we are being true to ourselves. Only then can we worry about pleasing others.'

'Thank you.' Kali looked at her shoes, which she should have removed before following him through the door.

'One of the reasons for covering yourself is that it helps you and others to focus on the beauty within. Before others can see it, you first need to find it yourself. When we find true happiness within, it will be reflected on the outside.' He pointed through the entrance to the magnificent marble pillars, and the stained-glass windows. 'There is always more within. I'm sure you could find a quiet place inside if you care to spend a few moments in reflection.'

Kali took the robe from him and removed her shoes, leaving them in the racks provided. As she slipped on the black robe and pulled the hood over her hair, she started to panic. Her pulse raced, and she broke out in a sweat. Her legs felt like jelly as she gripped the doorframe, gasping for breath. It was a flashback from another time, but she could feel the fear creeping up her spine as if it was only yesterday.

Kali was in her teens when she'd stepped out in front of a car near a shopping centre car park. She'd been thumbing a lift when a strange man stopped his car for her. Not hesitating, she had opened the car door and hauled in her shopping bags onto the back seat. Prattling without pausing for breath, she'd entertained the stranger, telling him about the bargains she'd bought. Kicking off her shoes, she'd offered him cookies, insisting he have the first choice from the large paper bag. Next, she'd dived into the bottomless shopping bag, pulling out various pieces of cheap jewellery. She added them to the many gaudy baubles already adorning her ankles, wrists, and hair. The stranger had listened to her garrulous banter, probably noting her bloodshot eyes, the unmistakable sickly-sweet smell of her breath.

Frantically trying to cool herself, she'd wound down the window and stuck out her head. 'I need a drink,' she'd said, bending down to find her water bottle. The driver had seized this moment to apply his brakes and grabbed a blanket from the back seat. As he threw it over her head, he chose what would happen next. She could still remember the dark, damp blanket with its strong chemical smell, the panic rising within her as she'd struggled to breathe. It was also a dark event that followed and, when she awoke, she was lying near a council rubbish dump on the outskirts of town. She didn't remember how she'd got home but probably she'd walked. As she recalled the incident now, the irony was not lost on her. After all this time, she still found it hard to believe someone could treat her so badly. To discard her like rubbish was unforgivable. She'd felt as worthless as the refuse people had dumped there, reeking of sour sweat and putrid decay.

She wrenched off the hood and wiped the sweat from her face with her hand. The holy man pointed to the taps for washing her face, hands, and feet. After splashing water on her face, she took a few deep breaths and slowly lifted the hood until it barely covered the top of her hair.

Following him to a quiet recess near the back of the mosque, she sat where the sun shone through a stained-glass window. From high above, it surrounded her in a circle of light.

'See if you can discover what you need to find.' He moved away, leaving her alone.

As she looked up at the golden dome with its intricate design, the ornate ceiling, and carved arches, she watched dust motes transform into magical beings as the sun caught them at the right angle. From within her dark cover of safety, she looked out at her surroundings. In her wider circle of light, she lost all sense of time but there was a state of calm and peace. It was something she could only describe as euphoria – a similar state of bliss she'd previously experienced with the help of drugs or alcohol. But today she needed none of those.

When she emerged from the mosque, she took off the robe and handed it to the holy man, who now sat outside the door. She barely managed a word of thanks before the tears started to well. Rushing through the door, she managed a quick, 'Thank you. I needed that. You've no idea how much.'

'*Assalam Alikum.* Peace be with you.'

'And, also with you.'

***

Jo opened her suitcase beside small piles of clothes she'd spread over the bed. She gently lifted the bundle of batiks she'd purchased at the longhouse, fingering the fringed thread along the edges. She placed them in her case, a memory of one of the most exciting days of her holiday. But would she remember it in months to come? Lately, she'd been forgetting more than she remembered.

As she unzipped the inner compartment, she smelt traces of another trip, another time. A hint of spicy heat and exotic aromas filled her nostrils. Smells of sun-ripened tomatoes, fresh coriander, ginger, and lemongrass invaded her senses, but was it Mumbai or Marrakesh? Red sunset skies against inspiring ancient ruins and vast towering fortresses, shimmering moons reflected on dark rippling water, but where was it?

During her flying years, she'd flown passengers to many exciting destinations, but today she couldn't recall the names or the words to describe them. She still felt something of the sensations though. When she saw images of bewitching people with soulful brown eyes and laughing faces, she was not frightened. As she gazed through a fog of mesmerising colours of saffron turbans and bright pink saris, she felt bewildered but content. Never scary, she found these people and places beguiling, enchanting. She remembered that much but that was all she remembered.

One small chink in the zip of her case reminded her of a previous adventure when her jewellery was stolen from her suitcase, but the details were now foggy, more like a dream. She recalled her grandmother's pearls were the only piece of jewellery that survived as they were stuck in this zip. She knew they'd survived the burglary because she was still wearing them. She became aware of Gareth behind her, pulling clothes out of the wardrobe and she asked him, 'Do you remember when my suitcase was broken into? Where did it happen?'

'Manila. The baggage handlers saw the jewellery as it was being x-rayed. They'd marked the case with chalk.'

'Was that all we lost?

'Yes.'

She remembered some of what she'd lost over the years. Her career, her plane, years of her marriage. But now she was getting some of it back. At least she and Gareth could make a new start. While they couldn't recapture the lost years of happiness, they could create new memories. But how long would she be able to hold onto them?

From where it had been nestling among the clothes in her case, she lifted a small bird that a young Iban boy had carved for her at the longhouse. Roughly hewn from the root of a tree, it was not an exact replica of the bird they'd seen that day. What type of bird was it? Hornet? No, that wasn't the name. She could still see it perched on the arm of an older man, its majestic black and white tail feathers inert. A girl was feeding wild figs into its large yellow beak, and its wide intense eyes tinged with vivid blue had stared back at her. But she couldn't remember what it was called. Never mind, she would ask Kali tomorrow. She would know.

The carved bird would help her remember a journey to a magical place that was once her home. She knew she would not be coming back here again but the important thing was she would not be leaving on her own. Gareth would be coming with her this time, and she didn't have to fear the prospect of a future living alone. She knew she had some difficult times ahead as her doctor had warned her about the symptoms. But she would have someone by her side to help her get through it.

263

Fearless and Dependable

'I can drop you off if you like,' Debra suggested. 'There's something I need to do but I can always pick you up later.' Sam wanted to revisit their old house, but Debra wanted to see again the workplace where she'd once spent her carefree days. She needed a moment alone for some peaceful reflection.

As time ran out for Debra, this was her last chance to recapture fond memories that had laid dormant for far too long. She wanted to drive past the college where she used to work, to absorb the energy she'd once felt, to remember the excitement she'd experienced as she'd walked through the wrought iron gates each morning, seeing the students and planning her day. She wanted to relive the way her pulse had raced as she stepped into the staffroom, the first glimpse of him, and the sound of his voice …

This time, she had no trouble finding their old house. It was the same road she'd driven along each day dropping Sam at preschool before driving to the college.

As she drove into the laneway, she looked at their old elegant two-storey house with its manicured tropical garden — such a contrast to the shared housing where Sam had lived in recent years. Sam pointed to the rows of pineapples growing along the sloping driveway, where the mango tree bursting with ripened fruit towered above them.

She caught sight of a young Malay woman in a batik sarong playing with a small boy near the front porch. The boy had his arms wrapped around a life-sized stuffed toy.

'Check out the tiger,' Sam laughed.

The small boy struggled to lift the tiger twice his size until his mother came to his aid. The stuffed toy was too heavy for one small boy to lift on his own. The boy and his mother looked up as Sam approached. They watched him hesitate at the gate.

'Excuse me, do you mind if I have a look around the garden? I used to live here as a child.'

The woman frowned and wrapped her arms more tightly around the boy but Sam prattled on with his friendly banter. Pointing to the mango tree, he told her how his father had built him a swing there and while it may not have been the original, rope still dangled from its branches. The Malay woman nodded and called out for her amah to unlock the gate. Sam walked up the sloping driveway to his old house introducing himself to the new occupant. She didn't accept the hand he thrust out, but she smiled without showing her teeth.

***

Debra hesitated before driving off. She took note of the way the Malay woman wrapped a protective arm around her son, the way she lifted him away from the stuffed tiger. Something about the life-sized animal reminded her of a time when Sam had also had such a toy. But Sam was a teenager at the time and had probably found it on a kerbside collection. His shared housing had mainly been furnished from kerbside discards.

At the time, he'd been living alone, and she often couldn't contact him as he rarely crawled out of bed. During one of his craziest outbursts, he'd glued Araldite over his front door locks to prevent anyone from entering. She'd had no way of knowing if he was still alive. One day in desperation, she'd lifted a couple of roof tiles and climbed down through the manhole. As she was about to leap from the ceiling to the floor, she stopped, dangling mid-air. In the doorway of the darkened room loomed a huge black animal.

Her pulse thumped in her ears like a freight train out of control. In her peripheral vision, the animal appeared real and threatening but there was no turning back. She had to push on. She took a leap of faith and landed shakily on the floor. Staring at her was a life-sized stuffed black panther. Unlike the elephant, who allegedly sits in the living room, this panther's presence was obvious. During the next few months, the panther became quite familiar to her, despite his many guises.

On one occasion, the panther greeted her wearing a business shirt, complete with tie and sunglasses. Another time he had written a message on the whiteboard propped next to him, which said, *what are you staring at?* She wanted to write a rude reply but who was she kidding? It would simply fall on deaf ears, and besides, the panther couldn't read. At times, she was so angry she wanted to scream. Other times she felt so depressed she avoided going around there. She'd consoled herself with the fact that this was not her child who was acting so strangely. It was the drugs. There were often days when she felt as if she was the one losing her mind.

But today she was holding it together.

As Debra slowly drove out along the laneway, she watched Sam through the wire fence as he pointed toward the swimming pool. No doubt he was telling the woman how his dad had built the pool and the surrounding decking. Their Chinese landlord had planted many trees before they moved into the house, as he wanted them to benefit from the fruit. Still bearing fruit, most of these trees were now twice the size. The Malay woman appeared to be listening to Sam, nodding with her head cocked to one side.

***

Sam turned to the small boy and asked him his name.

'Ismail,' he answered shyly.

'Ismail found a toy in the cupboard under the stairs,' the woman said. 'Perhaps it was yours.' She called to her amah who was sweeping the front porch. The amah propped her broom against the wall and went inside. Minutes later, she appeared with a small action figurine and held it out to Sam.

'Oh, my god. GI Joe. My father gave me that toy when I was about your age. Dad told me if I was ever scared to hold it in my hand. He said it would make me brave, like a soldier, fearless and dependable.' He nodded at the small boy. 'Thank you for finding him.'

Before he could stop himself, he told the strangers all about his dad. How he'd bought GI Joe for him when he was sick. It was as if the toy had unleashed many more memories he'd been storing inside.

'My dad loved to organise birthday parties for me,' he pointed around the garden. 'One was a pirate's party by the pool.' He laughed as he remembered the photos of his dad wearing a pirate's costume, with a patch on his eye. Once he started talking about his dad he couldn't stop. He told the woman how sad he was when his father died.

'You have lovely memories of your father. That is good. They will bring you much comfort, I'm sure.'

The swing in the mango tree also reminded him how much his father had loved to eat mangoes. 'Even when he was ill,' he told the woman, 'he couldn't eat enough of them.'

'We have plenty of ripe mangoes. Come,' she said, wrapping her arm around her son's shoulders and beckoning Sam inside.

She instructed her amah to chop the mango the way Sam remembered, the way it always fascinated him as a child. Slashing first one way then the other in a crisscross pattern, then popping it inside out like a football the same way his dad always did.

As Sam looked at the GI Joe, he thought about how generous his dad had been buying him toys and how much joy he'd brought into his life. His childhood was full of happy memories. He handed the toy to the little boy.

'Here, Ismail. You can keep him if you like. I had a lot of fun with GI Joe. I hope you do too. You probably can't buy them anymore. He's a relic of the seventies. I had lots of imaginary friends and no doubt you do too.'

As Sam handed over the toy, it occurred to him he no longer needed any props to help him face the world. He now felt brave enough to fight any demons on his own. There were real creatures in the world who deserved his attention, and he hoped to protect and nurture them. Maybe he would see some of these animals at the museum before he left Brunei.

***

As Debra drove past the front garden, the swimming pool looked sparkling clean, everything in the garden neat and tidy. The bamboo that provided a natural screen around the pool had been trimmed but the banana groves were heavy with large hands of fruit. The magenta bougainvillea, which once framed the front porch, had been trimmed back from the entrance. No doubt this family had a gardener who kept their garden in such a pristine state.

When she'd lived here, the garden was untamed and like her, not yet certain where it wanted to go. There was still room for reaching out into places that had not yet been explored. There were also secret nooks providing her with the privacy she'd needed at that time.

She stopped before turning onto the main road and searched for the golden sunflowers that once had turned their faces towards the setting sun. On the first day she'd arrived, Jo had told her the flowers were called *matahari*, named after the sun. It was also a nickname Rahim's mother had given him, but she'd shortened it to Hari or Harry. He had been her sun.

Debra remembered sitting on the deck at sunset as the swimming pool reflected the last shafts of sunlight across its surface. Fruit bats had swooped around the mango tree, circling in and out. Dusk was short and night fell instantly. Within a few hours, this beautiful tropical garden would be covered in darkness and the first sounds to break the silence would be the constant rhythmical clicking of cicadas and the drone of insects. She looked back at Sam in these serene surroundings. It was such a far cry from what they'd lived through in recent times.

Why do I keep returning to those dreadful times? Do I need to process those images before I can completely purge them from my mind? She'd kept them stuffed inside, never acknowledging, or releasing her pain. Now she must let them go.

Gripping the steering wheel, Debra forced herself to take a deep breath and let it all go. *It's now time to move on. No more glimpses into the past, no more demons to frighten me.* She relaxed her shoulders and loosened her grip on the steering wheel. *All is well!*

She took one last look at her old house and felt a sense of calm. They had many memorable moments living in that house – she didn't need to go inside and look around. She remembered the happy times with Alex and Sam.

A wave of gratitude swept over her, reminding her how lucky she was to have experienced this lifestyle. She imagined the small Malay boy sleeping in Sam's upstairs bedroom. His parents had probably given him everything money could buy. No doubt they had hopes and aspirations for what path they saw their boy taking. Would he be a doctor or a lawyer? Perhaps they would send him to the UK to study engineering. They had no idea what the future would hold for him, but they would keep on hoping.

As a parent, she'd become involved in a journey that wasn't hers to live. Sam hadn't asked her to sort through the debris, clean his mess, and discard the unwanted. She did it because it was part of the healing process in her own life journey. Like a lotus that blossomed out of the mud and murky depths, she, too, tried to salvage something positive from the wreckage. She attempted to find rationale in situations that were almost always irrational. But, at the time, Sam had no idea where he was heading, and she was merely a passenger on his train wreck journey.

She could have chosen to get off the train whenever she wanted, but if she alighted too soon, she would never have known there were better destinations ahead. Now she knew she could safely disembark, leaving him to face his own destiny. He would be fine, and so would she. She'd lived a life that was challenging but it was also exciting. It didn't matter what the future held. She didn't need to know. She could love her son and cherish him and that was enough.

***

As Sam walked outside his old house, he looked at Ismail who was waving to him from the window. Should he have kept the toy to remind him of his father? No. He no longer needed anything to remind him of his dad. His father was present in his thoughts every moment of the day. Besides, he hoped the toy would change the boy's life for the better. Like GI Joe,

Ismail would grow up to be brave; he would try harder, and he'd do all the things his father would want him to do.

Where the Path Leads

On the penultimate day of their holiday, Sam asked, 'What about the place with the bronze cannons?'

The one remaining place they'd not yet visited was at the bottom of Debra's list. It wasn't the display of antique cannons and menacing daggers that filled her with dread, but something darker, more deeply entrenched in her memory. She turned to Sam, hearing the eagerness in his voice but hesitated before answering.

'I guess we could have a look at the museum.'

'We don't have to go there, Mum, if you don't want to.'

'No, I think I need to go.'

They first stopped at the Centre for Arts and Handicrafts, where Sam questioned a young silversmith who hammered a silver bowl into shape. The craftsman showed Sam his paper design of swirling vines, the small tool he would use to manually etch the surface. As Sam ran his finger around the rim of the bowl, it emitted a faint humming vibration. He listened and watched this young craftsman who appeared happy to follow the path already laid out for him. He didn't need to question his future or where his path would lead him as he continued carrying out this ancient skill his father and grandfather had done before him.

Debra observed a group of women as they demonstrated the historic traditional craft of weaving gold and silver thread into cloth. She compared this finest cotton and silk to the simple cloth used by the Iban women in the longhouse, as they weaved the minutiae of their daily lives. This cloth of the

Brunei weavers, enhanced by man's most precious metals, was designed to be worn at weddings or royal and state functions. Not an everyday cloth to be worn by common people, it involved a time-honoured skill passed on from mother to daughter. The elegant centuries-old art form was to be enjoyed only by those who could afford the luxury of attending special events or auspicious occasions.

She moved in closer to the women at their looms as they prepared bamboo spools and calculated the number of strands needed for the cloth they would weave. As they untangled the common threads from the precious gold and silver, she wondered, was it enough? Did they ever wish for more? Or did the touch, and occasional flash of gold and silver compensate for what was lacking in their everyday lives?

Sam offered to drive to the final museum, and she gave him instructions on how to get there. As they drove up the sloping driveway to the car park, her pulse quickened. It was the car park behind the museum she dreaded the most. As a memory flashed into her mind, she relived the fear like spiders crawling over her skin. But while the fear was still there, it was losing the power it once held. She inhaled deeply as Sam parked the car close to the front entrance of the museum.

The bronze cannons still stood erect on the top of the brick wall, as if guarding the tropical gardens below. She pushed away past images of menacing faces with cigarette butts glowing in the dark. Instead, she focused on happier times and the myriad of magical memories associated with this place, the many times she waited for him, her heart full of love and longing.

Sam strode ahead, but now stopped and waited for her.

'What is it, Mum?' Gently he placed his arm around her shoulders.

She slowly shook her head. *How can I explain a place that holds such a mixture of emotions? How can I possibly describe how a secret meeting place for lovers had become a place of violence and fear?*

'I just want to look at these cannons.' She pointed toward them, her breath catching. On one of them, a part of the metal mounting had worn away with time creating a small opening beneath. It had become their secret repository, concealing their billets-doux, penned by two people in love. There was a time when it had offered them a portal into another world, where nothing else mattered.

She remembered Rahim telling her the history of Brunei's famous ornate bronze cannons. He'd said the *bedil* dated back to the fifteenth century. She now related this information to Sam.

'Nowadays they're purely for decoration. But originally, they were used to defend the battlements.'

They looked at the high stone wall separating the car park from lawns leading to the jungle and river below. A long set of steep stone steps led to a secluded tropical garden concealed from the road. The encroaching jungle had created a natural shelter around a solitary wooden bench. *Our bench.* The museum building had been extended since her last visit and a terraced restaurant now jutted out over the well-maintained lawns.

'Mum, life is going to get better, I promise.' Sam's dark eyes widened, his expression that of someone older and wiser. His new confident tone brought her a surge of hope, and she said what she'd wanted to say for a long time.

'Sam, regardless of what life has taken from me, I have always had you, and you are enough. I love you.'

'I know I haven't been much help but I'm here for you now.' He wrapped her in a hug, and they stayed that way, encased in their snug cocoon.

As they entered the old museum, Sam scanned the many exhibits, narrating to her what he read on each sign.

'A visiting curator from London is giving a talk on the restoration of the old bronze canons. It starts in ten minutes.'

'Oh, that might be interesting.'

Sam went outside for a cigarette while Debra stared at ancient gongs adorned with bronze gilded dragons. A display in varying sizes, each gong with its own unique sound. A crowd of people was moving past the gongs and gathering outside the lecture room where the talk was to be held.

A young woman pushed her wheelchair through the crowd before settling herself at the front of the lecture room. Sam and Debra followed her in, choosing seats towards the back. A dark-bearded staff member adjusted the screen and projector before introducing the guest speaker. The young woman began by giving an in-depth account of her work in ancient history at Oxford University before explaining her interest in the bronze cannons.

At the end of the lecture, a balding man with a German accent asked about her particular interest in Brunei artifacts.

She hesitated before answering him. 'Although I now live with my aunt in the UK, I used to live in Brunei as a child. We often return to the place of our childhood to complete unfinished business.' She had a natural smile, showing perfect white teeth with the slightest dimple in her left cheek.

When Debra looked at her, she had goosebumps. *Yes, it is often the ghosts of our past that bring us back.* As Debra stood to leave, she read the young woman's name badge: *Aleesha Ibrahim.* A common name in this part of the world but there was just the slightest chance.

Rahim had once jokingly referred to his youngest daughter as his clone. He'd said she shared his eyes and his mind. When she was young and Rahim was deep in thought, Aleesha would sit quietly beside him talking about the same topic, which mirrored his thoughts moments earlier. At the time, he'd found it uncanny.

Looking at the young woman in the wheelchair, Debra hoped Aleesha also shared her father's patience and determination. She looked as though she might need them. This young woman certainly shared her father's natural good looks. Debra hesitated.

'Excuse me. But was your father's name Rahim?'

'Yes, it was. Did you know him?'

'I used to teach with him at the college. Twenty years ago.'

'Oh really! Well, he's here now if you'd like to speak to him.'

All at once, her pulse sped, and she broke into a sweat. Her jaw dropped, and she stared open-mouthed. She tried to relax, lifting the handbag strap on her shoulder. Before she could reply, Aleesha looked over Debra's shoulder.

'Dad, this lady says she knows you.'

Debra had barely two seconds to take a deep breath and control the thumping in her ears and the trembling in her legs. She had less than two seconds to turn and look at the person she'd spent the last twenty years wondering about. Where had he been? What had he been doing, and why had he disappeared from her life? His image was etched in her memory, engraved on her heart.

When she turned, there was no doubt about the warm brown eyes staring back at her, his handsome face barely aged with only a few fine lines around his mouth. He gazed at her wide-eyed before his face radiated the same endearing smile she remembered so well.

'Debra? Oh, my goodness! What are you doing here?'

'I came for the reunion. When Jo invited me after Alex's funeral, I decided to come.'

'Oh, I am sorry. I did not know about Alex. I cannot believe you are here.'

The same balding German man asked Aleesha more questions, and she explained her project in detail. She didn't notice the way her father's eyes shone, or how he threw his hands in the air as if he didn't know what to do with them. She also didn't see Debra's flushed face or the way she frantically twirled the beads at her throat.

'Why don't you join us for dinner tonight?' Debra spluttered before taking another breath. 'Mike will be there. He'd love to see you. He's flying out early in the morning.'

'Oh!' he paused, looking towards Aleesha. 'Unfortunately, I have a family commitment.' He frowned as he whispered, 'I am really sorry I cannot get out of it.'

An ocean of disappointment washed over her. To have waited so long for this. To have finally found him but then to lose him again. The weight of the water crashing down on her drowned out any other sounds and she no longer heard what he was saying. Nor could she see as her eyes were smarting. As she blinked back tears, she mumbled incoherently.

'That's a shame. Never mind.' She started to back away, to distance herself, to disconnect from the source of pain. 'I'll tell Mike I saw you.'

'Yes, please do.' Worry lines appeared on his brow as he ran his hand through his hair, before plunging it into his pocket.

The crowd that had gathered around Aleesha was now crushing her in its throng. Rahim stepped aside to let people pass through.

Debra moved towards the glass sliding doors, wishing they would open instantly and take her to another place and time, a time when she was still contemplating if it was possible. Now she knew it would never happen. She watched Sam striding towards her after butting out his cigarette in the garden. She forced a smile and a casual wave.

Rahim watched her as the glass doors slid open. She was about to disappear from the building and out of his life. But outside the sun still shone, the sky was a perfect blue with not a cloud to be seen.

'Debra, wait!' He followed her until he drew close enough to whisper in her ear. 'I'm free tomorrow. Can you meet me here for lunch?'

'In the new café overlooking the bronze cannons?' She attempted to laugh.

'Yes,' he smiled. 'From the terrace, where the stone steps lead down to the river, to a secluded garden bench concealed from the road.'

The Muse

After Debra had left the college and his life, Rahim felt a huge emptiness that could not be filled. At least when he knew she was nearby he could quietly admire her from a distance. His memories were so vivid he could recapture every minute detail of her as she sat in the staffroom pretending to ignore him. He liked the way she played with her hair as she read, winding a curl around her index finger. He loved stealing glimpses as she moved her head to one side and a stray curl would catch in the collar of her blouse and then spring out as she changed position.

Rahim had added the college report he'd been writing to the pile on his desk. He spent most of the morning fiddling with each report several times before replacing them back on his desk. Despite these matters of urgency, he was consumed with thoughts of Debra and could think of nothing else.

After enduring four long weeks of self-imposed separation, they'd arranged to meet at their secret meeting place. He could not wait to see her, but a series of unplanned mishaps had taken place. His car had broken down, and by the time he arrived her life was in jeopardy, and she was about to fly to Manila to be with Alex. She had promised she would return soon, but she hadn't. All this had happened within a few days, and it was hard to get his head around it. He felt wretched knowing he could not ring her.

After the first shrill ring, he had grabbed the phone, expecting it to be his wife in Kuala Lumpur. He was surprised to hear his father's voice, the line full of static, obliterating half of what his father was saying.

'Is it Mahani? How is she?'

'Mahani is fine. This is about your favoured one.'

Visions of Debra immediately flashed through his mind. His father had found out about their relationship; his father, speaking a combination of English and Malay, his voice cracking as if he was trying to hold back tears. Rahim could hear every second word and then one word he did not expect to hear.

'Aleesha?'

'Yes, there has been a car accident. You need to fly here straight away.'

When Aleesha left for Malaysia with her mother the week before, she had been excited to be going to Kuala Lumpur. A reckless driver had changed everything and now she was lying injured in a hospital. As he tried to absorb this latest shock, he'd lifted the framed photo of his young daughter from his desk. All three of his beautiful daughters he loved dearly, but it was with his youngest he shared the strongest bond. She was the one who understood him best of all.

He'd rung the airline and booked a seat on the next available flight, but it was Debra he wanted to ring, to tell her his tragic news. He wanted to hear her comforting words, but it wasn't possible to ring her. By then, she would have been sitting by a hospital bed in Manila attending to Alex's needs. He smiled as he visualised her face and recalled the sound of her voice.

Before Mahani left for KL, Rahim asked if she wanted him to accompany her. She smiled and said, 'I understand why you need to stay here.'

There were times when he wished Mahani had been less understanding. At least then, he would not have felt as guilty about cheating on her. Poor sweet Mahani deserved to be treated with far more respect. She, too, would be sitting by Aleesha's bedside, worrying about their precious daughter.

As he'd thrown a few clothes into an overnight bag, he'd tried to think of how he could contact Debra. He'd placed his bag in the boot of his car and driven in the late afternoon traffic to the airport.

'Oh, Debra, where were you when I needed you most?'

***

'Would you like a coffee, Dad?' Aleesha was knocking on his hotel door.

At the sound of her voice, Rahim snapped out of his reverie. Here he was in the place where he'd first met Debra. He couldn't believe she was here now. Waking with the sun, he'd been pacing up and down the small hotel room, his mind full of questions and disbelief. It was hard to believe that across town, the same sun was shining down on her, and she, too, was waking to the same day full of hope and promise. In a world full of chaos, they'd managed to find each other.

After years of loss and anguish, they were alive and about to meet again in a few hours' time. He walked over to open the adjoining hotel room door.

'Yes, I would love a coffee.' He held open the door while Aleesha pushed her wheelchair through the doorway with practised ease.

'Are you hungry, Dad?'

'Yes, I have been awake for ages. I did not sleep well. How about you?'

'I had a good sleep. It's been hectic at the museum these last few days. I was exhausted.'

They chose a table close to the buffet and helped themselves to the breakfast food. Rahim poured them both another cup of coffee, placing hers in front of her.

'I hope you do not mind me meeting Debra for lunch. It is just that we have not seen each other in so long. There is so much …'

'I'm a big girl. I can look after myself. Besides, I'm sure Debra is far more exciting company than me.'

'We are just good friends.'

'Dad, you've been quiet ever since you saw her yesterday. And this is your third cup of coffee. You're nervous.'

'It was many years ago. Perhaps we have both changed.'

'Or perhaps you still have whatever it was that first connected you.'

The mysterious factor that had first connected them had taken them by surprise in a way no one could have predicted. The universe had thrown them together, bringing about an unexpected and unorthodox union of love. Those same unseen forces had later conspired to thrust them apart. But while it lasted, it had been a sublime connection of hearts and minds and what first brought them together was poetry.

Rahim was about to bite into his toast when Aleesha spluttered, and he dropped the toast onto the plate. She had been reading his mind again.

'Your poetry. She's your muse, isn't she?'

He stared at the toast, not knowing how to answer but he was conscious of the silence and his daughter waiting for a reply. 'It is difficult to explain.'

'I always knew there had to be someone else. The eloquence and passion in your words. They came from another place, another woman.'

'It is how we met. Our first love was Sufi poetry. We fell in love with Rumi.'

'Before you fell in love with each other? I understand, Dad. In fact, I think I've met someone special.'

'Really! That's great news. I'm so happy for you.'

'Yes, one of the curators at the museum wants to visit me in London. We've been writing to each other.'

'It is not surprising you wanted to come back here.'

'Well, I also wanted to check out our childhood home. As I've said before … it's the ghosts of our past that bring us back. Sometimes there's unfinished business to deal with.'

'Yes. And I need to deal with mine,' he said.

***

When Sam dropped Debra at the museum, she asked him to come inside and meet Rahim. They walked into the restaurant together. Rahim stood and extended his hand to Sam.

'My goodness, you have grown since the last time I saw you. I was sorry to hear about your dad.'

'Thanks. It's been tough but I have an amazing mum.' Sam wrapped his arm around her shoulders and kissed her goodbye. 'Nice to meet you again, Rahim. Mike said to give you his regards. He flew out this morning.'

'Oh, I am sorry I missed him.'

As Sam sauntered off, Rahim looked at his retreating back and shook his head slowly. 'Where have the years gone? He was such a cute little boy. Now he's a young man.'

'It's a shame we don't stay cute forever,' she said.

'I do not know. You have not changed much.' He smiled, first with his eyes and then his mouth.

A warming sensation in her chest spread to her neck and face. They sat opposite each other at a table, oblivious to everything around them. 'Tell me everything about the last twenty years, Rahim. Tell me about your family … your mother in England.'

'Sadly, she passed,' His eyes moistened, 'but I did get to see her before she died. My sister and I have reconnected. Aleesha lives with her in London. After Aleesha's accident, I came back to Brunei for a while, but it was never the same. Once you left and my family had gone, there was nothing here for me. Once my mother died, Sophie encouraged Aleesha to stay with her and it put my mind at rest. It also means I get to spend time living in the UK and part of my time living in KL with Mahani. My wife's health has not improved, and she does not want to leave Malaysia.'

Debra pulled out the red leather book of poetry from her handbag and held it out to him. 'You finally did it. I'm so happy for you. I know how much it meant to you. It was always your dream. Will you sign it for me?'

'I would love to.'

He slowly took a gold pen from his chest pocket and opened the book. He didn't need to think about what he was going to write. He'd been writing it in his head for years. In the middle of sleepless nights or as he woke with the rising sun, he'd been thinking of her and what he wanted to say.

> *Debra, you were the inspiration for my thoughts, the source of my river of words. You were the waking sun, the somnolent moon, and your words whispered to me in the wind. Each frangipani that fell reminded me of you. Only you could match my rhythm without knowing the tune or the steps.*

There was a time when just the sound of his voice was enough to uplift her, vibrate her heartstrings. They had enjoyed the same poignant melody with their bodies moving as one. She'd learned the difficult steps and kept pace with his tempo. But fate had her dance to a tragic tune she no longer knew and could not have predicted. She stumbled each time someone or something altered the familiar steps. And later, when those same omnipotent elements had wrenched them apart, they were ill-timed and unforeseen.

Her throat constricted but she didn't want anything to smother her momentary joy. As he wrote, she watched him and was once again struck by the pleasing shape of his exceptionally well-sculptured lips, and the way he rested his head on his hand as he wrote.

She knew that he would lift the pen and use it to brush away the hair from his eyes. He would look up at her smiling and it would be as if twenty years had been absorbed into the present. Before she knew it, she was once again enjoying the temporary madness, the fusion of two selves merged into one, and she was willing to risk everything for what she had known and loved.

CR

About the Author

Moira Yeldon lives in Perth, Western Australia but spent twelve years living in Brunei, Southeast Asia which inspired her to write this book. A love of writing motivated her to complete a course in creative writing and she has been writing ever since. This life-affirming journey has taken her along winding paths and off the beaten track, to many exotic locations such as the tiny Shangri-La of Bandar Seri Begawan where this story is set.

As a member of the Australian Society of Authors, the Romance Writers of Australia, the Society of Women Writers of Western Australia, and the South Fremantle Writers Centre, she regularly contributes articles and participates in writing workshops.

After graduating with a Bachelor of Arts from Murdoch University, she completed a Graduate Diploma in Education at Curtin University and lectured for many years in English language, communication, and literacy. She has taught Indonesian and Malay language and is also a qualified yoga teacher.

Where Dragonflies Dream is her third novel, and is a sequel to *Where Sunbeams Fall,* set in the same location twenty years later. Her first novel, *Chasing Marigolds,* a memoir inspired from travelling to India, was released in 2019.

She also publishes a blog that you can follow on her website at https://moirayeldon.com and has author profiles on most social media platforms.

www.ingramcontent.com/pod-product-compliance
Lightning Source LLC
Chambersburg PA
CBHW051253210726
48287CB00002B/473